SECRETS OF A
(SOMEWHAT) SUNNY GIRL

KAREN BOOTH

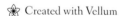

For every kid of divorce

CHAPTER ONE

MY SISTER AMY and I had more than twenty ex-boyfriends between us, a zillion stories about awkward first dates, and miraculously enough, only one declined proposal. Nobody was under the impression the Fuller sisters were saving themselves for marriage. Not even close. But I'd sort of thought we might be saving ourselves *from* it.

"Engaged? To be married?" I practically had to shout over the noontime rush at Big Time Diner in midtown—waitresses barking at bus boys, dishes clattering, customers yammering.

Amy worked her way out of her charcoal gray suit jacket, draping it neatly over her purse on the seat next to her. "What other kind of engaged is there?" She loved to answer a question with a question. If it was possible to be a born litigation attorney, that was my sister.

"I know. I know. I'm just..." I couldn't say more without my stomach lurching, which made me second-guess my lunch order. Matzoh ball soup might kill me. Or, in the absence of wine, maybe chicken broth could help wash down the news. The secret club I'd thought my sister and I had chartered was a sham. How long had she been planning her escape?

"I'm glad it's not just me. I'm speechless too." Amy fluttered her fingers, beaming at her diamond and platinum prize like she'd given birth to it. She tucked her neat, blonde bob behind one ear. I'd always envied her high cheekbones, but today they were straight out of a Technicolor film, blushed with every gorgeous shade of a ripe Georgia peach. She got the cheekbones, and the blush, from Mom.

"Speechless. Yes. That's the perfect word."

Patty, the waitress with the spiky persimmon-orange hair, slid white diner plates ringed in cobalt blue onto our table, putting my forthcoming paper-thin spiel about love and good news on pause, thank God.

"I still can't believe it. It's exciting, right?" Amy's voice reached a pitch like air squeaking out of a pinhole in a balloon. She picked up half of her turkey on rye with one hand, leaving the other hand—the bejeweled one—on display in the center of the table. It was no small feat. Big Time served some of the fattest sandwiches in Manhattan.

"It is." I nodded, as if that might make my lackluster performance more convincing. I sucked flat diet soda through a straw, stalling again. If only I'd had time to prepare some remarks. If only she'd given me some sign that she and Luke were this serious. I'd assumed she was sleeping at his place most nights because the sex was halfway decent. "I'm just..."

"You're just what, Katherine?" She was losing her patience for my lack of gushing, even while her ocean-blue eyes flickered with optimism as she gazed at the behemoth rock on her ring finger. Diamonds were beyond crazy if you thought about it—a nugget of dirty black carbon subjected to unbearable pressure and unthinkable temperatures until it had no choice but to turn into something sparkly and precious. A sunny person might call it a beautiful metaphor—even the ugliest thing could get better.

It just might take a few billion years.

"I'm wondering…" I innocently slurped my soup. *Don't say it.* "Did you know you were going to go back on our pact? Like all along?" *You are such a miserable excuse for a sister.*

She jerked her hand back. "The pact? Are you serious right now? You're supposed to be happy for me."

"I *am* happy for you." It came out as a plea to the universe. *Please let me be happy. Is that too much to ask?* "I'm ecstatic." I was going to have to lie until I could get on board with happy. I couldn't tell her how terrified I was. It pained me to think about her getting hurt and if anyone was going to hurt her, it was some dude she'd known for less than a year. Plus, Luke was a little too perfect—clearly spent a lot of time at the gym, had at least a dozen pet names for her, and was always celebrating tiny milestones. *Oh, honey. Guess what? This will be the tenth time we've gone out for Chinese food.* He had to be hiding something.

Then there was the not-small fact that our family tree had divorces hanging from every branch. The Fullers did not do well with the sanctity of marriage, and that led to divorce, which then led to heartbreak—for everybody, even the bystanders. If Amy's heart got broken, who would pick up the pieces? Me. And I was terrible at picking up pieces. I could never figure out how to glue them back together.

"That was almost nine years ago." Amy lowered her chin, forcing me to look at her. "It was your idea, and you were drunk when you said it. Remember? Cinco de Mayo?"

"Hey. We had fun that night."

"And you had five Margaritas."

"You weren't far behind me."

"Exactly why this is a stupid conversation. I only said yes to the idea that we should never get married and stay roommates forever so you'd shut up and get in your own bed."

It all came back to me. My head hurt just thinking about the hangover that came on May 6th that year. I didn't end up feeling right until June. "God. I got in your bed that night didn't I? I'm sorry. I should never drink tequila. Ever."

"Exactly." She punctuated her statement by pointing at me with a french fry.

"You know, I kept the pact when Jason proposed."

"And you have very big balls to turn down a guy in front of his whole family."

Jason was the one declined proposal. He'd invited me to dinner at his parents' house in Brooklyn, a lovely old brownstone so picturesque it was like something out of a romantic comedy. His family was Italian and vocal, nothing like mine: Scandinavian and choking on every slightly impolite thing. I hadn't even taken off my coat before his mom put him on the spot. *Look at her. She's beautiful, with the blonde hair and the blue eyes. She looks like a milkmaid. You'll make such pretty babies.*

It didn't stop during dinner. *Your brother is already married and he's younger. He's going to have children before you. It's not right. You should marry Katherine. She's a keeper. I can tell.* After the tiramisu was proudly presented for dessert, her mother's mother's recipe, she'd dragged Jason into the other room. I'd sat at the table with his dad and younger sister while we heard every word and could only exchange tortured smiles. I'd twisted the cloth napkin in my lap so tightly that I was embarrassed to give it back.

Ma, we're not ready to get married.

Just give her your grandmother's ring. You'll lose her if you don't.

My brain sputtered. *A ring? Oh, shit.*

What if she says no?

She won't say no.

The next thing I knew, Jason skulked into the dining room, followed by his grinning mother. He sank down to one knee and delivered the most dispassionate proposal a man had ever given. *Katherine, will you marry me?*

His mother gasped.

I wanted to cry.

And then I'd said what I had to. *No. I'm sorry.*

When I told Amy what happened, you'd have thought I'd fought off the evil empire, even if I'd crushed a guy's pride in the process. The truth was that Jason and I were not in love, and that was an inescapable point. I came from a long line of people who had not taken that seriously. I was certain I was never meant for marriage anyway—too screwed up, too much nightmarish baggage, some of which my sister carried around as well. I'd only been within spitting distance of love once, with an Irish hottie my sister knew very little about. That guy, the sexy heartbreaker, had been too much to hold onto.

"Look, Katherine. I'm not you. I can't spend every waking minute being pessimistic. I get enough of that at work. Please don't fault me for finding a guy and falling in love."

My shoulders dropped. "You're right. You're absolutely right. I want what you want. I've spent my whole life wanting you to be happy." That much was true. That part I didn't have to fake. I'd woken up every morning for the last thirty-two years hoping she'd have a good day, even before she'd been born. It was this thing in the very center of my brain, a drive planted at my conception. Had that ambition come from Mom? Was it God's way of keeping my sister safe? He had to have known our mom wasn't going to be around to do it herself.

"Thank you. I appreciate it."

"Now can we please order some pie? We're supposed to be celebrating, but I can't be late getting back to work." I flagged Patty, who nodded at me as she poured a silver-haired gentleman a cup of coffee and swiped a stack of empty plastic creamer cups from his table. "When are you going to tell Dad?"

"I'll call him tonight. He'll just start stressing about when the wedding is going to be and who's going to pay for it and where he should go for a tux. He'll probably book his train ticket as soon as we get off the phone."

Dad was always planning. He never wanted to be caught off guard. I could relate—Amy inherited supermodel cheekbones and I got a hatred of surprises. "Don't give him a hard time about any of it, okay? I'm sure it'll be emotional for him. You're getting married. It'll probably bring up stuff. You know. About Mom."

"Yeah. I need to psych myself up for that."

"Ladies?" Patty asked. "More ketchup?"

I grasped Amy's hand and held it up for Patty to see. "Look at what happened. My little sister. Engaged." There it was—my happiness. I guess I could muster it if I focused my attention outward. Note to self: stop thinking so much.

The sweetest off-balance smile you'd ever seen broke across Patty's face. She knocked my sister on the shoulder with her knuckle. "Look at you. Getting married. Is it the banker? The one with the tight tush?"

Crimson flushed Amy's face. "Yes. Luke. He asked last night. It was our eight-month anniversary."

"Which is why we're celebrating with pie." I was determined to hold on to this flash of happiness. I wanted to love it, give it a name, and keep it in my purse for later. "What do you want, Ames? Chocolate cream? Banana?" I looked up at Patty. "You know me. I'll have coconut."

Amy dabbed at the corners of her mouth with a paper napkin. "I don't know. I'm going to have to start thinking about fitting into a dress. Maybe french fries and a sandwich the size of my head is enough indulgence for one day."

Patty rolled her eyes. She didn't have much patience for healthy pursuits in her place of employment.

"She'll have the chocolate," I said.

"Got it. On the house. It's a big day." Patty sidled off.

"Hey, if you're worried about the apartment, don't." Amy pushed her plate aside. "Luke and I already talked about it and we'll pay my half of the rent through the end of the lease."

It hurt to know they'd already talked about my place in their new life, and that I would apparently be playing the role of difficult older sister. I needed to get used to no longer being consulted about things that involved me.

"You guys don't have to do that. I make good money." Better than good, actually. My position at the North American Color Institute paid great, thanks to a genetic gift that made me really good at my job—a one-in-a-billion anomaly called tetrachromacy. Most people saw a red rose as two or three shades of that color. But when I looked at that same rose, I saw two or three hundred colors. If I looked at something in the sunlight, the difference between hues was even more pronounced.

"It was Luke's idea, actually."

"You guys should save your money. Go on an amazing honeymoon. I'll get a roommate if I need one."

"I know you. You won't get a roommate. We're paying my half of the rent. End of discussion."

It was sort of adorable when she ended an argument with an assertion, like Dad used to when he was tired and grumpy and just wanted us to shut up so he could watch TV. Most of the time, Amy never wanted a disagreement to end. When we were little, Amy turned everything into a negotiation, some of which went on forever. Most of them had revolved around who got to be Barbie and who had to be Skipper, or who got to lick the beaters when we made brownies, but there had been big things we'd had to agree on, too. Like whether we should tell Dad that we were pretty sure Mom was cheating on him.

That topic had not been taken lightly, even though we were

ten and eight and unable to fully comprehend infidelity. We only knew it was weird that she invited a man to stay at our house whenever Dad was on a work trip. Gordon. Gordon who stayed over. Gordon who once wore our dad's bathrobe.

Hours of discussion, over the course of months, went into the decision to tell him. We ultimately made a list of pros and cons on a piece of the Hello Kitty stationery Grandma had given me for my tenth birthday. We'd been careful to consider every possible outcome. Well, almost every outcome. When you're a kid, and have a mostly happy heart, there were only so many horrible things you could imagine. We were much more inclined to believe that no matter what, everything would be okay.

To this day, I could recite every word Amy and I said to each other the final time we talked about it.

When do we tell him? When he gets back from his trip?

Yes. I'll tell him. I'm the oldest.

I could tell you what we were wearing that day—I had on a cherry red turtleneck and jeans, and Amy was wearing a celery green sweatshirt that said LOVE on it in rainbow letters. I could tell you what was playing on the radio, but not because I cherished the details. My mind refused to let go of that conversation and everything that happened over the forty-eight hours that followed. It liked to replay it all in my head, like a movie. With precision, it remembered every color.

Years later, when we were teenagers, I'd asked Amy if she remembered what we'd said to each other that day, our rationale, our thought process. Had I dreamed it? What had I overlooked?

"I was eight," she'd said. "I don't remember anything other than not wanting Mom to hear us."

I remembered that part, too.

Patty delivered our pie, two forks, and an extra stack of napkins.

"I won't live through the guilt," Amy said. "I can't give you a single reason to resent me for this."

"For what? Being happy?"

Amy scooped up a bite of whipped cream and chocolate shavings. "No. For leaving."

I stared down at the coconut cream pie, my absolute favorite dessert, and my sweet tooth refused to kick in. This was really happening. Amy and I wouldn't be together anymore. Everything was going to change, and I hadn't seen it coming. "I think I'll take this to go."

"After you made such a big deal about ordering it?"

"Yeah. Sorry. I'm swamped at work."

Amy yanked back the sleeve of her white blouse and eyed her watch. "Shit. I have to get back, too."

I settled the bill with Patty, Amy ate only half of her pie, and I tried to turn my thinking around. My bond with my sister was too important to let my temporary shock get in the way. I needed time. That was all.

Amy and I said our goodbyes out on the street, over the steady hum of traffic and car horns. It was the most beautiful fall day—the air was crisp and dry, albeit perfumed with the aroma of the hot dog cart on the corner.

"You sure you're okay?" she asked.

The sun was shining right in my eyes, and even with my sunglasses on I had to squint to see her. Something about that hint of warmth on my face, coming at me in a kaleidoscope of gold, made everything a little better. She looked like an angel in the sunlight, and in many ways, she was exactly that—a blessing. I grasped her by the shoulders to underscore what I was about to say. "I am better than okay. The person I love most in this world is getting married. It's not possible for me to be more okay."

She smiled and stepped in for a hug. "Love you, Kat."

"Love you, too."

"I'll try to be home in time for *Jeopardy*."

"Perfect."

I turned back and started the walk down to my office, while Amy went in the opposite direction. All in all, I felt pretty good for someone who'd eaten a Matzoh ball for lunch. Sure, I'd just received life-changing news, and it would take some work to keep from slipping down into the depths of worry, which was my biggest downfall. But I had to focus on the good. Amy and I would always be close. Nothing would ever take that away from us, not even a man. We had an unbreakable bond—we'd made it through the obstacle course of our childhood, together. And even though Mom wasn't around to be a part of our adulthood, I wanted to believe that she watched over us every day, her heart full of a mother's love.

And hopefully some forgiveness for me.

CHAPTER TWO

IT WASN'T fun to admit you came from poor marital stock, but it was the case with Amy and me. Our parents had taken good care of us, but they hadn't done a particularly good job at being husband and wife. Even though everything with their marriage ended with Mom, the trouble started with Dad.

You quit your job? Again?

I met this guy and he was telling me about a fantastic opportunity.

His list of seemingly unrelated professional pursuits was long—ad man, radio disc jockey, plumber. It drove Mom nuts, and understandably so, but she never even tried to exercise some patience. Never. That created tension, which only fed the feeling in our house that things were unsettled. Everything wasn't fine, even when they insisted it was. On some level, it made us feel like we couldn't truly count on either of them. Yes, there had always been food on the table and clothes on our backs, but kids see grown-ups as the barometer of familial peace. When there's open dissension, that means there's a storm brewing. In our case, Amy and I were in the calm of the eye.

Thankfully, Amy and I were nothing like Dad when it came

to our careers. We'd both managed to find our calling. She was a natural lawyer, able to argue for hours, running on nothing more than a Coke Zero and a handful of almonds. For me, I couldn't imagine doing anything other than being a color analyst, a job I was quite literally born to do.

"Hey, Katherine, can I get your help?" My boss, Summer Kimble, called out as I walked past her office, a few doors down from mine. It was after six, and everyone else had gone home for the day.

"Two secs."

Much of my day was popping into other people's offices and meetings to put out fires. I was known as the secret weapon. An art teacher discovered my quirky eyesight in high school, and with the help of her geneticist father, they reached the conclusion that I was a tetrachromat. It wasn't easy to explain, I only knew one way of seeing, but it helped me find the perfect career. During my first few weeks at NACI, it'd been a little embarrassing to be singled out for my vision, but over time, I came to appreciate how special it made me feel. Before I landed the job, I'd never felt singled out in a good way, aside from the few months I'd spent in Ireland—the only time I'd thought that maybe my parents' history had given me the wrong ideas about love.

Summer waved me into her office. "I just got the print samples for the Anthem Apparel catalog." She pushed her thick glasses up onto the bridge of her nose. "These don't look right. I don't know what happened."

I took survey of the trim, stylish women dressed in astronomically priced clothing. The catalog covers were indeed ghastly. These would not sell clothes—they'd end up straight in the recycling bin. "This isn't the paper stock they normally use." I flipped one of the samples to the blank side. "It has an ivory cast to it."

She held the paper up to the light. "Looks pure white to me."

Of course it did. She saw it as a solid field. I saw it as a mosaic of shades, and as anyone who's been to a paint store can attest, there are countless ways to convey colors. "It isn't. I'll call the printer in the morning to double-check. I can go down there if necessary."

"Thank you so much. Now I'll be able to sleep tonight." Summer sat back in her chair. She was a great boss. She never failed to express her appreciation. "Well, a little. Miles Ashby arrives tomorrow. Lord knows how that will go."

Miles Ashby was a hotshot from our UK office. He was coming to work out of the New York office for an unspecified amount of time. It was supposed to mean bigger clients and bigger accounts, but it was hard not to feel as though he was being sent to whip us all into shape. "I'm sure it'll be fine. He'll be blown away by how awesome we all are." I was sure of nothing of the sort.

"That's the spirit." Summer collected the papers on her desk. "Headed home?"

"Meeting my sister, actually. She has some big surprise planned." I'd been suspecting that tonight was a pity date, that Amy had noticed the way I got anxious every time she brought up the wedding. The truth was that things were happening very quickly. I'd assumed they'd tie the knot in a year, like normal people, but they wanted to do it in December. That was in two months. It was like they were dying to get married.

Plus, she kept dismissing my opinion of the bridesmaids' dresses, when all I'd done was point out that it wasn't fair she wanted to squash my already limited bust line into a strapless gown.

"Big surprise on a Wednesday?" Summer asked.

"There's some new Spanish place she's been raving about. Hopefully that's where we're going. I'm starving."

"Have fun."

I grabbed my purse and coat from my office, and ducked into the ladies room for a make-up refresh. There was no telling if I was dressed correctly. Amy had said to wear something cute, but as to what that meant, I wasn't sure, so I'd gone with a black turtleneck and pencil skirt, hair back in a ponytail, and my favorite knee-high boots. I'd describe it as 'quirky professor cute'.

I met Amy in front of the diner, our usual meeting spot since it was equidistant between our offices. "What's the plan?"

"You are going to love me after tonight." She clapped her hands together and grinned like she was up to no good. It was weird. It wasn't like Amy to be coy.

"I already love you." *This must be some pretty amazing paella.* "And was I supposed to wear heels? Is that what you meant by cute?"

"Remember how I told you that my firm was expanding our entertainment division to include music law?"

What exactly did this have to do with eating? Or with what she was wearing? "Can we talk about this over dinner?"

"No. Shut up. I'm trying to tell you the surprise. I'm taking you to see someone you know. Someone famous."

"I don't know anyone famous."

"Yes, you do. Eamon MacWard." She then said something about one of the attorneys in her office and tickets, but I was stuck on his name. "The show is sold out. People are scalping tickets for ridiculous amounts of money." She took my hand and led me to the street corner like I was a kid in need of a chaperone. "We're in the VIP section. Fifth row. And we have back-stage passes."

The light changed. The walk signal turned. Everyone around us proceeded to cross, including Amy. My feet, however, were stuck to the pavement.

She yanked my arm, then rounded back. "Katherine, come on."

A man bumped into us. "Watch where you're standing."

"Get your face out of your phone," Amy snapped back.

I'd known that Eamon was coming to New York. I'd have to be living under a rock to not notice his handsome face on one of the big screens in Times Square, or the way some of the women in my office had chattered about it. In fact, I'd been keenly aware of every time Eamon had played in the city over the last decade, ever since he became big enough to sell out concert halls all over the world. But I'd never gone to see him. It would've been too painful.

"What is going on?" Amy asked. "I thought you would be excited. Remember how you told me you met him in Ireland? We've never gone to see him together. I thought it would be cool."

"I thought we were eating."

"I've heard he puts on an incredible show. And he's so damn sexy. The Irish accent? Oh, my God. I could sit around and listen to him read the phone book."

"There's no such thing as a phone book. Not anymore."

"You know what I mean." She tugged on my arm again, but I didn't budge. "Come on."

I did not make a habit of keeping details from my sister. She was the one person I could tell anything, without judgment. I hadn't told her about Eamon when I returned from Ireland because she'd been stuck at home dealing with Dad while I was gallivanting in Europe. It wasn't until Eamon's first record came out that I casually mentioned I'd met him. Amy hadn't pushed me for more at the time, and I wasn't sure I could talk about him without crying. The more famous Eamon became over the years, the idea of suddenly sharing everything became exponentially more absurd.

I didn't just meet Eamon MacWard. We had a fling. A stupid hot romance where we almost never got out of bed, and when we did it wasn't for long. He made my toes curl. He wrote a song about me. Saying goodbye to him was one of the hardest things I've ever done.

"I need to tell you something," I mumbled.

"Can you tell me along the way? It's a good twenty blocks to the theater."

"Nope." I shook my head. "The closer we get to the theater, the dumber it's going to sound."

Amy dropped her head back out of exasperation. "You are officially making me insane."

"I didn't just meet him. I know him. I know him, know him."

Her eyes became so huge they threatened to swallow her button nose. "Like *sex*, know him?"

"It was a long time ago. Nobody knows. I mean *nobody*."

Amy squealed like a piglet. People turned around. "Oh, my God." She huddled up next to me and muttered in my ear. "My sister had sex with Eamon MacWard?"

The first time we did it, we were so hot for each other we didn't even use a condom. We were half-naked in his front hall. I was out of my mind.

"It's *Aim-un*. Not *Eem-un*. And shush. People will hear you."

"Sorry. *Aim-un*. And now you have to tell me everything."

I was in no way prepared to tell her this story right now—this was the sort of thing that required a comfy place to sit and at least one bottle of wine. Per person. "It was sweet and romantic. I was a kid." *Way to undersell it.*

"I want to hear everything later. Every juicy little detail."

Gleeful, she hooked her arm in mine and started walking with such force that I had no choice but to stumble along. She began to prattle on about the wedding, but I couldn't focus, not when I knew what—and who—was waiting when we arrived at the theater. Could I do this? I'd never even bothered with the question. I'd assumed the answer was no. If my vision was a one-in-a-billion fluke, Eamon MacWard was an even more rare kind of guy.

The first time I laid eyes on him, he was setting up to perform in a pub in the small town where I lived with my host family. It was a Friday. The place was packed, smoky, and loud. I managed to grab a stool at the end of the bar, with a direct view of the tiny stage in the corner. Eamon was plugging in an amp, tuning his guitar, and wrestling with a microphone cord in earnest. His thick, wavy hair, the color of warm, black coffee, fell to his shoulders. He was lanky, his legs a mile long in dark jeans. He wore scuffed work boots and a charcoal thermal, sleeves bunched at his elbows. Scruff peppered the fair skin of his square jaw. His brows were just as dark, but heavy. He was rough-hewn perfection. And I was transfixed.

I sat there sipping Guinness, unable to tear my sight from him while he nervously double-checked every little thing. I could tell he was talking to himself, which I found adorable. The tables in front of the stage were filled with people drinking and talking. They didn't notice a thing he did, which I couldn't comprehend. He was right there. And he was so worth watching. When he finished his preparations, he straightened to his full height, raised his arms and stretched, revealing a narrow sliver of his stomach. I had never been more turned on in my entire life. He caught me looking and peered back with his steely-gray eyes. Heat and embarrassment crept over me. It was like he could see inside my brain and knew exactly what I was thinking. He smiled. My whole world changed. For the first time ever, I had been glad I hadn't been prepared for something. I never would've believed it in the first place.

"Ma'am, your purse."

I looked up. The theater marquis flashed. *An evening with Eamon MacWard.*

Amy grumbled. "Katherine. She needs to inspect your bag."

The security woman radiated impatience.

"Oh, right." I scrambled to open the flap of my black leather cross-body bag, and let her rifle through my things. "Sorry."

"Next," the woman said.

We filed into the fancy lobby, walking on ruby red carpet past long tables of t-shirts, adorned with pictures of Eamon and his band. This was all too detached from the history I had with him—he was not a rock star when I knew him, although he was a star-in-waiting. I knew that much the instant I saw him in that pub.

It was such a long time ago—eleven years. Maybe seeing him perform wouldn't affect me much. I'd changed since then. Not a lot, but some. He'd probably changed a lot, so much that I wouldn't recognize him as being the same person. He'd gotten married a little less than two years after I left Ireland, which had sent me into a bit of a downward spiral at the time. He got divorced a year later, and that slightly improved my mood until I reminded myself that we were half a world away from each other, I needed to get over it, and no marital split was a good thing.

An usher showed Amy and me to our seats. My heart couldn't settle on a steady beat, behaving like a hyper puppy, saddled with too much nervous energy. I closed my eyes and took deep breaths through my nose while Amy and Luke exchanged texts that made her giggle. *It's going to be okay. It's just music. No big deal.*

When the lights went down and the crowd rose to its feet, I stood, but that one bit of upward momentum left me feeling like I was floating a few inches off the floor. His band filed on to the stage and he brought up the rear. It was just like him to arrive with little fanfare and have it met with an intense roar of screams and applause from the crowd. He waved. He smiled. And I fought to stay in the present, to not allow myself to think this was a dream.

Watching him as he strapped on his acoustic guitar and he squinted into the spotlight, I had to wonder if there was some part of him that sensed I was in the room. Were we still connected like we had been, all those years ago? My body was keenly aware of his presence—it was like I was in a tin bucket on a rolling sea, clutching the sides so hard that my fingers cramped, terrified of being tossed into the waves, even when excitement bubbled up inside my stomach. The temptation of the ride, however scary, was more fun than sitting on shore.

"Hello there," he spoke into the microphone, 'there' coming out like 'dare', his voice as rich and buttery as the best Irish short-bread. He'd said the very same thing to me that night in the pub. I was such a goner after just three syllables.

The crowed responded in kind, but I let the applause and voices fade. That wasn't what I wanted to hear. The drummer counted off the beat and the band joined in. Eamon's glorious hands stroked the neck of the guitar and strummed the strings, and it was as if his voice picked me up, lifted me straight into the air, and set me on a journey I had no idea I was so eager to take.

His music had always had a place between U2's ballads and Van Morrison's best love songs, but more sparse, which let his achingly beautiful, powerful voice take center stage. His lyrics stuck with you for days. Months. Years. Almost every song he wrote was about love or sex, with a Shakespearean slant—full of dark, romantic tragedy. Every perfect word and turn of phrase made you feel like you'd never be half as clever as him.

From the strong, upbeat songs to the gentle, acoustic ones, my heart swelled in the most familiar way, as if it had been sitting idly by over the last decade, waiting for him. I realized then that I could soak up a lifetime of his poetic thoughts and haunting voice and it still wouldn't be enough. A profound, but comfortable sadness came with that realization. As beautiful and incredible as he was, being with Eamon was like flying too close to the sun. Eventually, you'd have to steer yourself away.

Still, I was eager to hold on to every minute of his performance. I didn't want it to end, probably because it would mark a return to everyday life after a quixotic ninety minutes of escape. After two encores, time took its toll and Eamon his final bows. He walked off the stage, wiping his brow with a towel, and disappeared behind the curtains waiting in the wings.

Amy and I both collapsed into our seats. The house lights came up.

"Oh my God. That was amazing," she said.

"It was." I nodded, but it had been so much more than that. It stuck me with a cruel case of wanderlust, making me question one of the hardest choices I'd ever had to make. When I left Eamon and came back to the states, it had seemed like the sensible thing to do. He'd landed a major record deal. He had a world tour ahead. And Amy needed me—Dad had started drinking again.

"You're crying," Amy said.

I reached up to wipe my cheek. I had to prove that I wasn't, but my skin was damp with tears. "Only a little."

She looked me square in the eye. "He really meant something to you, didn't he?"

I shrugged. "It's emotional music."

"Come on, let's get backstage. I really need to pee and I'm

sure you're dying to say hi."

I grabbed her wrist as she rose from her seat. "We can't. We shouldn't. Backstage is just lame anyway, isn't it?"

"Um, no. It's not. Don't you want to see him and talk to him? Catch up?"

Catch up? I nearly burst out laughing. Nearly.

"You can tell him how much you loved his performance."

Been there, done that. The people next to us squeezed past and into the aisle. "I don't know if I can do it."

"Whatever happened between you guys was a long time ago. Water under the bridge. He probably won't even remember."

"That's so reassuring."

She grabbed my arm. The next thing I knew, I was shuffling behind her as she pushed people out of our way. "Coming through. Pregnant woman."

I didn't bother to protest since I detest crowds and her insane tactics were working, but I had to wonder if I looked like I'd put on a few pounds.

"Pregnant woman?" I whispered when we were in the hall leading backstage.

"I saw it in a movie." Amy pulled out the passes, and the security guard instructed us to put them on. My brain was running like a washing machine spin cycle, round and round.

What do I say to him?

Amy found the bathroom when we got back to the hospitality room. I followed her inside and quickly swiped away the mascara smudges under my eyes. I took about seven million cleansing breaths, avoiding my own reflection, which was just going to leave me unsettled. I straightened my skirt, my top. No cleavage to speak of, I was ill equipped for backstage. I really wished I'd worn something vaguely sexy. Damn my sister and her nebulous fashion advice.

My stomach growled, loudly, and I crossed my arms at my waist to muffle the sound. Eamon had made me forget about food tonight, event though I'd been famished. He'd had that effect on me when we were together, too. I lost my Freshman Fifteen, plus another ten. I'd needed no sustenance other than Eamon. Precisely why it felt like playing with fire to be around him.

Amy came out of the stall and washed her hands. "Ready?"

I wasn't.

Back in the hospitality room, we tried to act nonchalant and cool. There were about two dozen people in there with us, an odd mix of women trying too hard, scruffy looking rock guys, and a couple of teenagers with rolled posters and Sharpies. Not nearly enough room to hide. I still wasn't sure I had the guts to approach him. What if Amy was right and he'd forgotten me? What if I had to introduce myself? Surely I had never meant as much to him as he had meant to me.

I opened my mouth to say something mindless to Amy, and Eamon walked into the room. The chemistry of the air abruptly changed. I wasn't the only one to notice. Everyone did. The tone of voices changed, they pitched higher, and the conversations became rambling and painfully self-aware.

He was wearing the beat-up jean jacket he'd owned when I knew him. His hair was pulled back in a messy knot. He stopped to speak to a redheaded man with a fluffy beard. They smiled. They laughed. Eamon clapped him on the back. He was wearing sunglasses. Black ones, Wayfarers. It was too bad, because I'd really wanted to see his eyes up close one more time, but I understood it—rock star. He pulled it off so effortlessly, it was like everyone who'd done it before him was just copying his look.

This was all too intimidating. I couldn't approach him. Why torture myself? If I talked to him and had to explain who I was,

I'd never stop thinking about it. It would stick with me forever. I was there to remember the good times. The sexy times. There were a lot of those.

"He's coming over here." Amy rattled the words off so quickly that it came out as a single utterance. *Hescomingoverhere.*

"Would you stop grabbing my arm?"

I turned and Eamon was zeroing in on me, people in the room parting to make way. A few tried to talk to him, but his path to me was clear.

He swiped off his sunglasses and said it.

He said my name.

Right then and there.

"Katherine."

I waited for my head to hit the floor. But somehow, I didn't faint.

CHAPTER THREE

"KATHERINE."

It was like no one had ever said my name before, like he'd plucked it out of thin air. I'd forgotten the lilt of his voice when he said it. *Kah-thrin*. If I thought too hard about what it was like to have him mutter it directly into my ear, his soft breath on my neck in the middle of the night, I was going to leave backstage on a stretcher.

"Hi." *That's what you came up with? Hi?*

He pulled me into a hug, holding onto me for a few seconds. I'd also forgotten just how tall he was, probably because it was different when you were standing this close to him. He made me feel petite. I never felt petite. I took my chance and settled the side of my head against his broad chest, tentatively placing my hands in the center of his back and soaking up his body heat, all while remembering what his embrace had been like when we'd had to say goodbye. I'd drenched his shirt with tears. He'd kissed the top of my head over and over again. But he never asked me to stay. And I never asked if I could, even though I'd wanted to.

He stepped back and shook his head in disbelief. "This is

such a surprise." He sucked in his lower lip and licked it, leaving me staring at his mouth for too long. Kissing Eamon had been my hobby for four months. It was hard not to get caught up in remembrances. "How long has it been?"

I'd stopped counting at five years, four months, and eleven days. I was driving myself crazy. "At least ten years."

"Incredible. Absolutely incredible. I'm so glad you came."

Just say a few intelligent words. It doesn't have to be an Oscar acceptance speech. I shifted my weight and tried to figure out what to do with my hands. "The, uh, the show was great. Really good. Super good, actually."

"She cried," Amy added.

"Amy," I blurted.

"What?" She shrugged and smiled sweetly. "You did."

Eamon laughed. I'd forgotten what a freaking fantastic sound that was—throaty and sexy. "I'm glad you enjoyed it."

"This is my sister, Amy." I didn't add on any commentary about how she was thirty years old and still working on her manners.

"Ah, yes. I remember you talking about your sister a few times. It's nice to meet you." He shook her hand, but quickly returned his focus to me. I had to admit that it felt pretty good to be his center of attention, even if it made me nervous. "Katherine and I knew each other very well at one time." He said it to Amy, but he was looking at me, completing his statement with a bounce of his eyebrows.

"So I've heard." Amy had a far too flirtatious tone to her voice. Between that and the crying comment, I wanted to smack her.

"We need to catch up," he said. "The next show is in Boston, but we're not leaving until noon tomorrow. Come to my hotel and have a late dinner with me."

It was just like him to state his intention rather than ask a question—probably because he knew it would leave me with virtually no reason to decline.

"Yes. That is a *great* idea." Amy hitched her purse on her shoulder like she was ready to bolt. Who knew she was such an eager wingman? "You two catch up. I'll head home."

But I knew exactly where dinner and a hotel led...straight into his bed. As tempting as the idea was, as much as the women standing behind me, who were now clearly eavesdropping, would probably kill for the same opportunity, it wasn't a good choice. A night with Eamon would punch a gaping hole in my psyche. It would leave me longing for a life that wasn't wedged firmly enough in reality. "That would be really nice, but Amy and I are having Girls' Night. And I have a big day at the office tomorrow."

Amy swatted my thigh with the back of her hand.

He nodded, breaking me down with nothing more than a look. There was a softness in his eyes that made it feel like my legs were asleep. "Coffee then? In the morning."

His determination made me feel so damn good. It made me tingle. My body hummed. "I seem to remember you don't like to get up in the morning."

"I don't. I hate it. But I will for you." He reached for my hand, taking my fingers and wrapping them up in a familiar, calloused warmth. "It's true. I'll give up the little sleep I get for you. I owe you that much."

Damn him. That was about the sweetest thing he could've possibly said. "Eamon. You don't owe me anything."

A smile played at the corner of his lips. "Now you've done it. You said my name. You have to come to coffee tomorrow. I won't take no for an answer."

My face flushed with an odd mix of accomplishment and embarrassment. "Okay. Fine. Coffee. There's a diner not far from my office."

"I'm sure it makes me sound like a bloody spanner, but too many people."

Oh, right. Rock star. "It's pretty easy to be anonymous in New York."

"I know. But I want to talk. I want to hear your voice. I don't want to deal with interruptions."

Interruptions? What would we be doing that could possibly be interrupted?

"My hotel," he continued. "I'll have everything waiting when you arrive. Does eight work? Should give us enough time." He gave my hand a gentle squeeze.

I nodded in agreement, but that last thing he said was going to keep me up all night. Enough time for what? "Sure. Okay."

"Perfect." He pulled his cellphone out of his back pocket. "Give me your number. I'll text you the hotel info."

I rattled off the digits, probably a bit too eagerly. "I'll wait to hear from you."

"I'll send it when I'm done chatting and signing autographs." He still had my hand, and he used it to pull me close one more time, although he didn't have to try hard. He softly kissed my cheek. His stubble scratched my skin. It was the most glorious feeling.

"See you tomorrow."

"Nice to meet you, Eamon." Amy did that eye-bugging thing at me, and we high-tailed it out of there, back through the theater lobby and out onto the street.

The night air was bone cold, the sort of evening where you can't help but walk with your shoulders up around your ears. Amy put on her coat right away, but I decided I'd wait for a block or two. I needed to sober up and cool down.

"That was pretty intense, Kat."

"Which part?"

"The whole thing. The show. Meeting him. The revelation

that my sister who tells me everything had a thing with an actual rock star."

A breathy laugh crossed my lips as we stopped at the corner for the signal. "See how stupid that sounds? That's why I didn't tell you."

"I will always believe you. You know that."

The light changed and we marched through the crosswalk.

"But now you have to tell me something about you guys together. To make up for keeping the secret from me."

I'd known this was coming, but I was still getting used to the idea of sharing this secret. It was going to have to come out in a trickle at first. "One of his songs is about me."

She came to a dead stop and socked me in the arm. "Shut up. Which one?"

I laughed, for real this time, finally succumbing to the cold and putting on my coat. "Do you know *Sunny Girl?* He didn't play it tonight." I was relieved he hadn't. A few tears were one thing. That song might end with me in a puddle of my own emotion.

"*Straw blonde hair and a smile that never dies?* That's supposed to be you?"

Everything that had been funny a moment ago was now heavy with irony. Of course my sister didn't see me as *Sunny Girl.* No one but Eamon ever had. "Believe it or not, yes."

"Wow." She shook her head. "My sister is *Sunny Girl.*"

"Yeah, well, *Gloom and Doom Girl* doesn't have the same ring to it."

"Funny. That's funny. I feel like I'm seeing you in a whole new light."

"I was different with Eamon. I don't know how else to say it."

She nodded. We slowed our pace, even though it was cold. It was like neither one of us wanted the night to end, which was a little silly since we lived together, but I didn't say anything. I knew she'd text Luke the minute we got home and that would be the end of the conversation.

"Didn't you feel different when you left home and went to college?" I asked. "I know I did."

Going off to school had been a difficult decision for me. I'd spent eight years taking care of my dad and sister. It made me feel guilty to leave and not just because I wouldn't be there to make dinner or do the laundry. The truth was that I'd formulated my escape, starting the day the high school guidance counselor spoke to us about planning for college. She gave a talk about good grades, scholarships, and study abroad. She spoke of independence and getting away. That was all I'd needed to hear. From that moment, I hit the books, but never told a soul why I was studying so hard. There was no money to send me to college. If I wanted out, and I had, I knew I was going to have to work my way there.

"Yeah. I felt different," Amy said. "It was nice to be out of Chester, that's for sure."

"Exactly. I was just glad I didn't have to be one of the poor Fuller girls anymore. I could just be Katherine Fuller, Co-ed."

"Or Katherine Fuller, rock star groupie."

"He wasn't a rock star then. Not even close."

"That's hard to imagine."

"Seriously. We had no money. He worked part time as a carpenter just so he could pay for his flat, but otherwise he spent all of his time writing music and trying to get a record deal."

We walked for nearly an entire cross-town block in silence before she asked the question, "He doesn't know, does he?"

Amy didn't have to say that she was talking about Mom and the accident. "No. He doesn't." I was in high school when I'd stopped telling anyone about it. I couldn't keep reliving it, and everyone always wanted the gruesome details.

"Yeah. I still haven't told Luke. There's never a good time to bring it up."

I could relate, although with Eamon, it'd been a case of not wanting to ruin something perfect. Being with him was like waking up each morning to a blanket of fresh snow on the ground. A single footstep would destroy all that beauty.

"Right. There's never a good time." Another convenient excuse was that Eamon and I had spent such a huge percentage of our time together making love. And fucking. Those were two separate activities with him, which was part of the allure. Sometimes he'd seduce me for an entire day, with sweet smiles and soft kisses at the corner of my mouth. After hours of getting me worked up, he'd take my hand and lead me to his bedroom. A master of the slow burn, he'd caress my stomach, glaze his mouth over my breasts, and take strokes that were slow and deep, all while he burrowed into my soul with his gaze.

Then there were times when we'd be mid-conversation, making dinner or at the pub for a pint, and he'd wrap his arms around my waist and tell me he wanted me so bad he couldn't think straight. He fucked me on the kitchen table. Two or three times. We did it in a pub bathroom once, standing, while he held the door closed with his hand. There was no explaining the physics we'd used to make it happen.

"Oh. We're on Madison," Amy said when we got to the corner. "Let's walk this way. I want to show you something in the Vera Wang window."

"That's out of our way. Can we do it this weekend, during the day, when it's not so cold?"

Amy started across the street. "It'll take five minutes. Come on."

I did my sisterly duty and followed, but I wasn't thrilled with the change in subject. Everything these days circled back to the wedding.

When we were a few hundred yards from the Vera Wang storefront, Amy's feet began to carry her faster. "This. This is what I wanted to show you. What do you think?" She tapped the window as I caught up. On the other side of the glass, a faceless mannequin wore an exquisite white gown, with the perfect amount of poof in the skirt and just a hint of sparkle, like something Cinderella would wear. It wasn't an exact match for the dress our mom had worn, the one we'd only seen in photographs, but it wasn't far off.

I started to cry, silent and slow, my tears nearly freezing on my cheeks. My first thought of weddings was always the framed portrait of our parents that had hung on the living room wall at home. When I was five or six and I wanted to be a princess, our mom was a shining example. When I was seven or eight, it became the only evidence that our parents belonged together. Our mom was radiant. Dad looked so handsome in his tux. More than anything, they were a visual representation of true love. They gazed into each other's eyes like nothing else, and certainly *no one else*, mattered. It was impossible to imagine that they would end up the way they did.

Even today, if someone were to ask my opinion of the way marriage should be, I would want to have that photograph so I could say, "This is what marriage should look like. Two people who love each other more than anything. You stay together. Forever." But it wasn't so easy to point to the portrait anymore. My dad took it off the living room wall a week after my mom passed away, and banished it to the back of the coat closet.

"What do you think?" Amy asked. "Too much?"

I shook my head, my sights swinging back and forth between her and the dress. I choked back tears that could only be described as coming from a place of mourning *and* happiness. "It's perfect. You'll look amazing in it."

"It's so expensive."

"So? You should have the perfect dress. This is the perfect dress. I'll chip in if you need help paying for it." I never would have thought so a week ago, but I wanted that dress for her more than anything.

Amy cocked her head. "Are you feeling okay?"

I nodded eagerly. "Yes. I'm just emotional. Seeing the dress. Thinking about the wedding." It was really happening. And I had to stop holding my breath. "It's going to be such an amazing day and you're going to be the most beautiful bride ever."

"God, I really hope so. I have such a hard time picturing it."

"That's what bridal magazines are for. We'll figure it out."

For as many times as our aunts, uncles, and grandparents had been married, Amy and I hadn't been to many weddings as kids. Most of them took place in far-off, exotic locales like Illinois and our parents never wanted to drive that far. We did go to our Aunt Lucy's weddings, since she lived only a half hour away. Our Mom's sister, she has had five husbands, which always astounded me. How do you find five people to spend your entire life with? Even by the fifth husband, she was still having formal portraits taken. She just recycled the frame. I'd once made a joke that it was like walking past a movie theater, since you never knew who would be in that frame the next time you came to visit. I was never Aunt Lucy's favorite.

My phone buzzed with a text and I jumped. It was like the sound was plugged into my heart, like jumper cables on a car battery.

"It must be Eamon," Amy said, sounding frantic. "Read it, read it."

"Hold your horses." I fumbled with the buckle on my bag, and slipped my cell out of its hiding place.

Four Seasons, Rm 4908. Can't wait. XXX

Never before had a text made me so excited. Or sick to my stomach.

Amy craned her neck to see the screen. "Triple-x? Is that some sort of sex code between you two?"

I rolled my eyes, but it wasn't that absurd an idea knowing Eamon and me. "No. It's like kiss, hug. Except it's kiss, kiss, kiss."

"What are you going to wear for your coffee date?"

"It's not a date."

"It's a date. He was not about to take no for an answer."

Oh, crap. "I have no clue. You have to help me figure it out."

"Of course. Even if it takes all night."

CHAPTER FOUR

JEANS. After an hour of trying on clothes last night, Amy and I had arrived at jeans.

"You sure I shouldn't wear a skirt?" I asked as I tugged on my black wool coat and buttoned it up.

Amy rolled her eyes and jabbed the button on the Keurig to brew another cup. "I'm officially tired of talking about this. Your ass looks amazing in those jeans. Especially with the boots. End of discussion."

The boots had been my next question. Even with heels on, he'd still tower over me, but it would be less exaggerated, and I loved the way I felt small when I was with him. The advantages Eamon had were too numerous to count, but I didn't begrudge him a single one. "You sure they don't make me look like I'm trying too hard?"

"He's used to women trying. He probably won't even notice."

Too much of this made it difficult to swallow. The idea of trying, the idea of him not noticing, the idea that he was practically a different person now. I wasn't sure I was truly entitled to share the same air anymore. It wasn't that I was preoccupied with his fame, it simply felt like confirmation from the universe that he and I were not from the same galaxy. "I'm nervous." I had hoped it would make me less anxious if I said it out loud. Now it was worse. Every skittish cell in my body had completed mitosis and split into two.

"Yeah. I bet. I would be, too."

Gee, thanks.

Amy leaned back against the counter, still in her PJs, the nice ones from Garnet Hill with a colorful print of tiny Japanese fans. I was more of a sweatshirt and undies kind of girl. "I guess my question is, what exactly are you so worried about? What are you hoping to get out of this little exercise?"

I had no idea. It was the strangest feeling, being petrified by something you desperately wanted to do. I needed to see him and be alone with him, even when it brought back the butterflies. Mine weren't just regular butterflies, either. They breathed fire.

But what did I want to have happen? I'd thought a few hundreds times last night about what it would be like to have s-e-x with Eamon again. And was that what he wanted? Just an extra-hot trip down memory lane and nothing else? Or was there something important he wanted to say to me?

"Honestly, I don't know. I'm just going to go with it," I said.

"You. You're going to just go with it? You haven't thought about what you'll do if he kisses you? What if you feel like kissing him? I mean, you told me how amazing it was when you two were together, but you didn't say if you wanted him in your life again."

I wanted to laugh. That wasn't really one of my choices, was it? It wasn't even that I'd blown it with Eamon all those years ago. It had mostly felt inevitable. He and I were never meant to be together, and I didn't think we were capable of being just friends. That left us where we'd been before last night—two people walking the planet who managed to bump into each other, connected by a few hundred things we'd done together. It was a tenuous connection, those memories like the exhaust left behind by a spent tank of gas, or in our case, rocket fuel.

I stood there and stared at Amy, wondering how she always got me looking at things in a different way. Maybe it was the lawyer thing, turning an argument on its head. It was beneficial though, since I was chronically guilty of putting on blinders. She and I had only a few more weeks of these morning meetings of the mind. She'd be gone soon and I'd be forced to internalize my neurotic thoughts, and even worse, try to sort them out on my own. We would undoubtedly still talk every day, but it wouldn't be the same. It would be the way it was when I went to college, when the days and weeks apart started to dull the brightness of our sisterly bond.

"I have absolutely no idea whether I want him in my life again, but I'm sure he's just being nice. He probably doesn't run into old friends very often, especially not in the U.S." I popped up onto my toes and pressed my lips together. "I guess I should get going, huh?"

"Take a cab. Nobody walks up to the Four Seasons," Amy added as I reached for the doorknob.

I almost always did everything Amy told me to do, so I hailed a taxi out on the street. It made me feel more prepared, but as soon as my driver pulled up in front of the hotel, I learned the real truth. Nobody takes a cab to the Four Seasons. Everyone takes a limo, or at the very least a town car.

I climbed out and the doorman smiled at me thinly, like he knew I didn't belong there. Part of me wanted to pretend like he should know who I was, but I said thank you and shuffled through the revolving door. I pulled out my phone one last time to look at the text Eamon had sent last night. I'd be lying if I said

I hadn't read it a few dozen times. I'd be lying if I said it didn't make me nervous as hell.

I walked tall through the lobby, wearing my sunglasses. I didn't want to get stopped by security and have to explain that I was there to see Eamon. They probably wouldn't even let me explain. Between the cab and being there to see a rock star, I'd get shown the back door, where the bellmen took smoke breaks and homeless guys napped. Luckily, no one said a peep and I safely reached the elevator. Up I went, but when I arrived on his floor, it was only 7:58. I didn't want to be early, so I took half steps, like I was a teenager tiptoeing past her parents' bedroom in the middle of the night. One door away, I came to a full stop and waited for my phone to tick over to 8:00. I knocked. It was a heavy sound, definitive and final.

The door opened and Eamon poked his head out from behind it. "You're here."

"I am." I was just as amazed as he was.

He let me in and closed the door behind me. I then absorbed his state of dress. I wasn't sure what I'd expected Eamon to be wearing when he answered the door, but I had assumed clothes.

Nope.

"So sorry." His voice was sweet and breathless, and he was all smiles and bare skin, clutching a fluffy white towel at his waist. A nice towel, the kind you only get at an expensive hotel. His hair was dripping wet, depositing droplets of water on his shoulders and chest. I knew every contour of his trim torso, not an ounce of body fat, right down to that narrow trail of hair leading beneath his towel. It was a miracle I didn't attack him right there. "I slept through my alarm."

And I'm painfully punctual. "No worries." I laughed it off, wanting to be carefree Katherine, whoever in the hell she was.

"Come on in." He led the way, which left me to study his broad back and the way it narrowed to his waist, the way the towel hung loosely at his hips. Our coffee date might end up leaving a bigger scar than I'd anticipated. But that was Eamon—beautifully dangerous without trying at all.

His room was the uncommon meeting of pure luxury and a musician who wasn't keen on picking up after himself. Last night's clothes were in a pile next to the rumpled bed. I was foolishly relieved to see that only one side of the bed had been slept in. We hadn't really talked much last night, and I had no idea what the current state of his life was, let alone his love life. He could've had a girlfriend on the road with him and I never would've known. But he didn't. And I was stupid happy about it.

"So sorry. I really should've tidied up before you came." He began plucking clothes from the floor while tugging back the duvet, still holding up the towel, his hair hanging heavy with moisture.

"Eamon. Eamon. It's okay. You don't have to make things nice for me." I made the mistake of grabbing his arm, the one holding up the towel no less. We were mere inches from each other, nothing but white terrycloth and jeans between us. It took real, concerted effort not to touch more of him, not to rise on my tiptoes and kiss him, lean into his bare chest and let his wet hair brush the sides of my face. It took an iron will.

"I want it to be nice for you. And I'm pissed at myself for sleeping late."

I shook my head and let go of him, as hard as that was. "You worked your ass off last night. I'm surprised you can open your eyes before noon."

"You mean that? Did you really like the show? I couldn't tell last night. To be honest, I couldn't sleep because of it. I kept wondering if you were just being nice."

Oh, good God. Nice? "Eamon. I'm almost never nice. The show was unbelievable and incredible. Truly." I sucked in a deep breath, looking up into those cool gray eyes of his. Just watching the flutter of his long lashes as he blinked was so surreal. I was being pulled between two worlds—the past and the present. We could've easily been standing in the bedroom back in Ireland, talking about his show at the pub last night. He was ridiculously talented, but there was a very real part of him that questioned himself. It wasn't an act. He wasn't digging for compliments.

He smiled. "It only takes a few words from you and I feel better."

Knowing I still had the power to reassure him was almost too much to comprehend. Who had been reassuring him all these years? Or had he just forged ahead, feeling uncertain after every step? "Good. I'm glad. Because you should never feel badly about your music or your ability to put on an amazing show."

He shook his head. "I've had some bad stretches over the years. You just weren't around for it." His voice was rich with disappointment.

The air in the room went dead for a moment. *I wasn't around for it.* Had I let him down? I'd always felt like I'd let him off the hook.

He cleared his throat and looked down at his own bare stomach. "I should probably get dressed. In the bath, I suppose."

"Right. The bathroom." I was stuck with that feeling of wanting something desperately and knowing that what I craved was bad for me, if only because losing it made you feel hollowed out. Still, I wanted him to cup the sides of my face, dig his fingers into my hair, and kiss me. I wanted him to let the towel drop to the floor and I wanted him to want me naked. I wanted him to throw me down on the messy side of the bed and be reckless. I wanted him to weigh me down and let me feel him. Make me unravel around him and then roll me on to my stomach on the tidy side of the bed and do it again, this time from behind, with his arm curled under my belly, pulling my hips into his.

I wanted him to ruin me.

A knock came at the door. "That'd be room service," he said.

"I'll get it. You get dressed. You don't want to answer the door half-naked."

"Not that I haven't done it before." He laughed and disappeared into the bathroom, quietly shutting the door behind him.

I let in a young man with the name Edward embroidered on his uniform. He smiled, but was all business, charging into the room with the clunky cart. He earnestly began setting out plates, glasses of juice, a carafe of coffee, napkins and utensils on a table in a corner seating area. Leave it to Eamon to order way too much food for two people.

Edward turned and presented me with the leather folio. "Ms. MacWard? If you'll sign, I'll be on my way."

I looked at him, dumbstruck, then realized Eamon was standing there watching the exchange. He'd put on dark jeans and a plaid flannel shirt, but he'd only fastened one button so far and I was so close to blurting that he really shouldn't bother with the rest.

"I'll take that," Eamon said, signing the check and letting Edward know with a nod that he should clear out. "Right then. Breakfast. I don't know about you, but I could bloody use some coffee."

We sat in comfortable upholstered chairs and I watched as he filled the white room service mugs. This was so normal, it was still hard to wrap my head around. He reached for the tiny pitcher of cream, adding the just-right amount before handing me my cup. The coffee was delicious and hot, which seemed apropos considering the person who'd served it to me.

"I enjoyed meeting your sister last night. She's funny."

"Funny strange or funny ha-ha?"

"Humorous. She seems to enjoy embarrassing you." A few strands of his hair fell across his forehead as he removed the metal cloche from the plate before me. He knocked it back with a flick of his head.

"It's practically her hobby, but we've been close since we were kids. It just goes with the territory."

"What does she do?"

"She's a lawyer. And she's getting married in December. That's like a full time job right now. Or at least a preoccupation." I picked up a piece of toast and took a small bite, still feeling nervous and on edge.

"Good for her. And what are you doing for work these days?"

This. This I could talk about. "Do you remember when I told you about my eyesight?"

His face lit up with recognition as he scooted forward on the edge of his seat and tucked into his eggs. "Oh, right. Tetra something. The colors."

"Tetrachromacy."

"That's the word."

"Well, as it turns out, there's an actual use for it. I work as a color expert at the North American Color Institute. We consult with companies on product development, advertising, and marketing." It always sounded so dull, but I had no idea how to make it sound interesting. I only knew that it was. To me at least. "And what about you? How's the career stuff going?"

He let loose a heavy sigh. "It could be better, honestly."

"What? The house was packed last night and the crowd loved you."

"The last record did not do well. It sold about half of what the record before it did. So the pressure is on, you know? I need to write another hit." He dropped his fork for the sake of making air quotes. "I go into the studio in January. Upstate New York. We'll see. Hoping I can turn it around."

"I'm sure you'll do great. You always do."

He studied my face, making the creases between his eyes more prominent, then wiped his mouth with the napkin. "Maybe I need a change of scenery. I'd do anything to climb inside your head and see the world the way you see it."

"I don't know what to tell you. I can't really explain it. The world looks the way it looks to me. It's no more beautiful or ugly to me than it is to you."

"Somehow I doubt that's true."

"I could say the same thing about you. Writing music is mind-boggling to me. I could never do that. You put sounds into a pleasant arrangement and tell stories over the top of it. It's magic. I could never make beautiful things with words."

He took a sip of his coffee and shot me that disarming Eamon look, leaving me ready to surrender. "You make beautiful things with words every time you speak to me."

The heat rose in my cheeks the way an electric burner glows red. Forget temptation or desire, I needed him. He was pulling my very being straight out of the center of my chest. "I worry you think too much of me."

He shook his head. "Not possible. You've always had my number. You knew that from the moment we laid eyes on each other."

Once again, the air around us stood perfectly still. It still seemed impossible that I had his number the way he had mine. "It was a special time, wasn't it?" My voice was only slightly more than a whisper. The new direction of our conversation was peeling back the layers of my shroud.

"It wasn't the time. It was us. I knew that as soon as I saw you last night. I had wondered a million times if I'd built it all up in my head, but I knew last night that I hadn't." He pressed his lips together and choked back a quiet laugh. "Well, I didn't know it fully last night. We only got to talk. We'd need to do some other things before I could say with certainty that the magic is still there."

It was like a sprinkle of fairy dust fell on me. Magic wasn't quite the right word, but it was close. Add in some kismet and fate and alchemy. "We'll always have a connection. You can't undo what happened between us." That was exactly what I'd been feeling last night. There was an invisible tether between us, now pulling on me again. Maybe even pulling on him.

"Which is why I asked you to breakfast. I couldn't just see you last night and let you go." He nodded as if he needed to confirm this to himself. "I've made a lot of mistakes over the years and I'm not getting any younger."

"Don't be silly. You turned forty this year, didn't you? Don't tell me you subscribe to that bullshit about getting old. Forty is not old."

"It's not about the number. It's about the minutes I spent walking this earth without the one person I always felt understood me. Plus, there's no escaping the fact that you and I knew each other before I was anything to anyone. That means a lot. I know that what we had was real."

My brain was reeling so hard it was like I'd been kicked in the head. Looking into his eyes didn't help me decipher any of it. It only left me that much more vulnerable. "What are you saying?"

"I want us to know each other again, Katherine. For real. Like last time."

I must've blinked one hundred times in the span of ten seconds. "Really?" I knew how horrible it sounded as soon as it left my lips. "I'm sorry. I mean, really? Then why didn't you look for me? Ever." It wasn't like I'd been hard to find over the last eleven years. And he had means that I didn't. Didn't people hire private investigators? He could've at least spent twenty minutes with Google.

"Because I'm guilty of being a hopeless romantic. I always wanted fate to bring us together."

From any other man, this could have sounded sappy, but he was sincere. I could hear it in his voice. "Well, here I am. And there you are."

"I know."

I had a detail perched on my lips, but I wasn't sure I should share it with him. Call it embarrassment. Or maybe it was something else. "I wrote you a letter, you know."

His eyebrows drew together, forming a crease between his eyes. "You did? When?"

"A year after I left Ireland. I just..." Words were whizzing through my head. Some felt they were the most important and others were scrambling to hide. Loneliness and desperation were the strongest, drowning out everything else. "I missed you."

"I missed you, too. But I never got it. The letter." He cleared his throat and dropped his elbows down onto his knees, combing his fingers through his hair. "Damn. I never got it. That was right around when things started to get crazy for me."

"Your first big hit."

"Yeah. I wasn't even home that much. I, uh, I had someone dealing with my mail at that point. There was a lot of it. Bags and bags some days."

So that was what happened to it. My profound longing for him had landed in a pile of what were probably similarly worded sentiments—*I love you, Eamon. You're so amazing.* "I'm sure it was overwhelming. It must've got stuck in with the rest of your fan mail. Or maybe it got lost." I was feeling more pathetic about this with every word. Whoever had read that letter had probably seen it and thought I was some lovesick teenage girl.

"It's really hard to know what happened. But damn, I wish I'd gotten that. What did it say?"

I scrunched up my lips, wondering exactly how truthful I should be right now. So much time had passed. It didn't matter now, did it? However much it had hurt me at the time to write that letter and get zero response. Here he was, saying to me that he wanted to try to recapture what we'd had, but what did that even mean? Fate had always seemed more hell-bent on keeping us apart. "Just that I missed you and hoped you were doing well and were happy. That's all I really wanted for you. For you to be happy." Tears stung my eyes, emotion jamming up my throat.

He shook his head in disbelief. "That could've changed a lot of things. It could've changed my whole life, really. I got married eighteen months after you left."

"Yeah. I know. It was all over the newsstands here."

"And my daughter was born soon after."

"Fiona, right?"

His face lit up in a way I'd never seen before. "She's brilliant. Absolutely the best thing that ever happened to me." Eamon gathered his napkin in his hand and set it down on the table. "I'm sorry about the letter, Katherine. I don't know what else to say about it."

I waved it off. "Don't beat yourself up over it. It can't be undone now. Let's just focus on the future." Had I really said that? Me?

He smiled wide. "Yes. I want that more than anything." He gathered his napkin in his hand and placed it on the table. "But here's where it gets tricky. I thought about this for a long time last night. About what I was going to say today. I can only do this if you want it, too. If this isn't something you're really, truly willing to explore, I can't do it. I mean really try. Heart, eyes, and mind open."

I sucked in a deep breath, feeling my own shoulders fold up

around my ears. You know those moments when you have to ask yourself what you truly want? And the answer always seems just out of reach? This was one of those moments.

"Of course, my thought process was different last night," he continued. "I didn't know about the letter then. I'd always thought you'd just left and forgotten about me."

"I thought the same thing." The sense of loss was profound right now. It felt like a weight on my heart that might never go away.

He rose from his seat, leaned down and planted his palm flat against the side of my neck. His thumb rested in the indentation before my ear, fingers curled at my nape. "I never stopped wanting you, Katherine. I never stopped wanting this." His eyelids were heavy, and I knew exactly what that meant. A single glance at his lips and I could feel how soft they were before they landed on mine.

I wasn't prepared, however, for the way we both so fully surrendered to the kiss. His lips were like heaven, and I'd been away from them for far too long. I craned my neck and dropped my napkin to have more of him, clutching his shoulders and pulling him down. He dropped to his knees and we drove our shoulders into each other—the opposite of a tug of war, like we were trying to see if one of us could possibly get closer. He angled his head and took the kiss deeper. We weren't just hungry for each other. We were starving. Like neither of us had eaten. Ever. For a moment I was back in Ireland, young and feeling free. For a moment, I felt like me.

We wrenched our lips apart as if we'd been glued together. Our foreheads rested against each other, both of us breathless and restless. Dazed. I would've kept my eyes closed forever and just relived that feeling if I didn't want to see the things his face could tell me.

"After that kiss, I'd be an idiot if I said I didn't want to explore this." I had to lighten the mood. It was my defense mechanism. My impulse when I was overwhelmed.

Eamon laughed quietly and dropped back, sitting on his heels. "I'd do anything to take you in that bed right now."

So do it. "I'd be lying if I said I didn't want you to." I bit down on my lower lip, hard, just to tell myself that this was really happening. My breath picked up again. My pulse throbbed in my throat.

He shook his head, his hands gathered in his lap almost as if he was praying. "I can't do it. This second chance means too much to me. I feel like it'll ruin everything if we sleep together."

I supposed somebody had to be the responsible adult in the room, but it was still a total letdown. "So now what?"

"Finish breakfast and I send you on your way. You have my number. If you want this, you call me. And if you don't, then don't."

"Well, why wouldn't I want it?" Was there something he wasn't telling me?

"I don't know the circumstances of your life, Katherine. I want this, but I can't barge in and tell you I think we should pick up where we were a decade ago. Call me if you're serious. We'll spend a few weeks talking on the phone, getting reacquainted, and I'll see you when I come back to New York. By that point, we should have a pretty good idea of whether or not this will work. And if not, at least we had the chance to reconnect."

"That's it?"

He nodded emphatically. "That's it. I don't want to mess with fate."

CHAPTER FIVE

BELIEVE IT OR NOT, I actually managed to go to work after I left Eamon at the Four Seasons. I wasn't much use though, which was not good since Miles Ashby, the UK's golden boy, had arrived. Unfortunately, Miles was just as arrogant as his reputation and name suggested. I hadn't had any direct contact with him yet: I just stood in the conference room while he, his starched shirt, and his head of non-moving hair talked about us coming together as a team and hitting home runs and every other bad sports analogy you could imagine. It was all a bit ridiculous. Mr. Ashby didn't look as though he'd played a sport in all his life.

Afterward, I returned to my office and tried to get lost in some of my projects, but I was too stuck on everything Eamon had said about trying and being serious. Had that really happened to me? Had he really said those things? Even more important, had he meant them? Right now, there were far more questions than answers.

I got home around six, and Amy came barging through our door a half hour later. She kicked it shut behind her, tossed her bag and keys on the chair, and bugged her baby blues at me. "So? Eamon? What happened?"

I'd had a good eight hours to process the breakfast date, and I still wasn't totally sure. I swallowed a sip of my wine and set my glass on the coffee table, deciding it was best to start small. "It was great."

"That text you sent me was the worst, by the way. Had a good time? What does that even mean?"

"What was I supposed to say? And you were at work. I didn't want to bother you. You're always giving me shit when I send you long, rambling texts."

"For this, I would've cut you some slack." She planted herself on the couch next to me and flipped her pumps from her feet. They tumbled under the coffee table. "So, again. Tell me. What happened? How was it?" She nearly went full-on chin-hands with me. I had to admit I loved the chance to gossip with her, but this was so personal, it felt too raw to gush and squeal. A lot had happened. Heavy stuff of consequence.

"It was great. But strange. But also awesome. What do you want to know? The highlights?"

"The sex lights."

"There was no sex. But there was a kiss." Was there ever. Hours later and my lips were still asking me what the hell happened. "And he answered the door wearing a towel."

"Get out." She crossed her legs and started bobbing her foot. "You are such a lucky bitch."

"I know. I don't even know what I did to deserve it." How did it feel to suddenly talk about a secret as if it had always been public knowledge? Whatever it was, that was what talking to Amy felt like. Eamon had gone from hiding in the recesses of my mind to being fully out in the open.

"A kiss? On the lips? How was it?"

"Yes, on the lips. I wouldn't call it a kiss if it was on the forehead. I'd call it a peck or I wouldn't even mention it."

"If he kissed me on the forehead, I'd call it a kiss. I'd tell all of my friends that Eamon MacWard kissed me on the face."

"Nobody says that. The cheek, yes. The forehead, the nose. Nobody says 'the face'."

"You're stalling. Just tell me."

I sucked in a deep breath. Of course I was stalling. So I told her everything...the towel...the room...and although I didn't tell her every last word he'd said, I did tell her some things.

"Why didn't he ever look for you?" she asked.

"He said he was waiting for fate to bring me back."

Amy closed her eyes and flopped back on the couch. "Oh my God. I'm going to die of romanticism. He said that? I would literally pass out."

The detail of the letter was still bothering me. It was impossible not to wonder how things would've been different if he'd seen it. And that left me with one indisputable fact: I'd reached out to him and he had not done the same for me. "He did. He said that. So, anyway, he, um..." I took a gulp of my wine, not the way you're supposed to drink it. It not only didn't have time to wash over my palate, I'm pretty sure I skipped the tasting part altogether. "Do you want some?"

"Yes. I can't believe you waited this long to offer it to me." She hopped up from the couch, plucked a glass from the rack above the kitchen peninsula, and was back in three seconds flat. She finished off the bottle with a generous pour. "He what? He went down on you? You said there were no sex lights."

"You need to get your brain out of the gutter."

"Hey. I've been practicing law all day. Just tell me." She rounded the coffee table and sat again, tucking one leg under the other.

"He said that he wanted to try again."

"Katherine..." Amy's face was frozen in this bizarre state of poetic wonderment, like we were in a Hallmark commercial. She was completely silent, she didn't move at all, as if she'd decided we should mark this moment with entirely too much stillness. "That's so amazing."

"Is it though? Is it really? Maybe it's better if we let sleeping dogs lie. What if it's a big disaster? There was something nice about the way we parted the first time. Nobody was mad. Nobody was throwing things or slamming doors. We were just sad."

"Just profoundly sad?"

I nodded as if I thought that was a good thing, even knowing I'd ended up with an emotional hangover for years. Eamon had left his mark on me. There was no undoing that. "Yeah. It was."

"I don't know how you could be happier with sad than with angry."

"I wasn't. I'm not." Was I? Was I happier with unhappiness? Or had it become my default setting, so that was the comfortable place?

"Where did you two leave it today?"

"He said the ball is in my court. He's going to wait for me to call him. He doesn't want to do it if I'm not serious about it."

"Wow."

"I know. It's such a guy thing to say."

She shook her head and blew a disgruntled exhale from her lips. "I swear, sometimes you are so dumb I want to have you tested."

"What? It feels like he's putting it off on me and I don't know how I feel about that. Like how serious can I commit to being? All that time apart from each other and now we've spent a grand total of an hour together. Does that mean anything?"

"So you want to let what might end up being the love of

your life walk away without trying?"

"You make it sound so idiotic."

"Because it is." She took my hand, and directed her gaze at my fingers. She washed her thumb back and forth across my knuckles. It was hard not to notice what was different about this scenario—her big, fat honking ring. "Look. I get it. If anybody gets it, I do. What you and I went through was not normal. What Mom and Dad went through was not normal. All of it has messed with our heads, especially when it comes to relationships. But at some point, you have to look past it."

"I thought you were going to say I have to let it go. Everything with Mom."

Amy released my hand and reached over to the coffee table for her glass. "I've decided that letting it go is unrealistic. It's always going to be there. And acting like the cheating and the accident didn't happen is a mistake. All we can do is try to see what's on the other side of that. It will never go away."

Maybe that was my problem—I was still clinging to this irrational hope that someday, it would all suddenly become okay and acceptance would sink in. Or maybe I was hoping that someone would tell me I'd imagined the whole thing. There were parts of that day, things that were said that still hadn't come to light, one thing in particular that I hadn't shared with anyone. It was still locked away inside my head, the things Mom had said. I suspected that continuing to hold on to them might be part of the reason I had such a hard time moving forward, but the secrets from that day were not easily shared. People would get hurt. And all these years later, I was still wrestling with whether it was all true, or just angry words from a mom who felt betrayed by her oldest daughter. Her baby. "I guess I see what you're saying."

"At some point, I had to realize that Luke wasn't trying to trick me or hurt me or torture me. He was just trying to love me.

He wanted to be with me. And that it's okay for me to say yes to that. It was okay to let it be as simple as that."

"And you think I should do that with Eamon."

"I think you'll regret it forever if you don't."

I slumped back on the couch and rested my hands on my belly. "I guess I have a lot to think about, huh?"

"I still can't believe you never told me about him. I always thought that we would tell each other everything."

The weight of her words was impossible to ignore. If anything, it felt as if they were designed to chip a chunk out of my heart. "Have you ever had a secret that was so bizarre that it didn't feel real? Like it didn't feel possible, so you just didn't tell anyone at all?"

Amy sat back, deep in thought. "I don't think so. But I don't feel like bizarre things happen to me. Most things seem pretty self-explanatory. And Eamon is not a bizarre secret. He's an amazing one."

That hadn't been what I was getting at, at all, but it wasn't fair for me to veil what I was saying. I had to just forget it like I had for twenty-two years. What good would it do now, anyway? I could live with the burden a few more decades and let it die deep inside me. It wouldn't have to hurt anyone that way. It could just quietly go away.

"So? Are you going to call him?"

"I think so, but I'm not entirely sure. I think I'll wait a day or two. He's busy, anyway. I'm sure he'll hardly notice."

"Don't act like a lame guy. Don't play hard to get."

"I'm not doing that. At all."

"It sounds like you are. Just call him, Katherine. Just call him."

———

I WAITED three days to call Eamon. That seemed reasonable, despite Amy's assertion that I was acting like a lame guy. I didn't want there to be anything rash or desperate about me making this phone call. Still, the pressure was on. This was my agreement with the notion of trying. This was a commitment, and it was weighty given our history. There were expectations, tacit and not. I never wanted to hurt Eamon. Ever.

The call rang five times and then I got his voicemail. *It's Eamon. Leave a message, will ya?*

"Eamon. Hi. It's me. I'm sorry it took me so long to call." Why, exactly, had it taken me so long? Was Amy's persuasion that slow acting? "I've been crazy busy at work—"

The other line beeped. I looked at the screen on my phone. It took a few seconds for it all to compute—hang up and accept new call.

"Katherine. So sorry." Eamon had that breathless thing going on again. Just like that morning at the Four Seasons, he was always rushing about, a bit disorganized, like a very sexy absentminded professor. "Couldn't find my bloody phone."

"Slow down. It's fine. I'm here."

"I didn't want to miss you."

I sighed so heavily you'd have thought he was reciting lines from *Wuthering Heights*. "You're so sweet when you're like this."

"Like what?"

"Concerned about me."

"I'm always concerned about you. Even when I was an ocean away, I was concerned about you, Katherine. We talked about this the other day."

"I know. I know. It's just so damn sweet. You always know the perfect thing to say."

"You give me too much credit, but I'll take it."

I lay back in my bed, staring up at the ceiling. Amy was in

the other room packing, an activity I tried not to think about too much. She was going to be gone in fewer than ten days, but I didn't want to dwell on it. Nor did I want to abet it, although if she were to ask for my help, I would've absolutely done it. She merely hadn't asked yet, so I'd let it be. "So. What are you doing?"

"I'm at the hotel, staring at four walls. I spend entirely too much time doing that. We head to the venue in thirty minutes."

"That doesn't sound very exciting. I guess I thought that being a rock star was exciting."

"I'm not a rock star."

"Yes you are."

"No. I'm not. Only assholes think of themselves as rock stars. I'm a songwriter. A performer. I'm a musician. Not a rock star."

I rolled over to my side and pulled my knees up. "I never thought of it that way. I guess I figured that if you were famous for music, you were automatically a rock star."

"Fame is a bloody sham. You know that, right? It's about as empty a thing as there is in the world. People spend their days trying to get it and when they do, they realize it's nothing of substance."

"Ah, but you didn't want to go to the diner for breakfast that morning because of that thing that supposedly has no substance."

"I didn't want to go to the diner because of the pain in the ass it can be. How much fun would we have had if we were sitting there trying to have the conversation we had and we were constantly getting interrupted by people wanting a picture or an autograph?"

"Don't those people pay your bills?"

"They do. And I love my fans. Truly. I do. But I'm like anybody else. I need a break. I need my privacy. And that morning with you was too important to me. I had a lot I had to say." He sucked in a deep breath. "I had a lot I'd been rolling around in my head, practicing. For years. I didn't want to blow it, especially when I wasn't sure you were going to stay."

He had certainly been on edge when I'd arrived that morning. Was that his big worry? That I'd up and leave? "Eamon. How could you think that I wouldn't stay? And I don't believe you when you say you've been practicing. That's not possible."

"It's more than possible. It's the truth."

A stretch of silence passed between us while I prepared to make a second run at the question that kept eating at me, the one I'd asked that morning at the Four Seasons. "If everything you said meant that much, and you were that eager to say it, I still don't understand why you didn't try to contact me." All I could think about was what I'd been like over the last eleven years. It had taken a long time to heal from the loss of Eamon. It had been a bumpy road to get Dad sober and happy, and for Amy and I to both finish school, be reunited in the city, and find our jobs. In many ways, life wasn't good again until Amy and I were back together. We understood each other. We never had to explain. There was no replacing that closeness, precisely why her moving out made me so uneasy. Would things get bad again? Would Eamon break my heart? Would I end up breaking his? It was hard to see rays of sunshine in my future, even when I felt so lucky to have Eamon back in my life. I couldn't escape the feeling that it harkened the end of something.

"I thought about it. Many times." He cleared his throat and left me again with a morass of silence. "But I told you the other morning. I felt like I had to let the universe tell me if this was meant to be. I wanted us to drift back together. Just like we did in the first place. It was total chance that you walked into the pub the night we met."

"People meet like that all the time. It doesn't have to be fate."

"But do people have what we did, Katherine? Do most people ever get a fraction of what we had together? I don't think they do."

"I don't know how to answer that. It's like my eyesight. I don't know another way to see."

"Okay. Well then, answer me this. Was there a guy after me? A guy who came close?"

I nearly snorted into the phone. The answers on my lips was *unfortunately yes* and *hell no*. "There were some guys, yes. But none of them could hold a candle to you. If that's what you're asking."

"Did they make you laugh like I used to?"

"Not really." Even the amateur stand-up comedian hadn't been able to make me laugh like Eamon could.

"Did they bring you coffee in bed?"

"A few did."

"A few? How many are we talking about?"

"Are you seriously asking me that? I don't even want to think about how many women you've been with over the last eleven years."

"Don't forget I was married for part of that. I was always faithful to her."

That was a whole separate can of worms, but it didn't feel right for the first phone conversation. Things were still so tenuous between us. "Good to know."

"What about the sex?"

I clamped my eyes shut and my face grew hot. "What about it?"

"Sex with the other guys. Was it as good as it was with me?" His voice was a low, sexy rumble and I swear to God he was exaggerating his Irish accent, just so he could kill me.

"What do you think?"

He waited to answer and I braced myself for it, eyes closed, breath heavy. "I think it wasn't the same at all. I think none of them knew to walk up behind you in the kitchen and kiss your neck. I don't think they had the nerve to slide their hand down your belly and into the front of your panties and touch you exactly the way you like to be touched. I know for a fact none of them made you come while you were doing dishes."

That memory was as vivid as any between us. With my eyes closed, I could nearly feel my one hand gripping the edge of the cool porcelain sink with one hand, while the other wrapped back around his neck. The pads of my fingers slid over the delicate hairs at his nape while I gently dug my nails into his warm skin. His erection was pressed hard against my ass while his lips skimmed my neck. One hand was under my top, teasing my nipple. The other had me at his mercy, moving in deft circles. "That's not sex."

"You nearly crumpled to the floor when it was over. And I seem to remember we had sex a few minutes later. In the hall. Against the wall."

Was it possible to pass out from having a former lover retell a past sexual encounter? If so, I was about to do exactly that. "It was amazing."

"We couldn't get enough of each other, remember?"

"I do remember that. Very well. But we were young and horny. You can't forget that."

"I was twenty-nine. I had things pretty well worked out by the time you came along."

Amy popped her head into my room. I bolted upright in bed and slapped my hand over my phone. "Hey. What's up?" My face was on fire. The rest of me felt like I'd vacationed on the surface of the sun.

"Talking to Eamon, finally?"

"Yeah. I won't be much longer."

"Take your time. By the flush in your cheeks, I'd say you're having fun." Her eyebrows bounced.

She really thought she was so damn smart. "Did you actually need something?"

"Just wanted you to look at some of these clothes before I give them away. We can do it later."

I slumped back down in bed. "Give me ten minutes. And close the door, please." I removed my hand from the phone. "Sorry. Amy needed me for a second."

"Hi, Eamon!" Amy shouted before making her exit. It was like being in high school all over again.

"Your sister says whatever she wants, doesn't she?"

I laughed. "Yeah. But I love her."

"How are the wedding plans coming?"

"Good. Fine. They're keeping it small, so it's been pretty low-key so far."

"And how do you feel about it? Your younger sister getting married."

"It's great. I like her fiancé. He's nice."

"That's not the most ringing endorsement I've ever heard."

I'd thought it sounded pretty good. "You know I'm not like that, Eamon. I don't gush about much. It's just not my thing."

"I know nothing of the sort. You were always happy and enthusiastic about everything when we were together. I didn't call you *Sunny Girl* for nothing."

I wanted to tell him that I'd been *Sunny Girl* for only a short time, when I was with him. Would a second time with Eamon bring *Sunny Girl* back to life? Ff that happened, could I maintain it? That was my biggest fear about Eamon encapsulated. Did he just have a thing for me from eleven years ago? That version of Katherine had never told Eamon about her past. She hadn't given him even a whiff of her bad memories. That

Katherine had blinded herself from them, if only to have what she'd waited years and years for—a chance to be less complicated. "Amy still isn't sure that song is actually about me, you know. She thinks there's a good chance I'm lying."

"Remind me to tell her when I come back to New York at the end of the tour." He cleared his throat. "If you'll have me, that is."

I blushed again. "So you're definitely coming back to New York?"

"Always has been. I record in January and most of my band lives in the states, so there's no reason to go back home."

"Well of course I'll have you. I want to see you. That's why I called. You told me to call only if I'm serious. Remember? If I wasn't ready to try. This is me trying."

"Good. That's all I wanted. Truly."

"So when would you get here?" I rolled back on to my side and swished my foot back and forth across the duvet. I'd never thought of myself as the type for phone sex, but Eamon was making me reconsider everything. "I hope it's not too long. Now that I've seen you, I'm anxious to see you again."

He sighed on the other end of the line. "Three weeks."

"So forever, basically."

"A lifetime." He laughed it off. "We'll make it work. Lots of phone calls. Maybe some late night ones. When I'm alone and need to unwind after a show." His inflection was leading me right down that phone sex path. I was going to have to brush up on my dirty talk, practice saying "cock" out loud without giggling.

"After Amy moves out. She's very nosy. She's probably out in the hall listening right now."

He chuckled again. "I'm sorry, but I have to go. We're leaving for the venue."

"Okay. Have a good show."

"Talk tomorrow?"

"Talk tomorrow. Definitely."

"Bye then."

"Bye." I hung up and simply stared at my phone. For all of my stupid trepidation over the decision to call him, I was so glad I'd done it. I felt as light as air.

"I wasn't listening. I happened to be walking by," Amy said from somewhere beyond the confines of my room. I noticed then that she hadn't closed the door all the way.

"You're terrible," I called. "A grown woman deserves her privacy."

"Not with her sister around. You should know that by now." My door swung open and there was Amy with an armful of magazines. She waltzed right in, uninvited, and dropped an avalanche of bridal mags onto my bed.

"I always hoped you'd get some damn manners one day. Apparently not."

"Let's talk bridesmaid dresses." The bed shook when Amy flopped down next to me. "I picked one out and want to see what you think."

"Yay. Can't wait."

"You don't have me around for that much longer. We should get as much of this wedding stuff out of the way as we can while I'm still living here."

The end of Amy and Katherine, roommates, was coming. Things would never magically wind their way back to the way they'd been in this apartment, the way they'd been when we'd shared a room at home. Being close to Amy was the only thing that had kept me together all these years. Well, aside from Eamon. But he'd been his own kind of drug. And I still wasn't sure it was a good idea to start using again.

But damn, I really wanted to.

CHAPTER SIX

IT WAS MORE than twenty years ago, the day after Mom's funeral to be exact, when Amy moved her stuff into my room. The three of us—Dad, Amy, and I—were clinging to each other, but we girls had become especially inseparable. We were too scared to be apart, too freaked out by everything that had happened. We were little rabbits jumping at noises and always looking over our shoulders, ready to scamper off to save ourselves.

Amy had no idea I was carrying around a separate set of worries. She thought the horribleness had passed and we were simply dealing with the aftermath, adjusting to our new sad life. Amy had no idea I was convinced Mom's boyfriend, Gordon, was going to come and take her. Just her. She was the special one.

The move-in had been my idea. Amy eagerly agreed and Dad acquiesced. The man loved having a project, and the truth is that he would've done anything for us during the days and weeks immediately following the accident. He was our rock, treating us to whatever we wanted at the grocery store and reading us stories before bed. He was Super Dad. It wasn't until later that he fell into hundreds of tiny pieces.

With some extra muscle from the high school boy who lived next door, Dad moved Amy's bed across the hall. I coordinated the careful migration of Amy's kitten poster collection to my walls. Dad added an extra shelf to the inside of my closet and since we were only ten and eight, he stepped in when we struggled with space planning. It only took one day to create our new sisters' refuge, and Amy and I lived like that for another eight years, through zits and training bras, homework and breakups. We were together until I went off to college.

I'd slept well the first night we shared a room. Amy and I were both knee-deep in exhaustion, which was the only thing that could drive out the too-fresh memories of the events that had turned our entire world upside down. The second night, however, wasn't so easy for me. It was like the ghost of Mom was visiting me, but not the sweet and loving version of Mom. It was the angry one. The last version of her I ever saw. She stomped around in my head, blaming me for everything.

You're sad? Well, too bad. You wouldn't be so sad right now if you'd just minded your own business. What am I always telling you girls? Worry about yourself, not everyone else.

I could see the azure blaze of her eyes and the flame red in her cheeks, just like the day she'd died, when she'd screamed at me to get in the car. If I lived another day on this earth, I never wanted to see that expression in anyone's eyes again. I reached into my bedside table drawer that night, pulled out the flashlight I used for reading and stuck it under the covers. It provided just enough glow for me to see, so I did what any normal, hopelessly paranoid ten-year-old would do—I watched my sister sleep.

She was so beautiful when her mouth wasn't running a million miles a minute. Her complexion was perfect, her golden blond hair draped across her cheek, her mouth in a tiny "o". Somewhere in my wound-too-tight mind I decided that this was how I could keep Amy safe. I would keep watch over her every night to make sure I wouldn't lose the person I loved most in the world. Eventually, I fell into a routine—I pretended to be asleep, carefully listening to her breaths until they became slow and perfectly even. I would then get out of bed, double check the locks on the windows, and make sure the shades were closed as tight as possible. I'd climb back under the covers and keep an eye on Amy for as long as I could stand it, before my body would eventually wave the white flag of surrender and slip into sleep.

To pass my time awake, I thought up ideas for booby traps to capture Gordon if he tried to get into our room. Unfortunately, most of my ideas were the stuff of Wile E. Coyote and involved things like anvils. I was ten. I had no clue where to get an anvil. It kept me up, though, and most important, Amy stayed safe and sound. There was no way I could've lived through another loss like the one we'd just endured. All these years later, I still felt that way—I couldn't live through another family tragedy. No more loss.

"Getting down to the nitty gritty, aren't we?" Amy's fiancé, Luke, stood in the hallway of our apartment outside her room, slugging down the remnants of a bottle of water, the flimsy plastic crinkling in on itself. He flashed his super sweet self-assured smile, the one that always made me think of Ryan Gosling memes. *Hey girl...let me rub your feet while we watch Downton Abbey.*

"We're getting there." Amy folded in the flaps on another box and handed it to him while I packed up the last of her books.

Sweat dripped from Luke's brow. He'd been working hard all afternoon, up and down the stairs of our building with armfuls of my sister's stuff. His heather gray t-shirt said *This is*

What a Feminist Looks Like. It clung to his pecs like it couldn't bear to let him go. The guy was buff, ridiculously good looking, and certainly knew his audience—I'd give my sister that much. "I'll take this down right now. I've got a few things to rearrange in the truck, so I might be a few minutes."

I wasn't sure if it was a good thing that they'd opted to not hire movers. It was certainly giving me more time with Amy, but it was also making it a horribly long and drawn-out process. There was a part of me that just wanted today to be over so I could start getting used to the new normal.

"The books are all packed up now. Do you think Luke can take the bookshelf down on his own?" I folded in the flaps of the cardboard box and sat back on my haunches.

"I'm not sure I want it anymore. It doesn't really go with the decor of his apartment."

I tried very hard not to roll my eyes at the concept of Luke's second-floor walk-up in Brooklyn having decor. "You've had this bookshelf since we were kids. Grandpa and Dad made it for your room when you were born."

"I know who built it, Katherine. Sometimes it's nice to get a fresh start, you know?"

I bunched up my lips and choked back a sigh. She was getting huffy because she was tired. Moving was a real test of everyone's patience. "Okay. I'll hold on to it. I'm pretty sure you're going to change your mind anyway."

Amy crossed her arms over her chest. "Did you seriously just say that to me? You're sure I'm going to change my mind?"

"It's a nice bookcase. And it's sentimental." I got up from the floor and wiped the dust from my knees.

"Oh. You were talking about the bookcase?"

"What else would I be talking about?"

Amy looked away from me, staring out the window, blinking like crazy. The sun was setting, getting ready to duck behind the buildings across the street. The light made me second-guess what I was seeing—glistening, dewy teardrops.

"Ames, are you crying?" I walked over to her and put my arm around her shoulder. Amy never cried. She was tough as nails, tougher than me for sure.

"What if this is a mistake? What if things don't work out?" Her voice was croaky. "I love him, but we don't really know each other that well. Maybe this is moving too fast."

Now she was asking these questions? At least I didn't feel so guilty for the torrent of doubts that coursed through my head that day at the diner. I pulled her into a hug. "First off, you love him and that's all that matters. I'm proud of you for taking this leap and listening to your heart."

"Are you really proud? You're not mad?"

I rocked her back and forth, our cheeks pressed against each other. Amy was two inches or so shorter than me, so I had to stoop a bit. "I'm not mad. I could never be mad at you. You know that." There were a lot of other things attempting to run out of my mouth, but I had to hold it all in. The minute I started confessing my own unease and sadness, it would be hard to make it stop. And it would be even harder to take it back. "I love you and I'm happy that you're happy. Luke is amazing. You'd be crazy not to want to be with him. You guys will do great. I know it."

"I wish I knew for sure. I wish I didn't question every damn thing. It's not a good way to live."

Welcome to my world. "It's okay to question things. The important part is that you didn't let it paralyze you. You're taking the leap. That's the way to live your life." Maybe that was what I needed to do. Take more leaps. Stop shuffling through everything. "Just focus on the wedding and you'll do great. It'll be an amazing day. And you know you love it when you're the center of attention."

"Yeah. I do like that." She laughed quietly. "It'll be nice to see Dad for a happy family occasion. It's been a long time since we've had one of those."

"Everything okay?" Luke asked. "I can come back if you need me to."

Amy wrenched herself from my embrace. She wiped away a tear with the back of her hand. "No. I'm fine. Just sister talk."

The concern that crossed his face was so warm and genuine I had to wonder how the guy had managed to stay single for so long. "Tell you what. It's been a long day," he said. "How about I run down to the Thai place across the street and get us all some dinner?"

Amy's expression brightened like someone had just flipped a switch inside of her. I was such an ass for doubting Luke. He was a good guy. Of course he was. My sister was whip smart and almost as skeptical of people as me. She would've taken nothing less. "Oh, my God, yes. I'm starving. And that way we can have one last dinner together before we head out."

"Katherine? You in? My treat," Luke said.

"Of course. Sounds great. I'll open a bottle of wine."

"Perfect." Luke pressed a kiss to Amy's cheek. "Pad Thai with shrimp; extra peanuts and cilantro?"

Amy nodded. "You know it."

He turned to me, his earnest blue eyes leading the way. It was uncanny how well the color matched his well-worn jeans. "Katherine?"

"Chicken Panang. I don't need any extra anything. Just the normal way."

"Mild, medium, or spicy?"

"Medium."

"Got it. I'll be back in a few." With that, Luke was out the door.

"See?" I asked. "He's so great. You're a lucky bitch."

"That's my line, Katherine. It just doesn't work when you say it."

I shook my head. "You don't know what you're talking about. Now let me get the broom so you can clean the floor in your room before you go."

We worked on tidying up while Luke was fetching food. When we were done, we stood together in the doorway of her room, admiring our handiwork. Except for the bookshelf, and Amy's bed, which she didn't need anymore, everything was gone. A clean slate.

"What are you going to do with this room now?"

I shrugged. "No clue. Leave it empty for now. I'll figure something out." I knew very well that this apartment was too big for one person. I was going to have to move when the lease was up in April.

"Maybe Eamon could set up his guitar stuff in here."

"I guess. I don't really know how long he's staying when he gets here. A month or two, if we make it. Then he goes to record and after that, I'm guessing he'll go back to Ireland." The thought of going with him back to Ireland held some appeal, but it could only be for a short time. I didn't think I could separate myself from Amy. What if she and Luke decided to have kids? I had to be there to be amazing Aunt Katherine, the one who lets her nieces and nephews have chocolate ice cream for dinner and never enforces bedtime.

"Did he not say that he didn't want to pursue anything unless it was serious?"

"Well, yeah, but..." As the words came out of my mouth, I realized exactly how dense I'd been, so focused on the idea of him coming back that I hadn't thought about how long he might stay. I hadn't entertained the idea that it might be forever. As far as I knew, his ex-wife and daughter still lived in Ireland. I needed to ask him a lot more questions.

"But what? You two are going to need to talk about this. Soon."

I sighed. I'd been focused on the prospect of phone sex. Now I had to think about more important issues. "Yeah. You're right."

"Food's here," Luke called from the other room.

"Let's eat. You can stress out about Eamon later," Amy said. "After we leave."

"Can't wait."

I followed Amy out into the living room and into the kitchen. Luke was unloading the cartons of take-out, lining everything up on the counter. Amy got out the plates and silverware while I opened the bottle of wine, a light-bodied French red I figured would go okay with our meal. Luke handed over Amy's Pad Thai, which was perfectly arranged on the plate, lime wedges and all.

The three of us settled in the living room, the only place to eat in our apartment. I let them take the couch and I sat on the floor in front of the coffee table with my legs curled up under me. Amy poured the wine while I made note of how adorable she and Luke looked together. They were going to make very pretty babies, with squeezable cheeks and thick hair. I couldn't wait for that to happen.

"Cheers." I held up my glass. "To the happy couple and new beginnings." I wasn't sure exactly where that had come from. I only knew that I wanted Amy to leave on a good note. I didn't want her to feel bad about any of it.

Amy knocked her head to the side and jutted out her lower lip. "Thank you. Thank you for everything. For helping today, and for being my maid of honor, and for agreeing to help with wedding planning."

"Yes, thank you. I don't know what we would do without you," Luke added.

"Happy to do whatever you guys need. I'm there for you." I loaded up my fork with curry and took a big bite.

"So, Katherine, are you ready to meet my family at the engagement party next week? They can be a bit of a handful," Luke said.

I choked. And then I sucked in a lungful of Thai chiles. The heat registered first in my brain. *This is not medium. This is Chernobyl.* My throat was engulfed in fire. My eyes flooded with water. I slurped down some wine, but it just spread the heat. I flapped my hand, fanning the air in front of my lips. As if that was going to help. "Water. Need water." I scrambled to my knees and ran into the kitchen, fighting back the urge to stick my face under the faucet. I poured myself a glass of water and downed it, but it only helped a little.

"Drink milk," Luke said, nearly as frantic as I was. "It will help to dilute the capsaicin."

"I don't have any milk," I gasped. Even breathing hurt right now. "I have half and half. I'm not drinking that."

"Ice cream?"

I nodded furiously as I poured myself another glass of water. Luke lunged for the freezer, grabbed the carton of coffee gelato and dug out a heaping spoonful. I let him feed it to me like I was a little kid, but the instant it hit my lips and tongue, I felt so much better. My shoulders dropped. Relief. "Oh, my God. Thank you so much. I have never eaten anything so hot in my entire life."

Amy walked into the room. "Everything okay in here?"

I took another bite of gelato. "Yes. Luke saved me."

"For a minute there, I was worried you just didn't want to talk about the engagement party," she said, not seeming the least bit concerned about the fact that her sister had just nearly died from Thai food.

Between this and the scene in the bedroom, it felt like she

was waiting for me to be a downer about her wedding. But I refused to be that person and I was not going to let her goad me into it, either. I would not rain on her parade. No way, no how. "Are you kidding? I can't wait for the engagement party. I'm really looking forward to meeting Luke's family."

"My parents are so excited. It's all they talk about. My aunt and uncle are flying in from Omaha. They wouldn't miss this for the world." He nodded and smiled, continuing to feed me ice cream. I just went with it, watching as the expression on his face never wavered from true enthusiasm. "My brothers and my sister will be there, of course. I have two cousins coming, one from Florida, one lives in New Jersey. Then there's my best man, and the other groomsmen of course, and some old friends from school and some of my neighbors."

"On our side, it's you and the other bridesmaids," Amy said.

"Great. Sounds great." I managed a smile, even though my lips were still throbbing. I was going to have to start psyching myself up for this. A room full of strangers who were about to become family? This was going to mean questions. Likely lots of questions. About our parents, our childhood—precisely the reason I avoided those situations.

"We tried to keep it small. Just like the wedding."

It made me wonder what the size of the final guest list would be. This did not sound small. "Don't worry about me. It's a happy time. It'll be fun." I smiled again. In any normal family, yes, this would be fun. For Amy and me? Complicated. I had to give my sister credit for attempting this at all. "Should we get back to dinner?"

"Do you want me to run down to the Thai place and get you a new order of Panang?" Luke asked.

"You're sweet, but no. I'm not really hungry. I'll have another glass of wine while you finish eating, and let you guys be on your way."

I kept to drinking while Luke and Amy finished their dinner. We talked about the wedding, about their notion that this wasn't going to be a large affair, just a small intimate gathering at the country club Luke's family belonged to. Of course, they lived out in Westchester County, so I already knew it was going to be all kinds of swanky. Another step into the unfamiliar, when the familiar had become perfectly comfortable. Maybe that was my problem.

I cleaned up the dishes while Amy and Luke gathered the last of her things. Then it was time to say goodbye. I didn't want to prolong my agony, so I just hugged her. "I'll talk to you sometime this week," I said.

"Shut up. You'll text me tomorrow and it'll make my whole day."

I smiled through the tears, not wanting to let her go. "Deal."

She stood back and grabbed my shoulders. "You'll always be my sister, Katherine. Moving out won't change that. Nothing can change that."

"You're right." I nodded. "Nobody can take that away."

CHAPTER SEVEN

THE FIRST GUY I went out with after I left Ireland was Dan. Dan, the Doomed. Everything Dan did was measured by the yardstick of Eamon MacWard. It wasn't his fault that he didn't look as good in jeans, or couldn't really pull off five o'clock shadow all day long. There was no blaming him for his perfectly average voice or the fact that he didn't make my heart flutter when he walked into a room. No, it wasn't fair that Dan had so much to live up to, but sometimes life just isn't fair.

I'd hesitate to call Dan an actual boyfriend, even though we dated for nearly two months. Dan was a stand-in. Our relationship never moved beyond sex, and just like an addict, I wanted it all the time. Dan was always on board, and he tried. Good God, he tried. But what Dan and I had wasn't going anywhere. I was too busy trying to show myself that what Eamon and I had shared was merely physical, and therefore, easily replaced. I'd been epically wrong.

Kissing was the most unfortunate part with Dan. He was greedy and desperate like he was worried he'd never get another kiss in his entire life. There was no finesse. There was certainly no artistry.

Slower. Don't rush.

But I want you. I want you to know how much I want you.

It's okay. I know.

Another thing about Dan—the way he talked to me was too wishy-washy. I didn't want a man to pussyfoot his way around with me. I wanted him to tell me everything. Eamon was always sweet, but when he made up his mind about something, there was no convincing him otherwise. He was determination wrapped up in a ridiculously sexy package.

I really want to fuck you, Katherine. The man could walk into a room, look me in the eye, and say that out loud with no prompting, and it seemed perfectly normal.

Oh, really?

Unless you tell me no, yes.

I see. Being coy was my only way to keep on even footing with Eamon, but it was all a ruse. He always had the upper hand. Or at least it had felt that way.

Are you going to tell me no?

No.

No?

I'm not going to tell you no. I can't tell you no. You know that.

I still like to hear you say yes. He'd whisper it right into my ear, his breath hot against my skin. The whole charade was so pointless, but I enjoyed the hell out of it. I lived for it.

Yes, Eamon. Yes.

I wasn't the only woman who adored Eamon. Not by a long shot. Millions of women did. The bulk of them had experienced only the proverbial tip of the iceberg—they'd listened to his music, seen him perform, or ogled his photo in a magazine. That was the public Eamon. It was only the tiniest hint of what made him sexy, intriguing, and utterly beguiling. That was where the sense of playing with fire came from. If someone could love and adore him from afar, how was I supposed to do it up close when everything about him was so damn over-whelming?

I was still searching for that answer. I suspected I might never find it. I might have to learn to live with not knowing.

———

THE NIGHT of my sister's engagement party, I had Eamon on speaker again. "If it wasn't for my sister, I wouldn't be going to this party at all."

"Of course not. It's an engagement party. What other reason would there be to go?" Eamon was on the same practical answer plan as my sister.

"This is my way of telling you I'd rather be doing anything other than this. Anything." I knew exactly how messed up my attitude was. I hadn't seen Amy in days and it was starting to feel as though my heart was shriveling up. I found myself wondering what she was doing, whether or not she was okay, all the time. It took everything I had not to text her ten times a day. But because my despair was born out of her leaving to get married, I felt no inclination to go to the engagement party. This was going to be a celebration dedicated to the very thing that was making me unhappy.

I sighed. "I'm going to have to get drunk."

"Do *not* do that. You'll regret it. And you'll piss off your sister."

"Fine. I won't get drunk. But I'm texting you from the bath-room if it gets really bad."

"I'll likely be on stage at the time, but sure."

"So you won't actually text me back in the middle of a show?"

"Something tells me the people paying money to see me perform might take issue with that."

"But I need you," I joked. Where would I be right now if Eamon hadn't come back into my life? Drowning in tears, most likely.

"I fucking love hearing that." His voice had gone to that low place, the one that made the earth stop spinning.

"It's the truth."

"I need you, too."

I plopped down on the bed and crossed my legs. "No you don't. You're one of the most well-adjusted people I know."

"Doesn't mean you haven't made me a lot happier over these last few weeks."

And I was here all along, you big dolt. "That's very sweet. You've made me happier, too." Of course, that was relative only to my normal state—worry and pessimism intermingled with blips of cheer.

"Can I call you after the show tonight? It might be late. Some old friends are coming and they'll be hanging around a bit after the show."

He'd managed to keep ties with other people, apparently, just not me. "Call me whenever. I'll leave my phone on."

"You'll do great tonight," he offered.

"I'm not worried about that. All I have to do is show up." *It's the way I'll feel when it's all done that I'm worried about.*

He laughed quietly. "All right then. Talk later?"

"Talk later." I hung up and dropped my phone on the bed. Once again, the quiet of the apartment moved in on me. It threatened to swallow me up. No music from Amy's room or the TV on. It wasn't normal for New York to be quiet. It was unsettling. My phone beeping broke through the silence. A text from the car service Luke had booked for me. I tossed a few things into my bag and replied that I was on my way down.

Downstairs, the black SUV stuck out like a sore thumb. My neighborhood was nice, but it wasn't car service nice. Luke's parents lived out in Westchester County, and I'd braced myself for just how highbrow their neighborhood would be, but nothing could've truly prepared me once we crossed over into the land of tree-lined streets and smooth pavement. Sprawling houses poked up from behind high walls and gates. Luke's parents had graciously left their wrought-iron cage door open, so my driver didn't have to deal with the security system. A handful of cars were parked in the driveway—BMW, Jaguar, Porsche. I was about to rub elbows with the well-heeled of suburban New York. I hoped they were ready.

I straightened my coat after ringing the doorbell next to the grand entrance. I could already hear merriment inside.

"Katherine, you're here!" Luke seemed genuinely surprised when he answered the door, but I could appreciate his attitude. I was pretty impressed as well. "Let me get your coat."

"Hey Kat." Amy rushed to the front door.

My heart leapt when I saw her. Her cheeks were flush and full of color. Her smile came easily and was absent of any irony or skepticism. My influence had already worn off and she looked all the better for it. "Hi, honey," I croaked when I gave her a hug. Damn, I knew I'd missed her, but being around her put a much finer point on it.

"Come in. We have a ton of food and Luke will make you whatever you want to drink." She was wearing an adorable ice blue party dress, with a fitted bodice and short full skirt. She looked like a slightly slutty Disney princess.

Luke passed my coat to a woman waiting off the wings of the foyer. "It's true. Whatever you want."

"A Negroni?"

"Up or on the rocks? And is there a particular brand of gin you prefer?"

Luke was *not* messing around. "Up, please. Hendricks if you have it."

"Of course I have Hendricks. I wouldn't dream of having a party without it."

Of course not. "Thank you so much."

Amy grabbed my hand. "Come on. I want you to meet everyone. I've told everybody all about you."

I stopped myself from saying the words fighting to make their way from my lips. *And they still want to meet me?* "Can't wait to meet your future in-laws."

We started down a long hall. Overhead, soaring barrel ceilings dripped with chandeliers. Beneath our feet, a black granite and white marble checkerboard made our heels click with every step. Family portraits of suspiciously airbrushed people sat in fat gold frames on the walls. Everything screamed history and money. Longevity. Permanence. Perhaps that was part of the great appeal of Luke. This was the opposite of our upbringing.

The hall opened up to large carved pillars at least twelve feet high and a palatial room with a roaring fireplace at one end, a grand piano and a lavish display of opulently upholstered furniture. Milling about in the space, a gathering of well-coiffed men in V-neck sweaters and khakis grumbled and laughed.

I tugged on Amy's arm. "Where are the women?"

"In the kitchen. We'll go in there in a minute."

"Don't you think that's a little strange?"

"Why is it strange?"

"It's weird. The way they separated the men from the women."

"Nobody separated anyone. That's just the way it happened. You have been to a party before, haven't you? This is what happens."

Something about this screamed misogyny and patriarchy and quite possibly toxic masculinity. "I still say it's strange."

"Katherine, what is your problem? Please don't ruin this party for me."

"I'm just asking a question."

The introductions were fine, albeit uncomfortable, but most of that was likely coming from me. What year were we living in that the dudes were in one room and the women in another?

After I met Luke's dad and brothers, his uncle, several of his cousins, and the groomsmen, Amy walked me into the kitchen. Luke's mom, Cindy, was the first person we encountered. She was just as much of a perfect physical specimen as her son, with blindingly white teeth and the posture of a person who has done dance her entire life. "Katherine, we want you to know that you're about to become a member of our family, too. Just like Amy." Something about the comment, however gracious, made me think she was perpetually widening her social circle.

"Oh, well, gee. Thanks. That's very sweet of you." I forced a smile and glanced at Amy, waiting for the moment when she'd roll her eyes, the signal that we would get to laugh about this later.

That moment never came. Amy admired Cindy in utter adoration. "I'm getting the best mother-in-law ever."

Cindy's chin dropped and her lower lip stuck out. "And I'm getting the daughter I always wanted."

"Don't you already have a daughter?" Granted, I was still sorting out the family tree, but Luke had definitely mentioned a sister.

Cindy tossed back her head and laughed, cupping my shoulder with her hand. "I can tell we have a real firecracker on our hands."

Amy smiled in eager agreement. "She's a real barrel of laughs. Especially at parties."

I forced a beauty pageant grin. Or at least that was what it looked like in my head. "You know how much I love large social gatherings."

I surveyed the massive kitchen, a sea of white marble and

double ovens populated with women who spoke while hardly moving their jaws at all. When in the hell was Luke going to show up with my cocktail? I needed some gin and Campari to loosen me up for more fake pleasantries.

Amy paraded me around the room, which put my pageant contestant practice from a few moments earlier to good use. I met Luke's aunt, Jan, who was clearly cut from the same cloth as her sister, Cindy, except quite self-absorbed, the sort of person who tells you all about herself before she thinks to ask a single question about you. Thankfully, the groom showed up with my drink, which took the edge off. Next time, I wouldn't wait so long. I'd start drinking in the car.

Luke left to join the men in the other room, which made me a bit sad. He was a known quantity, always even-keeled and easy to be around. Plus, my sister was acting so unlike herself it was hard for me to be in the same room with her without slugging her arm and asking what in the hell was wrong with her. We hadn't shared a single inside joke or made fun of anyone yet, not even Aunt Jan, who would *not* stop talking about her seven Pomeranians, each named after a member of 'N SYNC or The Backstreet Boys. By all accounts, Justin Timberlake was quite a rascal.

I'd met two of the three other bridesmaids before at work functions for Amy's law firm and they were nice enough, but after ten minutes, I ran out of things I could think to ask about practicing law, so those conversations fizzled. I just felt all too uncomfortable, like when you're wearing a blouse with a scratchy tag or undies that won't stop riding up. I wasn't meant for idle chitchat and it was always impossible to explain to anyone what I did for a living, which added an extra layer of awkward to everything.

"So you're like an interior designer." Aunt Jan had hunted me down to tell my an adorable story about how Joey Fatone is always gnawing on one corner of her very expensive designer couch, but apparently decided to humor me with a discussion of something in no way related to herself.

"Not quite. I'm a color analyst. I help companies put together color schemes for things like ad campaigns and corporate branding."

"So you're a graphic designer."

I shook my head. "I don't do any actual design." Once I reached this point in the back-and-forth, it started to sink in just how easily I could disappear and it wouldn't matter. What I did was like a wisp of smoke—fleeting, difficult to quantify, and I suspected would not be missed when it was gone.

"Katherine has superhuman eyesight when it comes to colors," Amy explained. "It's remarkable. A one-in-a-million anomaly."

"Well, it's not superhuman so much as it is uncommon. I can see a million more colors than the average person. It's my job to identify particular colors that might be especially harmonious or pleasant. Or sometimes schemes that are jarring or make people uncomfortable. There's a real psychology behind it."

"Katherine's working on the new Anthem Apparel catalog. It's very exciting."

Somewhere above her head, a light bulb went off for Aunt Jan. "Oh, I just love their cardigans. You must pick those crazy names they use. Like when you buy a sweater and it's called cornflower, not just light blue."

No, that's not what I do either. "Sort of."

Eventually, Amy and Jan launched into a lengthy discussion of where Amy and Luke were going to go on their honeymoon and I wandered into a quiet corner of the kitchen, where a young woman with dyed magenta hair and heavy eyeliner was sitting on a barstool drinking a glass of red wine and staring at her phone.

"Hi. I'm Katherine. I'm Amy's sister."

She looked up from the screen. "Oh. Hey. I'm Shelly. Luke's sister." She turned her phone over and set it down on the counter.

I knocked back the last of my drink to disguise my shock. This was Mr. Perfect's sister? The outcast girl in the corner? I immediately liked her. "Your mom was talking about you. I guess she just never got around to introducing us. She's pretty busy with the party."

"My mom was most likely *not* talking about me, but I appreciate your willingness to lie to make a stranger feel more comfortable. It shows a great deal of empathy on your part."

Apparently I'd better buckle up for this conversation. "She mentioned you if that makes you feel any better." She'd also called my sister the daughter she never had, so there was no telling what sorts of skeletons Shelly might have. I didn't want to pry, but if I happened to stumble over a few bones, it would at least make the evening more interesting.

"That's something. For sure." Shelly pulled out the empty barstool next to her and patted the seat. "Join me."

"Now let me get this straight. You're the youngest in the family?"

"Yeah. The three boys and then me. There's nine years between me and Luke. Mom really wanted a girl, so she made one last attempt. I'm a senior at NYU."

"Your mom got her wish. That's nice. It seems like most people who try that always end up with another child of the same gender."

Shelly took a sip of wine and seemed to ponder the glass when she set it back on the counter. "I don't know if my mom actually got her wish, but she can tell people she did and I think that's all she really cares about. My parents have a knack for getting whatever they want."

I was busy wondering what Shelly meant by that first part when her dad waltzed into the room. No one seemed to be horribly scandalized by the fact that a second man had made his way into the kitchen. That was reassuring. I hadn't completely stepped into a 1950s time warp. "Can you give me the lay of the land with your family?" I asked it out of the corner of my mouth. The last thing I needed was for Amy to hear me.

"There's not much to tell. Everyone is normal and boring. Even worse, they're all happy being that way. Frankly, it makes me sick. That's why I end up hanging in the corner. I can't sit through one more conversation with Aunt Jan about Howie D and her precious little personality."

"Interesting. So Howie D is a girl."

Shelly cocked an eyebrow. "You name your dogs after boy bands, you're going to have to bend some gender rules or deal with a lot of doggie testosterone."

"There has to be some family dirt." I leaned back in my seat and surveyed the group of women. Almost everyone had the same hairstyle—a longish bob with highlights. "Somebody has to be on their second or third marriage or sleeping with someone they shouldn't be."

"It would sure make family gatherings more interesting, but I come from a long line of monogamists."

And I came from a long line of people who seem to take liberties with that. I knew for a fact that my Aunt Lucy had cheated on every one of her husbands with the guy who eventually became the new Mr. Aunt Lucy. "Interesting. Is your family Catholic?" I was always looking for a reason why people were able to stay with the same person without any bumps in the road, although that was a bit silly. Amy or I had never cheated on a boyfriend. We'd managed to keep things together. Neither of us had gotten married though. That was the next big test.

"Nope. It's just the way it's played out. Everyone seems

adept at finding their soulmate. My parents have been married for thirty-six years and they're showing no sign of stopping." Shelly and I looked at them, and nearly on cue, her dad patted her mom's ass, and she feigned disapproval, swatting him on the arm and telling him he was terrible. Everyone who witnessed the exchange found it hilarious. *That Cindy and Tom. What a couple of rabble-rousers.*

"What about you? You find your soulmate yet?"

Shelly was immediately fighting a smile. "Maybe. We'll see. We've only been together for about a month."

"Well? Who is he?" Hot guy from one of her classes? Better yet, super hot older professor?

Shelly scanned my face like she was looking for something. "Promise you'll keep this to yourself? You can't even tell your sister."

"Yeah. Of course. I'm very good at keeping secrets." If only Shelly knew the lengths to which I would go to hide some things.

"Not a he. She. And my family doesn't know." Every family has a secret somewhere. It was a fact of life. And just like the secrets in my family, I sensed that this was causing pain. Shelly was a very relatable jumble of happy and sad. "You asked for the family dirt. I guess that's me."

I shook my head. "No way. You're awesome. Secrets and dirt are not the same thing, anyway." I scanned my brain for some nugget of wisdom. I'd been through my fair share of relationships. Surely all of that life experience, a million mistakes made, could benefit someone. "You know, it's okay to enjoy a relationship without it being under the microscope of family. Especially at the beginning when everything is so new and perfect and you know that feeling will go away at some point. When things settle in."

"That makes so much sense."

Sure, I was echoing my exact attitude about Eamon and why I'd never told Amy about him. "I think it's best to worry about what's between you and your new love and worry about your family later. You're so young. You're just starting to know your own heart. You don't have to figure it all out now."

"Thank you for saying that. Before you came over, I was sitting here stewing in my own juices, wishing I could find a way to tell my parents."

"It's probably more than wanting to just tell them, huh? You want them to accept you. That's the big fear, right?"

"As much as my family makes me nuts, I do want their unconditional love."

"I've only known your parents for a short while, but everyone seems lovely and full of affection for each other."

"As long as you don't rock the boat." She jabbed the kitchen counter for effect. "It's okay. I'm not ready to talk about my girl-friend yet anyway. There's something about it that makes me want to keep it to myself. The minute I start bringing anyone else into it, it could be ruined very easily."

"Makes sense." Perfect sense, actually.

"Does it? Or am I making excuses because I don't want to deal with it? I can't decide which one it is."

"It's normal to worry about what your family will think. I did something similar once. I fell in love and didn't tell anyone. Not even Amy." I never told Eamon I loved him, either, at least not in person. That letter I sent him a year after I got back from Ireland contained the confession, but he'd never read it. He still didn't know, but what was I supposed to say now? *I loved you eleven years ago and I could probably love you again, but I'm afraid it won't last. I nearly died the first time it ended.*

"Was it a long time ago?"

"It feels like it was a lifetime ago."

"And what happened?"

Now it was my turn to blush. Just thinking about Eamon made my skin hot. "I thought it was over and then he reappeared in my life. Sort of like magic." Except that it wasn't really magic, was it? There was a logical explanation for what had happened. The magic that I had once hoped for, Eamon reading and replying to my letter, begging me to come back to him, never came to fruition. But the way it had happened was better, especially now that I knew that his proposal all those years ago had been for real. I might not be sure I was ready for love now, but I had undoubtedly not been ready then.

"I hope everything works out."

"Me too." As to what "working out" meant, I didn't know. The world seemed to think it was the picket fence, but I wasn't convinced.

Shelly smiled. "Thanks for the advice. I like talking to you. I can see why your sister loves you so much. You were all she talked about before you got here."

"Really?" I watched Amy as she chatted away with her future mother-in-law. How I could ever question my sister's love was beyond me, but I did sometimes. Seeing her in this setting, I had to wonder if I'd been holding her back all these years.

———

In the car on the way home, I called Eamon. "I hope this is an okay time to talk. I really needed to hear your voice."

"I love hearing you say that. And yeah, this is a good time."

"You don't need to sign the boobs of random women with a Sharpie?"

"I'm done with the boob signing for today. Thank God. I nearly got a cramp."

I laughed nervously, watching out the window as we started

to escape upscale suburbia and enter the realm of normal people again. "Very funny."

"I hope you know I'm kidding."

I didn't really know that, so it was nice to hear. "Good. That makes me glad." I realized then that I'd already gone from being the woman who wasn't sure this was a good idea, to the woman who didn't want to share him with anyone else. Those women were not entirely compatible. I was going to have to stick to one, for my sanity and his.

"How did the party go? You don't sound drunk, so it must've been at least tolerable."

"It was okay. Everyone was really nice, but I definitely did not feel comfortable. Their whole family is like pod people. They're all so happy and normal."

"Why does that make them pod people?"

"I don't know. Because that's nothing at all like my family? And there's no family dirt, which I find a little impossible to believe."

"You went digging for dirt at your sister's engagement party?"

"Hey. You're the one who told me not to drink too much. I had to entertain myself somehow."

He unleashed the laugh I find most disarming. In my head, I could see his off-kilter smile. "There's always dirt somewhere. Trust me."

"That's what I was thinking."

It got quiet on the other end of the line and I wondered what he was thinking about or whether he was maybe tired. I would've given anything for him to be waiting for me at home right now, rather than thousands of miles away. I couldn't escape the loneliness of that fact.

"Katherine, can I ask you something?"

"Of course. Anything."

"What exactly is it about that situation that makes you so deeply uncomfortable? Your sister getting married. I know it's not just that you feel like you're losing her. There's something more to it, isn't there?"

It felt like my heart was doing a bad impression of an old clock, ticking away at an unreliable pace. There was so much about this for me to unpack, probably because I'd devoted so much of my life to keeping it hidden. "My parents didn't have a great marriage and they did a lot of things to hurt each other. It's hard as a kid to witness that. It definitely sours your opinion of the institution."

"I suppose."

"Am I being unreasonable?"

"No. You're not. I just think that's not the only way to look at it. Some people might go through that and decide that they can do better. Maybe that's the way your sister feels."

Was he right? Had Amy taken things one way while I'd run with it in the opposite direction? She'd definitely seemed comfortable at the party, acclimated to the idea that marriage was this normal thing normal people did, and that she was a member of that group. Maybe I needed to accept that just because I saw her one way, and I saw myself the same way, perhaps I'd been completely wrong. After all, she had been younger than me. She'd witnessed less than I had. And of course, she hadn't been the catalyst for the ultimate bad. She hadn't set the demise of her own family in motion. Amy didn't have to live with that.

"Maybe you're right. Maybe I need to stop looking at it like that." I knew then that I needed to get my attitude straight. Amy deserved better than a maid of honor who was being a complete pain in the ass.

"I could be wrong."

"Nope. It's a great suggestion. You make me a better person, you know. You always have."

"Do you really think that?"

I thought back to the way I'd been with him the first time, so full of sunny optimism, not at all the way I was right now, but I could admit it was a place I wanted to get back to. "I do, Eamon. I really do."

CHAPTER EIGHT

THE QUIET OF the apartment had become insufferable. I found myself turning on the TV the minute I walked through the door after work every night, just to fill the void. I'd turn on game shows, Jeopardy if I got home in time. Amy and I used to love to watch it together. Now I watched just to see faces and hear people talking. It was inexplicable to me. I'd never liked people all that much. I abhorred idle chitchat. But still, I found myself seeking it out. I'd even struck up a conversation with the cashier at the bodega down the street the other night. As if that guy gave a flip about whether or not I'd had a hard day at work.

Dinner every night was also an adjustment. I'd forgotten how depressing it was to cook for one person. The portions never worked out. You always ended up with too much food. So then you had to address the leftovers. If you hated what you'd made, you were still going to have to eat the rest later. I didn't like to waste food. Too many people in the world were starving and suffering for me to go around tossing it in the trash.

Tonight, I didn't have the energy. I'd had a bad run at the office over the last several days. Mr. Ashby was already proving to be a pain in my ass, or as he would say, arse. Unlike quite literally every other person I worked with, Miles put zero stock in my abilities. He'd said that my eyesight was both "curious" and "convenient". When I showed him the changes I was suggesting to next year's color forecast, he didn't trust what I was telling him, nor could he see what I was showing him. It was like trying to negotiate with someone in a language you didn't understand. I'd ended up slinking out of that meeting with my tail between my legs, feeling wholly unsure of my purpose at NACI. If Miles thought I couldn't do my job, how long would I be able to keep it?

So I made a peanut butter and jelly sandwich for dinner, poured myself a glass of wine, and curled up in the chair in the corner, the one with the best view, out the back of my building. The sun had already set, and the sky was a field of inky layers—indigo, violet, and sapphire, all of it glowing from the ever-present lights of the city. Dead tired, I nearly fell asleep while staring out the window, but then my phone dinged and I jumped.

Can you talk?

I grinned at the text and washed down my last bite with wine. Eamon didn't have a show tonight, but he did have a rehearsal with his band to work on songs for the new album. He'd said it could end up going until the wee hours. I called and he picked up right away. "I thought you were working late tonight," I said.

"I did. I'm done."

"Wait. What time is it?"

"After ten."

"That's not late for a rock star."

He laughed. "We've talked about those words, darling."

I shook my head and sank back in the chair, pulling my knees up to my chest and resting my feet on the edge of the seat. "I'm tired. I stayed at work way too late."

"Does that happen a lot?"

"Thankfully, no. In fact it almost never happens, but I have a new boss and he's putting me through my paces."

"I don't like that tone in your voice."

"I'm fine. It's just work. It's no big deal."

"Glad I never had to get a real job. I don't know that I could handle the stress."

"But songwriting is stressful. You told me yourself. There's a lot of pressure to write a big hit, right?"

He cleared his throat. "Yeah. Huge."

"How's it going with that? The writing."

"It's coming. Slowly, but that happens. I'll get it done."

"Ten songs by the end of the year, right? How many do you have done?"

"Why do I feel like I'm being interviewed right now?" His voice had taken a turn, almost defensive.

"I'm just curious. It's fascinating to me. That's all. And I want to be supportive."

"I have three good ones, but that doesn't mean I only have to write seven more songs. I write and write and then we pick the best songs to record. Ten is the minimum. Ideally we'd go into the studio with at least twelve solid options."

I thought about asking how many of the three were solid, but I didn't want to push him or make him upset. He was supposed to be my respite. "I'm sure you'll write something amazing and mind blowing and the world just won't even believe how brilliant you are."

"Right now, I'm just going for the world thinking I haven't lost my touch."

There was that uncertain edge in his voice again. Was this just the bad side of living a creative life? Constant doubt? It was hard to believe that with all his commercial and critical success that he would ever feel that way about himself or his work. "As someone who's seen you perform recently, I can absolutely say that you haven't lost your touch. At all."

"Performing songs that people already love is easy. Creating new stuff and enduring that moment when you find out whether or not they like it is the hard part. But it could be worse. At least I don't have to wear a tie and go into an office every day. No offense."

"None taken. Women haven't really worn ties to work since the '80s, you know."

"I meant the office. I never had to do that."

"My office isn't as bad as some. I could never do what my sister does. Go into a law office every day? Forget it. She works with a bunch of assholes. I know. She set me up with a few of them."

"Now why would your sister set you up with an asshole? You two clearly love each other very much."

"Don't be fooled by her cute exterior. She can be mean and spiteful when she wants to be." I scratched my leg and looked out the window, the phone cradled between my cheek and shoulder. It was late and I was dying to get out of my work clothes. I climbed out of the chair and padded into my bedroom. "I have to put you on speaker for a minute, okay? I need to change clothes."

"Really?"

I pressed the button and placed the phone on my dresser. "Yes, really. Do you hate speaker phone that much?" I took off my skirt and shook it out, then put it back on its hanger.

"Not what I'm talking about."

"Oh." I froze with my arm still in the closet.

"I'm talking about you taking off your clothes while we're on the phone."

I had to wonder if this was a regular thing for Eamon. He

seemed to be awfully drawn to it. "Is this a tour thing? Like you're bored so you want to have phone sex?"

"No. This is a Katherine thing. I've actually never done it before."

The way the heat rose in my body was entirely unfair. How was I supposed to even stand up under these circumstances? I sank down onto the bed. "I'm supposed to believe you're a phone sex virgin?"

"I'm not in charge of making you believe anything. And how difficult could it possibly be?"

"I wouldn't even know where to start."

"I was thinking I'll just say every dirty thing that was going through my mind the other morning when we had coffee."

I flopped back on the mattress, dying to hear more. "Were there a lot? Of dirty things going through your mind?" I gnawed on my thumbnail.

"Too many."

My breath hitched in my chest. I'd had myriad filthy things racing through my head that morning. Had he had more? He'd seemed so focused on everything but anything sexual, except maybe at the end when he'd said he wanted me in that bed, but didn't think it was a good idea. And of course, we'd had that kiss. "So tell me." I could hardly believe I was being so daring.

"Well, I certainly didn't want to go into the bathroom and put on pants."

"I didn't want you to do that either." My face flushed with heat—such an innocent string of words with such naughty implications.

"What did you want me to do instead?"

"Take off my clothes and throw me down on the bed."

"Hold on. You're going too fast." It sounded like he dropped the phone. "Okay. Sorry. I'm back."

"What was that?"

"Had to take off my pants."

"Oh. What about your shirt?"

"Wasn't wearing one."

Goose bumps raced over the surface of my skin. Had this been what he'd wanted all along?

"What are you wearing, Katherine?"

Damn. His voice. I clamped my eyes shut while the sound of my own name echoed in my head. "A blouse I wore to work."

"And?"

"And panties. And a bra, of course."

"Tell me more."

I had to look down my own shirt. I couldn't remember what I'd put on that morning. "The bra is white. Well, it's more of an ivory color."

"You gotta give me more than that, darling. Silk? Satin? Lace?" Everything he said came out in a low, sexy rumble.

"The bra is a sort of soft fabric. I'm not sure what it is, really. Microfiber or polyester or some sort of blend."

He laughed under his breath. "You're terrible at this."

"Hey. This is my first time and I'm trying. I liked it better when you were telling me the dirty thoughts that were going through your head. That worked better for me."

"Fair enough. Let's make a deal. You take off the rest of your clothes and I'll talk."

That sounded like the best deal ever. The anticipation was almost too much to take. It wasn't like seeing him for real, getting to touch him and hold him and have him do the same to me, but right now, in my sad and quiet apartment, this was heaven. "One minute."

I tossed the phone onto the mattress, pulled my blouse up over my head, unhooked my bra and got rid of my panties light-ning fast. If he asked about those, I would have to lie and tell him that they matched the bra. Plain pink cotton wasn't probably going to excite him too much. "Okay. I'm done." I got back on the phone and tore back the covers, settling in on the bed with my head on the pillow. "I'm ready."

"Good. Because I've already got my cock in my hand."

I blinked about five million times in two seconds. Eamon was *not* messing around. "Oh. I see." I frantically scanned my brain for a logical thing to say, but was drawing a complete blank. I tried to think of what other sexy women might say, but the only person I could come up with was Ms. Moneypenny from James Bond. I'd stayed up too late watching *Octopussy* the other night. "Are you hard?" I came a little too close to calling him James.

"I haven't been this hard in a long time, darling. I wish you were here. I wish I could have you on your knees, with your gorgeous lips wrapped around me."

I was so close to calling bullshit on his claim that he was a phone sex virgin, but this was *not* the time. "It's been a long time since I've done that to you."

"Too long. But I thought about it when you were at my hotel the other morning. I thought about how much I liked recip-rocating."

My eyes were half-closed, my mind conjuring images of him and the way it felt to have my knees up by his ears, his hair in my hands, his lips on my body. There wasn't much better in the sexual arena than having Eamon go down on me. He was so damn patient.

I reached down and touched myself, flinching for an instant. My skin was so hyper-sensitive right now. I tried to replicate what he could do, the delicate circles he would wind with his tongue. It wasn't exactly the same, but it was the closest I'd been in forever.

"Are you wet?" he asked.

"I am." I sucked in a breath and rocked my head back and forth on the pillow. "Talk to me."

"After you left the other morning, I was hard as a rock. I had to wank off, and I thought about you the whole time. I thought about burying myself in you and making you say my name."

I smiled softly, floating in and out of consciousness. I was close. The tension was coiling, but it felt so damn good, I was trying to skirt the climax. "Was it good?"

"I came all over my chest. I had to take another shower."

I could see him in his hotel room, sprawled out on that beautiful bed, his glorious body right there. Dammit I'd missed a lot being in the fucking elevator. "And how about now? Are you close?"

"Very."

I decided that I had to help him along. My body was getting fitful and I couldn't wait much longer. I wanted that peak as bad as anything I'd ever wanted. I needed it. "Are you thinking about fucking me?"

"I'm thinking about bending you over the couch and holding your hair in my hand. I'm thinking about making you mine."

That was it. The proverbial dam broke. Judging by the noises Eamon was making on the other end of the line, he'd gotten his happily ending as well. I began my eventual descent back down to earth, but Eamon's voice was buoying me, keeping me in that place where everything is blurry, but you absolutely don't care.

"Everything all right?" he asked.

"Yes. Very. Can you give me a minute to run to the bathroom?"

"You could just put me on speaker."

"I don't want you listening to me pee."

"There was a time when there were no secrets between us, remember? I knew absolutely everything about you.:

Almost everything. "Fine. Suit yourself." I hoisted myself out of bed and grabbed a t-shirt from my dresser and stumbled into the bathroom, nearly like I was drunk. I placed my phone on the edge of the sink and pressed the speaker button. "You there?"

"Just barely. But yeah."

I pulled the t-shirt on over my head, laughing to myself. As insatiable as he could be, he was also the guy who crashed after sex. "I hear you. I think I'll sleep well, which will be a nice change of pace. I haven't been sleeping well at all lately." I muted my phone and flushed the toilet. I didn't need to let him hear *everything.*

"Too much on your mind?"

"I'm just not used to being alone. That's all. I haven't lived by myself in years."

"But I'll be there soon. I don't want to invite myself, but I'm hoping I can stay with you."

This was all too surreal, the casual admission that Eamon was really, truly going to come back into my life. "Of course you can. I'd actually sort of assumed that you would."

"Good. Because it'll be far less fun if I'm staying in a hotel."

"Something tells me you'd just end up staying over anyway." That was exactly what happened in Ireland. Once we'd had one night together, neither of us ever wanted to be apart.

"Won't be long now. Only a few more more days."

I ran some hot water in the sink and washed my hands, then grabbed a washcloth to clean my face, only glancing at the mirror to make sure I got the mascara. "How long do you think you'll be able to stay?"

"Of course, it depends on how long you want me, but it'd be great if I could just stay. Until we decide what we want to do."

I turned off the water and left the mirror foggy from the

steam. I didn't need to see my rosy afterglow. I could feel it. "So, indefinitely?"

"Uh, yeah. But only if that works. I'm back November fifth. My daughter and my ex are coming to New York for a few days about a week later. I'd love for you to meet them. And for you to be able to spend some time with Fiona. She'll love you."

It wasn't Fiona I was worried about. I wasn't sure how I felt about meeting Rachel, his ex-wife, the woman who ultimately replaced me. But I'd have been lying if I'd said I wasn't curious to see what was there, to at least paint in that part of his past. I'd constructed a lot of backstory in my head about them years ago, all in an attempt to convince myself of the reasons Eamon and I were not meant to be together. But I had no idea if any of it was even remotely true.

"I'd love to meet Fiona and Rachel. It's Rachel, right?" I knew damn well his wife's name. Why I was pretending to possibly not know was beyond me.

"Yeah. They've moved to the states full time. They're living in Philadelphia now. Rachel got remarried six months ago."

The puzzle was starting to come together. "Were you thinking of moving here, too?"

"Why? Does that make you nervous?"

Hell yes, it made me nervous. The long-distance thing had been one of my outs. "I'm just trying to understand what your plan is, Eamon."

"My plan is to see where things between us can go. Then I'll see where Rachel and Fiona end up. With my touring schedule, I don't get nearly enough time with Fiona and she's growing up so damn fast. I don't want to miss out on any more than I have to."

"Sure. Of course."

"But it's not just that. I need to see if you and I can make this work. That's why I said I couldn't take up with you again if you weren't serious."

"I don't know why you act as though I'm incapable of being serious. Like where does that come from?" I switched off the bathroom light and headed back to my bedroom. "I was very serious when we were in Ireland. You were my whole world then."

"You say that, but I asked you to marry me and you laughed it off."

"You did not."

"That night in the pub. A few weeks before you left."

"Are you serious right now? You did not ask me to marry you. You said *marry me* and then you took a drink of your beer. That was not a proposal."

"Maybe I was trying to protect myself. Which was probably a good call, since you laughed."

"Of course I did. We were always joking around. You never mentioned it again."

"I was dead serious, Katherine."

My head was swimming. Of course it was—I truly had thought he was kidding. We'd been in the middle of a crowded pub. We were both at least a little drunk. And I was twenty-one years old, nowhere close to being ready for marriage, whereas he was a year away from thirty at that point. "Shit. I'm so sorry." I plopped down at the end of the bed and ran my hand through my hair. This was a classic example of just how far out of my depth I was with Eamon. "I had no idea you were serious." My brain wouldn't stop churning out scenarios of how differently my life would've played out if I'd known he wasn't kidding around.

"To be fair, I should've forced the issue. I see that now. Which is why I might've been a little heavy-handed the morning we had coffee. I just didn't want there to be any ambiguity."

"You didn't want me to laugh."

"How would you have answered? All those years ago. If you hadn't thought it was a joke?"

"I don't even know how to answer that question. I was so young. I had my family at home."

Painful silence hung in the air and I again flopped back on the bed, staring up at the ceiling.

"It was stupid of me to ask in the first place. It was probably more stupid for me to bring it up now. It was a long time ago. We can't fix the past."

Everything he was saying was designed to let me off the hook, but the reality was that none of it made me feel better. I would've said no. I never would've said yes, and if I told him that now, it would hurt him unfairly. It was hurting me right now just to think about it. That would've been the end. But I knew my own heart and was very well aware of the way the idea of marriage made me feel. Some people might feel like marriage made their whole world open up. For me, it meant nothing but the beginning of the end. The moment you're trapped. No one gets out happy or alive.

"I'm super excited for you to get here. And you can stay for as long as you like. As long as you can put up with me. That's probably a better way to say it."

"I've waited a long time for this chance. I don't think I'll have any trouble putting up with anything."

"Well, good. It sounds like you'll have some writing to do while you're here. But that should work out since I'll have to go to work every day."

"The perils of a day job."

"Hey. Not all of us can be a rock star. Wait. Sorry. Musician."

"That's better."

"Hey. Maybe I'll inspire another song."

He didn't reply right away, which made me horribly embarrassed. Why did I have to say stuff like that? Eamon couldn't force his creativity in any particular direction and it made me sound like I was fishing. "You never know. I'm hoping I can get everything written before I get to New York. That would be better for me."

"But then what would you do all day? Sleep?"

"That and convince you to stay home all day."

I laughed softly and settled back into bed. "Yeah, well, only a few more days of phone sex."

"I enjoyed it, but it wasn't the same."

"Yeah. I want to be able to kiss you. That was always my favorite part."

"I think that was my favorite part, too."

CHAPTER NINE

ON THE FRIDAY after the engagement party, Amy and I each took the day off from work. It would've been an understatement to say I was excited to see her. After the party and my subsequent conversation with Eamon, I really was determined to prove that I had turned my attitude around. I couldn't pretend to be enthusiastic about the wedding. I had to throw myself into it. I had to be psyched. As maid of honor, it was my duty to do nothing less. My role in this wedding would set the tone for my relationship with my sister for the rest of our lives. I needed her to look back at my efforts fondly, not as though she was dragging me across the finish line.

We met at the diner for breakfast, and Patty was our waitress.

"What'll it be for the bride-to-be and her big sister?" Patty winked at me as she impatiently tapped her pen against the order pad.

"I'll do the diner breakfast." I'd made a point of getting a full night's sleep. Today was a big day. "Scrambled eggs. Bacon. Sourdough toast." Apparently it was also a day for eating like a lumberjack.

"Egg white omelette," Amy said. I suspected she'd been eating like a bird. She looked skinny. Or smaller. Or maybe just different.

"Two coffees?" Patty asked, but she didn't really need to.

"Please," we answered in unison.

Patty headed back to the kitchen. Amy and I looked at each other for a minute, not saying anything when one of the other waitresses delivered our coffee and cream. I wanted her to take the lead. I wanted her to pull out a three-ring binder full of pages torn from bridal magazines. I wanted her to give me a to-do list a mile long. But she wasn't doing any of that. She was just sitting there. Being quiet.

"What's on the agenda today?" I stirred cream into my coffee, and decided to force the issue, pulling the supplies I'd brought out of my bag. "This is the calendar I made to keep me organized." I turned it around and pushed it to her side of the table, opening the front page. "I'm pretty proud of it. I went to Kinokuniya and dug around in the stationery section for an hour." That was one of my favorite stores in the entire city, a beautiful three-level Japanese bookstore across the street from Bryant Park. "I got the blank pages and this pretty silver binder. I even made the cover." I closed it up and there was my master-piece—Luke and Amy, December 16, in my admittedly less than stellar handwriting, with a multitude of hearts fanning out around it. Middle school me would've been duly impressed.

"I have a calendar," she snipped. "Why would you think I don't have a calendar?"

"It's not that I thought you didn't have one. This is mine. To keep me organized for all of the stuff you need me to do. I just thought it should be pretty."

"It's weird."

"Why would you say that?"

"Why are you being like this?"

"Like what, exactly?"

"So over the top. It's not like you." She sat back and wrapped her arms around her waist.

She wasn't wrong. It wasn't like me. But I was trying, dammit. Didn't I deserve some credit for that? "I want to do a good job. You're my sister and I love you. I want your wedding to be everything you want it to be."

Patty motored over with our food, sliding the plates onto the table. "I'll get you ladies a refill on coffee. Anything else?"

I shook my head and forced a smile. "No. Thank you. We're good."

Amy spread her napkin out on her lap. "Okay. Just don't go overboard. Big, fancy weddings are so old-fashioned."

Was that meant to be a slag against my art project? Or maybe my age? Either way, I didn't appreciate it.

"We want everything to be low-key and low stress and simple," she continued. "Tasteful."

The bad sister part of me wanted to point out that although I had yet to visit it in person, something told me that Luke's parents' country club was likely to be as far from low-key and simple as I was lacking in enthusiasm for attending events held at country clubs. But it was her wedding. I needed to cast aside my own agenda. And my opinions. And pretty much anything else belonging to me. I took back the calendar and tucked it inside my bag. "Sorry. I was just, you know..." *What? Feeling psychotic?* "Excited. But I want whatever you want. So tell me what we're tackling today."

"Shoes and the dress. You've already seen the dress, but I want you to come for my fitting. I've picked out my shoes, and they're on hold, but I want your opinion."

It didn't sound like she needed my help with much of anything other than standing there and validating her choices. Maybe the rest would come later. "Sounds fun. What else?"

"We have to pick out the flowers."

"Oh."

Amy looked up from her breakfast and I knew exactly what she was saying. The flowers were going to be tough. Really tough. If she were still alive, the flowers would've been Mom's domain. No questions asked.

"I have an idea of what I want already," Amy said. "But you can tell me if you think it will look okay. Obviously you're the expert when it comes to color and it's one of the only pops of color we're using. Everything else is white and silver. Very subtle. Classic."

"Does that mean you decided to go with silver for our dresses?" Right before Amy had moved out, she'd shown me her choice and I had done my best to dissuade her.

Amy finished her bite of food and dug through her bag. "Yes, I went with silver, but this one is different from the one I showed you." Finally, she handed me a page torn out of a magazine. This was more like it. "I already sent the link to the other bridesmaids. You have to order it online. I spoke to the company and they said that it shouldn't need any alterations. The bias cut is very forgiving."

I nearly spat my coffee across the table. My sister was not only putting us in silver satin, that so-called forgiving bias cut was a freaking bullhorn for figure flaws. Just thinking about it made me regret my decision to have toast. I should've skipped the carbs. But I couldn't say anything. "Pretty. Very pretty. The, uh, other bridesmaids already have the link?" Why in the hell had I not been consulted on this choice? That was going to be my silver ass walking up the aisle, not hers.

"Yeah. I wanted to talk to you about your dress first. I wasn't sure you would want to wear the same thing they're wearing. Sometimes the maid of honor has a different dress. It just has to be silver. And satin."

I wasn't about to spend the next several weeks hunting down a dress that met her criteria. Keeping things simple right now was the best course. "I want whatever you want. If you want us all to be matching, I'll get this. Is that what you want? For us all to look the same?"

"You don't have an opinion?"

"I want whatever you want."

"Okay. I want you to all be matching."

"Sounds great. Send me the link or I'll write down the info." I tried to hide my growing disappointment. This wasn't the way I had envisioned this going. It was starting to feel like today was a token. Like my sister was throwing me a bone. "Walk me through everything else you need me to do. Address invitations? Coordinate the DJ? You know I make the best dance playlists. I can be a flower girl wrangler. Kids love me. Give me a job and I promise I'll do exactly what you want."

"Luke's mom is running with most of that. I'm letting her call the shots."

"But you said she was making you crazy."

"I mean, they belong to the country club and I guess she's thrown tons of amazing events there. Luke's two brothers both got married there, so she has it pretty dialed-in by now with the catering and the rentals. It's sort of a family tradition at this point and I don't want to rock the boat, you know?"

Yet more of Luke and his perfectly perfect pod-person family taking over everything. I picked at my food. "What about a shower? I can throw you a shower."

Amy looked up and wiped her mouth with the napkin. "We got a ton of gifts at the engagement party. And..." Her shoulders dropped and she stared out the diner window.

"And what?"

"Luke's sister is already throwing me a shower."

"Shelly? She's in college. What does she know about

throwing a shower?"

"I have no clue, Katherine. Am I supposed to ask someone for their credentials when they tell me they want to throw me a bridal shower?"

"You didn't even give me the chance to organize one. You know I'd do a good job. I'm super organized."

"And who exactly would we invite, Katherine? Our friends? We have almost no mutual friends. Our family? There's nobody on Dad's side and we both know mom's side is a disaster. I can just see Aunt Lucy being a total embarrassment. She's always making comments about how much money people have. The second she meets Luke's family we'd never hear the end of it. And we both know there's no way we can invite Grandma Price."

Just the mention of Grandma Price, our mom's mom, and I couldn't eat another bite of my breakfast. At least I no longer needed to worry about a few slices of bread coming between me and my bridesmaid's dress. Grandma Price had been absolutely horrible to Dad, Amy, and me after the accident. As horrible as a person could possibly be.

The thing everyone knew about Grandma Price was that she had a highly formed sense of justice. She was also obsessed with Agatha Christie books, re-reading them over and over again just in case there was some tiny clue artfully hidden in the text that she'd somehow missed. She hated the idea that anyone would ever get away with anything, which made it zero fun to go to her house. If you stole a cookie out of the cookie jar, you had better be prepared to pay for it with your life.

Grandpa Price had been a police detective, a small-town sleuth tackling school vandalism and the occasional rash of newspaper theft. After work every day, he would tell Grandma everything that had happened, even the stuff he wasn't supposed to because he was in the middle of an ongoing investigation. The instant she got the call from our Dad that her youngest daughter had been killed in a car accident, she and Grandpa rushed right over from three towns away, demanding to speak to the police.

That was when things got crazy. Our local detective was a police academy buddy of Grandpa's and showed our grandparents everything—the statement from Dad, an account from me since Amy's injuries gave her a reprieve on reliving the nightmare, and the photographs of the scene. Amy and I never saw the pictures, but I didn't need to imagine what they looked like. I'd lived it.

After their visit to the police station, our Grandparents came to the hospital where Amy had been admitted and just spent the night. They charged into her room, all hellfire and damnation, demanding an explanation from our father. They said that the police had told them and shown them everything. Dad did his best in the situation, but Amy and I were both in rough shape—Amy, physically, and me, mentally. Grandma pressed hard for a chance to speak to me alone out in the hall. I was terrified of her, of every horrible thing she'd been hissing at our dad, but more than anything, I didn't want to leave Amy's bedside. That massive hospital bed practically swallowed her up. She was so out of it that she couldn't even keep her eyes open. For as scared as I was before, during, and after the accident, I was equally petrified at the hospital.

But Dad made me do it anyway. He said it would be good for me to spend some time with my grandmother. He sent me out into that hospital hallway with her. I will never forget the way she grabbed my arm the instant we were out of sight of my father, or the way she marched me down to the bank of elevators.

"Where are we going?" I'd asked, up to my neck in panic.

"The hospital chapel. You have some praying to do. You

need to tell God that you're sorry." She didn't let go of my arm. When we got to the ground floor, she pinched harder to corral me off the elevator.

"Sorry for what?" It was a legitimate question. I'd just been through something no kid should ever have to go through and there she was, telling me to apologize?

"For telling your father. You caused him to misjudge her. God is the only judge, Katherine. And children have no place telling a grown-up's secrets."

That last part was what really put me over the edge. I stopped in my tracks and wrung myself out of her grip like a wild animal. "She should've kept it a secret. She shouldn't have dragged me and Amy into it."

I'd braced for a violent rebuttal. Grandma Price had yelled at me many times before that day. She was the Shakespeare of stern talking-tos. But instead, she started to cry. She leaned back against the hideous mint green wall right there in the middle of the hospital and slid all the way to the floor, crumpling in a heap. Visitors walked by and stared at us. A nurse stopped and asked if we needed help, but Grandma shooed her away.

I have no idea why, but I ran to her. I wanted to comfort her. She was so obviously hurting, and I wanted someone to share my own pain with. "Grandma. It's okay. We're all sad." With every inch of my adult self I could still remember what it was like to sit on that linoleum floor and wait for a hug from my grandmother. Maybe a few kind words. *I'm so sorry, sweetie. You're right. Come here.*

"I lost my daughter and I feel like I lost my granddaughter, too."

"Amy's going to be fine, Grandma. She just has a broken wrist and a concussion."

That was when the anger returned. The color in her eyes was like something out of a movie about demons or monsters. It

SECRETS OF A (SOMEWHAT) SUNNY GIRL   111

wasn't human. It wasn't normal at all. "Not Amy. You. I lost you yesterday, Katherine. I can't look at you ever again. All I'll ever see is my dead daughter."

I couldn't remember what happened after that. I must've either blacked out or blocked it from my memory. The only thing I could recall was what happened when Dad and I went home that night, my suitcase and Amy's were waiting on the front porch. Apparently the police had brought them back to the house.

"What are these?" Dad asked.

It broke my heart to have to tell him. "Mom packed our suitcases before she made us get in the car to go to his house."

He cleared his throat. "So she really was taking you to live with him."

"That's what she said."

I had no idea what had happened to Mom's suitcase until we walked into our eerily quiet house and very quickly learned that every last thing that belonged to her was gone—her clothes, her shoes, her jewelry. And apparently her suitcase. Grandma took every picture, leaving behind only one—our parents' wedding portrait. As definitively as our mother was gone from our lives, so were the physical reminders. She was less than a ghost. It was almost like she'd never existed. Amy and I were the most substantial evidence of her time on earth, and we were both battered by it.

A few days later and in tears, Dad put the wedding portrait in the front closet. We never got anything of Mom's back from Grandma. Not a damn thing. She denied she'd taken everything, but it had to have been her. She'd had a key to the house and all the motive in the world. Amy and I had tried several times over the years, but we only met up with a big brick wall.

"No. Probably not the best idea to invite Grandma Price," I said to Amy, pushing my scrambled eggs around on my plate. "It would just upset Dad and I don't think she's doing well anyway. Aunt Lucy posted about it on Facebook."

"Good God, Katherine. You're friends with Aunt Lucy? I've blocked that whole side of the family. No good comes from digging up the past with them anyway."

"We don't dig up the past. I post funny cat videos and she shares tasteless memes and I mute her most of the time."

"Whatever. My point is that you don't need to throw me a bridal shower. Luke and I don't want a lot of hoopla. Really."

My stomach growled, but I pushed aside my breakfast. I had to find some great way to play a role in the wedding. I had to do right by my sister. "What about the whole something old, something new tradition? I was thinking about that last night. I could be in charge of that."

Amy shrugged. "I wouldn't be off to a very good start, would I? It's hard when you don't have anything old."

"You have me." I smiled.

"You're not old. You're just grumpy."

"Grandma Price has all of Mom's stuff. Including all of her jewelry. There was that pearl necklace Mom used to wear whenever we went somewhere nice. The double strand she wore on her wedding day. The one from their wedding portrait."

Amy and I had spent hours upon hours staring at that picture, studying it. It was, after all, the only remaining photographic evidence that our mother had ever existed, outside of the clipping of her obituary that Dad had kept in the desk in his study. Grandma had taken everything else, even the pictures of our summer vacations and Christmas mornings.

Often, when Dad was out of the house, either mowing the lawn or perhaps running an errand, which was usually a trip to the liquor store, Amy and I would clamor to pull the wedding portrait from the depths of the coat closet. We would sit on the hardwood floor, poring over this glimpse of a happy past. We analyzed our mother's facial expression, looking for clues as to why she might later become so very unhappy. We admired the way her golden blond hair curled at her temples and the way her long veil cascaded down her back. We even dared to pose theories about what our lives might be like if things had been different. If she had lived. I never really cared for that part of the conversation because it sent the guilt crushing down, but Amy liked to talk about it, so I would put up with it until we'd hear Dad's key in the front door and we'd scramble to return the photo to where it belonged—leaning against the wall behind the coats, facing away.

"Do you think she still has it? The necklace?" Amy asked.

"I don't know. But we could ask. I could send Aunt Lucy a message and see if she can get it for us." I had no idea what misguided part of me wanted so desperately for Amy to have something of our mother's for her wedding, but I did. That had always been such a hard part of trying to heal after Mom's death. Neither of us had a single thing to hold onto, which made it really hard to remember the good times. Despite the way things ended up, there had been good times. There had been happy days.

"You're opening a whole can of worms that I don't know if I'm eager to open. How do you even broach the subject without Aunt Lucy asking whether or not she'll be invited?"

"Is she invited?"

"I haven't decided."

I waved Patty over with a nod. My coffee cup was empty again. "I'm not sure how I bring it up. Let me think about it."

"Anything else I can get you ladies this morning?" Patty asked.

"That's it. Thank you." I plucked the check from her hand before she could put it on the table.

"I miss seeing you two for lunch," Patty said.

Yeah. Me too.

"We'll get back to it soon. As soon as the wedding is over, probably. Between planning and work, I'm swamped," Amy said. I hoped she was being sincere. Some semblance of our old normal would be a nice change.

Patty was hailed by a customer a few tables away and I mumbled goodbye.

"Let me think about Aunt Lucy. I'll come up with something. I'll get you that necklace."

"Please don't make a big deal of this. I can ask Luke's mom if she has something old. Or I can buy something at a vintage shop."

Amy was trying to keep the involvement from our side of the family at a minimum. I couldn't exactly stage a protest. If anyone understood why she felt that way, I did. "Please let me do this one thing. Okay?" Now I was determined, not only because Amy deserved this but because maybe this would be a chance to patch things up with my grandmother. It had been so many years. Maybe it would give me a new perspective on everything that had happened. That might help me tell Eamon. It might help me see myself in a new light. I wanted to be able to do that. I was tired walking around the world feeling like a semi-fulfilled adult. I wanted to be a fully actuated one, and that meant putting to rest at least some of what had happened in my childhood.

"Do you think I should invite them to the wedding?" Amy asked.

"I think it would be a nice gesture. They probably won't come. But at least you would've made the effort."

Amy pressed her lips into a thin line and pulled out her phone.

"What are you doing?"

"Adding their names to the guest list."

Maybe this could be a good thing. "Now I know what to tell Aunt Lucy if she asks."

Amy rolled her eyes. "Right. Now let's get to the shoe shop. If I'm not on time to my fitting at Vera Wang, it'll be murder trying to get a new appointment."

I slid out of the booth and followed Amy out of the diner. It was a chilly day today and threatening rain. "Cab it?"

"I say we walk. It's only about ten blocks."

And so we did, although those ten blocks consisted of three avenues across before we turned and walked seven streets south. We didn't talk much and I didn't really know what to say. Amy was being so weird about the wedding. She was not being herself, but it wasn't like I had anything to compare her behavior to, so I just let it go.

The visit to the shoe shop was quick. They sold only bridal shoes, which could've meant a long visit since they seemed to have about one million choices, but Amy had already made her selection—super blingy and sky-high. I was, once again, about to call bullshit on her tirade about low-key and unassuming, but Amy had always loved cute shoes. Who was I to deny her? She paid and we hustled over to Vera Wang, making it in the knick of time.

I sat and waited as the shop woman got Amy set up with the proper underpinnings. I wasn't quite prepared for the moment when she came out of the dressing room though. I'd already told myself it was okay to cry. I was basically the stand-in for our mother at that point, and it not only made sense that I fall apart at some point during the day it would be expected of me. I just hadn't planned on sobbing.

"Good Lord, Kat. Get a grip." Amy stood on the carpeted pedestal and admired herself as the folks from Vera Wang did their thing with Amy's hem.

"I can't help it." As surreal as that night had been in front of the shop window, this felt even more like a dream, like it wasn't really happening. And yet, I knew it was. The feeling that our mom should be here right now was overwhelming. She should've been here to see her youngest daughter looking perfect in her wedding dress.

"Does that mean you like it?"

"It's even more perfect on you than it was in the window."

Amy pulled up the skirt just enough to show off the shoes. "I think these work well."

"Yep. Also perfect." I nodded, slowly regaining my composure and grabbing a tissue from the generous box sitting on a side table.

"Good. Two more things I can cross off my list." Amy looked accomplished, and most important, she looked happy. Maybe she'd be in a better mood the rest of the day.

"Did you want us to pull some necklaces to try with the dress?" the saleswoman asked.

"No," I blurted. "I mean, no, thank you. We have a family necklace we're hoping she can wear."

"I see."

"It was our mother's," I added. "She wore it the day she was married to our dad."

"It sounds wonderful," the saleswoman answered, seeming wholly disinterested. She was probably pissed at me for cutting down on her commission.

I walked up to Amy after the seamstress announced she had everything she needed. "You look absolutely beautiful. Luke is going to flip."

"Do you really think we should count on the necklace? Maybe I should just pick something out to be safe."

I shook my head. "No. I will get that necklace if it's the last thing I do."

CHAPTER TEN

THE MOOD of the shopping trip with Amy took a noticeable turn when we left Vera Wang and there was only more stop to make—Maggie's Floral. Mother Nature had gone for the purely theatrical and moved a bank of gray clouds in over the city, shutting out the sun, and casting everything in an eerie blue. It sure as hell felt like the arrival of Mom's ghost. Flowers were her specialty. She should have been here for this.

"Do you want to stop and get a coffee? Maybe frozen yogurt? A cookie?" I asked, sensing that Amy might want to put this off. I could be totally onboard with that.

"No. Maybe we should save that for after. I'm still pretty hopped up on caffeine from breakfast anyway."

Amy was going for the "let's just get this over with" approach. I admired her fortitude in the face of what might be her greatest bridal hurdle. "Great. Then lead the way."

The sky was threatening to open up, sprinkling raindrops on us, so we nabbed a cab as soon as we could. Once again, things were quiet between us, but this was one of those symbiotic sister moments. Neither of us had to say what we were feeling or thinking. We were battling the same inner conflict, wanting so desperately to be able to saunter into Maggie's Floral and revisit happy memories of our mom. But we both knew it would never be as simple as that. The good was too inextricably tied to the bad.

When Amy and I were kids, our mother worked at Taylor & Daughters Flowers, a few miles from our house. She'd actually started there when she was pregnant with me. She even went into labor while working the counter, her water leaking all over the gray-and-white checkered linoleum floor. Our mom lived for that job. Amy and I loved the shop, too. It was pure magic.

A hippie lady named Sarah Taylor, who wore long flowing skirts and jangly bracelets, owned it. Ms. Taylor didn't have any actual daughters, but she resented how businesses had "& Sons" tacked on to the end of their name like that was supposed to make them more legitimate, but daughters were never discussed. I'd heard Sarah say many times to her customers that the women who worked in the shop were just like her daughters, and she tended to hire women who were, by her own admission, a bit lost. Apparently our mom fell into that category, a community college dropout with an interest in art, but no real talent for things like paint or sculpture. But she had an eye for color and design and she became a master with flowers.

For as long as I could remember, Amy and I spent every Saturday at the shop. It was a necessity when Dad was out of town on a work trip, which as we got older, was pretty much every week. It was like a fairytale, with big windows that faced the street, the sun streaming across the long wood counter marred with deep gouges from scissors and clippers. There was this unavoidable feeling that anything could happen there, but it never seemed foreboding. It felt more born of possibility.

The smell in the shop was like nothing else—sweet and fresh and heady, like a garden in the middle of summer, but even more potent. If there were lilies in the shop, the fragrance always made me a bit sick, but Amy loved it. She would run into the back room and stick her face into the profusion of blooms. If the lilies were open, she'd end up with stains of orangey-brown pollen on her cheeks and nose. Mom was always busy doing arrangements and assisting customers, so it was my job to help Amy get cleaned up. It always took a lot of rubbing with rough brown bathroom paper towels. There were invariably tears and accusations that I was a mean older sister, followed by a stern reminder from me that if she would just stop doing that, I wouldn't have to scrub her face clean in the first place.

Saturdays were big days at Taylor & Daughters—wedding day. Much of the work would've been done Friday, but there were always a million last minute things to do. Mom was the one who made everything come together. She ensured the flowers were still looking their best, replacing any blooms that might have drooped overnight. Wanting no bride to ever be disappointed, she double and triple-checked the order, then packed everything up in the big white delivery van. That's how Mom became involved with Gordon. He was the delivery driver for Taylor & Daughters, hired when I was one year old. Gordon and Mom had known each other in high school. They'd even dated. Right there, in the charming shop that Amy and I loved so much, was where their affair began.

The cab zipped up to the curb and jerked to a stop in front of Maggie's Floral. Amy collected our things while I paid the driver, and we made our way inside. A tiny bell chimed when Amy opened the door. An older woman with kind violet eyes emerged from the back room. "Can I help you?"

"Yes. Hi. I'm Amy Fuller. Are you Maggie? I called about flowers for my wedding. Mrs. Mayhew recommended you. She's my future mother-in-law." Amy was rambling and her voice was tight. I knew she was feeling just as overwhelmed as I was—the sights and smells made it feel like we'd been thrust into a movie made of our own memories.

"Oh, yes." Maggie smiled. "This must be your sister. The one with the special eyesight?"

Amy slipped out of her coat, draped it over her arm and turned to me. "Yes. This is Katherine."

"It's not really that special," I said. "I mean. It's not like it's a talent. I was just born this way."

"Your sister told me all about it on the phone. She's very proud of your abilities."

I could feel a blush creeping across my cheeks. It felt good to know I was the only one who could help Amy in this way, but it didn't take away the bittersweet edge of picking out flowers. "That's my sister. Always bragging about something." I elbowed Amy and she tittered nervously.

Maggie pulled out a large three-ring binder and placed it on the counter in front of two stools. She sat on the opposite side. "These are some bouquets I've done for other brides. I find it best to start with the bouquet and work everything else from there."

"Our mom always said that," I said. "When she worked with brides. She worked at a florist when we were little."

"How nice," Maggie offered. "Will she be helping with the wedding?"

An even darker pall crept over the scene. I never should've brought her up. That had been stupid of me. "She passed away when we were kids."

"I'm so sorry." Maggie's voice had taken on a somber and heavy tone.

"Thank you." Amy now seemed more annoyed than anxious. "Let's pick something out."

Amy and I were both quiet as church mice as we looked at page after page of bouquets. I chimed in when she asked for my opinion, which wasn't often. There were just a lot of silent head-shakes or hums of "maybe" and the occasional hesitant nod. By the time Amy had reached the end of the book, she hadn't found anything she liked.

"Maybe we could look at some actual flowers," I suggested. "Come up with some ideas?"

Just then, another customer came in. "Sure thing," Maggie said. "Everything is in the back room in floral buckets. Feel free to go into the cooler, too. I'll be back after I'm done helping this customer."

Amy and I traced down a narrow hall lined with shelves of clear glass ginger jar vases standing like soldiers.

"Now this is more like it," I said when we arrived in the back room. I zeroed in on some beautiful dark purple calla lilies.

"So now you're going to say something?"

"What's that supposed to mean?"

"I asked your opinion and you hardly said anything."

"I was letting you take the lead. Was I not supposed to do that?"

"I need your help, Katherine."

"Do you? Really? Because I felt like our entire conversation at the diner was about you *not* needing my help. And then we go to Vera Wang and it was pretty clear you don't think you can count on me to get the necklace. I don't need you to humor me. If you don't want me involved, just tell me."

Amy sucked in a deep breath and shook her head. "Do you know what I want?"

"I don't, Ames. I really don't."

"I want to be a normal bride, arguing with her mom about who should get invited and whether we should have chicken or fish. Instead, I get Luke's mom, who just wants to take every-thing out of my hands, like I have horrible taste or am completely clueless about what a wedding entails."

Maggie appeared in the back room. "Everything okay?"

Amy looked petrified, which was saying a lot. She wasn't embarrassed by much. "Just a little sisterly squabble. I'm so sorry."

"Oh, honey. I wasn't trying to listen, but what I overheard is nothing but perfectly run of the mill. This room has seen brides throw fistfuls of carnations. I'll leave you two to it. Just come and fetch me when we need to talk flowers." With that, Maggie retreated back to the front of the store.

"I'm sorry, Ames. I'm sorry Mom's not here to help you. If I could make her appear, I would. If I could conjure her out of thin air, I would." The underlying current of this was that I was the reason she wasn't there. I had been the cause.

"But you can't. Neither of us can." Right there, in a few short words, was the essence of the pain Amy and I fought on a daily basis.

"Look. I want to do whatever you want me to do. If you want me to argue with you about the menu, I totally will. If you want me to tell Luke's mom to back off, I will. Whatever you want, I'll do it."

Amy nodded slowly, scanning my face. "I think more than anything, I just need you to be my rock. Like you always are. Like you always were. I don't think I know how to function without you being there for me."

Tears clouded my vision of my sister. "I will always be there for you. Always. Happy or sad, you and I can get through anything, right?"

Her head bobbed up and down, and now she was crying, too. "Yep."

"We can do whatever you want to do today and we can set aside whatever you don't feel like doing. This is your wedding. We don't have to accomplish everything today. We'll have some time after Thanksgiving."

Amy went in for a hug, resting her head on my shoulder. "Thank you. I know I'm pathetic right now."

"You're getting married. You're supposed to be pathetic."

"I thought I was supposed to be on top of the world."

"That's just the movies."

After our talk, we called Maggie to the back room and we chose a gorgeous combination of deep purple calla lilies and red roses wrapped in silver satin ribbon for Amy's bouquet, and a smaller version for the bridesmaids. Amy seemed pleased, and much more relaxed. Maybe she'd just needed to freak out at me. I was okay with that.

We said our goodbyes out on the street. "I'm so sorry I was a bitch in there. It's just a lot to deal with," she said.

I pulled her into a hug. "I love you. You know that, right?" Despite the permanent off-putting smell of New York, I could still draw in the sweet fragrance of her shampoo, which brought me back to the days when we were roommates and I'd walk into the bathroom after her shower only to discover that she'd used all of the hot water. There was something so comforting about that smell.

"I know. And I love you, too. I promise I'll be less of a pain next time I see you."

"When will that be?"

She shrugged. "I don't know. I have to go out of town for a work thing next week and Luke's parents want us to go with them to their house on the shore of Maryland. I'll have to look at my calendar."

I donned my requisite sisterly smile. "Okay. We'll figure something out."

"Eamon's coming to see you, soon. Right?"

"He is." It was the sole bright spot right now.

"Cool. I'm sure you're looking forward to that. Maybe Luke and I can have you guys over for dinner after he gets into town.

That would be fun. Luke's actually a bit of a fan. Although he's a total music geek to begin with."

"I didn't know that."

"Yep." She nodded then looked at her phone. "I should go grab my train." In a flash she kissed me on the cheek. "Love you. Talk to you later."

I stood there on the sidewalk and watched her walk away, her blonde hair swinging back and forth. I decided to soak up the anxiousness that came over me when she left. I had to get used to it. There was so much more of it ahead.

I opted to walk back to my apartment, relishing the cold damp air and the sense that winter was coming. Before we knew it, Thanksgiving would be here, and then the wedding. Hopefully Eamon and I would still be in one piece by then. I not only didn't want to go to my sister's wedding by myself, I wanted to make something in my life work.

As soon as I keyed into my apartment and threw down my stuff, I pulled up Facebook on my computer and prepared myself to write a message to Aunt Lucy. I had about fifty false starts before I decided on the most direct approach.

Aunt Lucy,

I'm writing because Amy is getting married right before Christmas. You should get an invitation soon, although I'm not sure when she's sending them. As you know, every bride needs something old, something new, something borrowed, and something blue. Amy would really like to wear our mother's pearls as her something old. As far as I know, Grandma Price has them. Is it possible for you to play intermediary with getting it for Amy? That would be a huge help to me. If you need me to speak to Grandma directly, I will do it, but I thought I'd start with you since you see her more regularly. I hope all is well with you.

Love, Katherine

I didn't particularly feel a lot of love for my Aunt Lucy, but warmth seemed like the way to go for now. I shut down my laptop and did the only thing I could do. Poured myself a glass of wine, made myself a quick dinner, and curled up in bed with a book, waiting for Eamon to call.

Like clockwork, he rang at eleven. "Only two more days," he said right away.

"Crazy, isn't it?" I snuggled up under the covers in my very non-sexy pajamas. After the day I'd had with my sister, I was not in the mood for an iPhone booty call.

"It's actually less than forty-eight hours. I should get to your place Sunday morning."

"Sunday morning? Wow. I thought you were flying in from San Francisco. Don't you have a show Saturday night?" I started mentally going through the list of all of the stuff I needed to do—laundry, shopping, shaving.

"I had my road manager get me a seat on the red eye. I didn't want to stay in SF and get up in the morning. I'd rather just land and get to your place right away."

I still couldn't believe this was happening. All these weeks of talking, and the waiting was about to be over. "Sounds perfect. I can't wait."

CHAPTER ELEVEN

AT TEN ON SUNDAY MORNING, Eamon showed up at my apartment dressed as the man in black. Black bomber jacket, black jeans, charcoal wool scarf wound around his neck. His dark hair was pushed back from his face, showing off his now-feral beard. His eyes crinkled at the corners when he smiled. I could see how excited he was to be here. This unbelievable man was happy to see me.

"Hi." I didn't know what else to say. I was so painfully aware of what we both wanted first from each other—everything we stopped short of doing at the Four Seasons.

He carefully set down a battered acoustic guitar case along the wall just inside the door. His canvas duffel didn't get the same treatment, forcefully flung across the floor. "I hope you had the sense not to make any plans today. We are not leaving this apartment." His voice was rough and my head dizzied with the possibilities.

Plans. If only he knew. The sheets had been washed. Every square inch of my place was immaculate. I was not only wearing really nice underwear, it was a matching set. "I'm not dumb, you know."

"Wasn't saying you are. I didn't want to take off your clothes and have you tell me you got tickets to see *Hamilton*."

"Don't be silly. It's still impossible to get tickets."

He smiled wide and uncoiled the scarf. "Funny. You're funny." He unzipped his jacket. My breaths got shallower with every tiny stretch of his skin. He looked skinny, and that made me want to feed him, but dammit, I had to focus. All the while, he didn't take his gray eyes off me. He wrapped one arm around my waist, dug the opposite hand into my hair, and nearly made me collapse on the floor with a whisper of a kiss on the corner of my mouth. There was tongue—the sweetest amount, except there was nothing sweet about it. The subtext was nothing but hot sex.

"I don't even get a hello?" I wanted to continue to be amusing or at least get my bearings before this happened. Why couldn't I shut up already and rip off his clothes?

"This *is* my hello." He reached down and grabbed my ass, pulling my hips into his.

I smiled as our lips drifted closer together. "I like your hello. I like it a lot."

"My hello misses you." Skipping a real kiss, his mouth roamed to my neck. I closed my eyes and gave into his apparent need to torture me. Every inch of Eamon was meant for making me feel good. He was going to remind me of it. With meticulous detail.

"Good. I missed your hello."

He sucked in a breath through his nose. It was the sound of a desperate man. "I missed everything about you, Kat." He kissed my cheek, my temple, my forehead. "Your hair. The way you smell. Your smile. Your glorious neck."

My heart nearly melted. He always knew the perfect thing to say. I smoothed my hands around his waist and tugged up his flannel shirt, exploring his back, every muscle and channel familiar. "I missed everything about you, too." I could've produced a complete inventory in no time of the many, many things I had missed about Eamon.

His mouth finally landed on mine and I went blind. I knew exactly what it felt like to kiss him, but somehow there was an element of surprise. How could anything feel so good? I was sinking and floating at the same time. The kiss made the last one we shared look like a first date. Gone was the backwards tug of war. We knew how to do this to each other. We knew exactly how our bodies fit together.

My hands fumbled with the front of his shirt. The desperation and anticipation of the last few weeks—hell, the last decade —burned through me like a spark zips along a fuse. I was a botched up mess with his buttons, like my hands couldn't remember how to work, but multitasking with Eamon—kissing and undressing him—was no small feat. I was on sensory overload.

I forced the final button through the hole and pushed the shirt past his shoulders. He caught it in one hand and tossed it onto the chair in the corner. When he curled his fingers under the hem of my sweater and lifted it over my head, everything went from being familiar to new. And back again. The excitement, the tunnel vision, the way the rest of the world disappeared when I was with him came roaring back like it had been waiting in the deepest corners of my mind. Waiting for its chance. Any doubts I'd had about recapturing what we'd once had were gone. It was still there. It was right here. All around us.

He pulled me closer, our bare stomachs touching as we stumbled across the room. "I don't know where I'm going." His voice came out as a burst between kisses. "Show me."

"Oh. Yeah. Sorry." I took his hand and tugged him down the hall, past Amy's empty bedroom, and the bathroom, to my room.

He smiled when we stepped inside. "Much better." He

perched on the edge of the bed and reached down to untie his boots. He was watching me while he plucked at the laces, but I was watching him, too.

The sun streamed in through the window, catching threads of silver in his hair. His boots and socks were gone now and I stepped between his knees, slipping my fingers through his long, somewhat tangled locks. "You've got some salt and pepper in here now."

"Mostly salt in some spots. That's what eleven years will get ya." The rumble in his voice was back, working its way into me. It was like my own personal dog whistle. It shook me awake every time he spoke.

"I like it. It's sexy."

"You fancy the old man with the long hair?" He peppered my belly with kisses while he unhooked my bra and pulled it down my arms.

I laughed and sank down to my knees, resting my arms on his thighs. "I do. He's ridiculously hot."

He leaned closer and kissed me, squeezing my ribcage with his legs and cupping my breasts with his hands. How was it possible that all these years later, the calluses on his hands would feel the same way, perfectly hard and rough against my nipples? A sharp gasp left my lips.

"I love it when you make that noise," he mumbled against my lips.

"You're torturing me."

"No, darling. I just want you to feel good."

As if I could feel anything less right now.

He threaded his arms under mine and hoisted me back onto the bed, on top of him, my legs twisted between his. He groaned as I let my full body weight rest on his, and he wrapped his leg around me and flipped me to my back. He stretched out alongside me. His warm lips found my breast, sucking on my nipple, flicking at it with his tongue. Oblivion was already in my sights.

I unbuckled his belt, unbuttoned and unzipped his jeans. He did the rest of the job for me, pushing them and his boxers past his hips and onto the floor. I rolled him to his back and kneeled between his legs.

"Don't start this while you're still wearing clothes, Katherine. You're going to frustrate the hell out of me."

I smiled and popped off the bed, dispatching my jeans and panties. "Better?" I asked, setting a knee back on the mattress. I didn't wait for an answer before I took him in my hand, his skin so smooth and hard against mine. Again, our blissful history swirled in my mind, the untold times we'd done this together.

He clamped his eyes shut and knocked his head back on the bed. I stroked him. Firmly, but not too hard, and all I could think about was how I wanted to make him happy, but more than anything, I wanted to feel him. Inside me. This was everything I'd thought about that morning we had breakfast. Everything I'd fantasized about over the last few weeks. Everything I would've killed for after I left Ireland, when I had to lie in my bed at night and try to sleep, all while my brain wouldn't stop remembering the magic of every moment with him.

I didn't bother asking if he had a condom. I opened my bedside table drawer and plucked one from the box. I rolled it onto him. One step closer to what I wanted. And then I stretched out next to him. Goosebumps dotted my arms. There was nothing else holding us back. No more clothes between us, no more space, no more distance. The universe had pulled me back into the arms of the only man my heart wanted the way my lungs wanted to breathe.

He pushed my hair from my face and kissed me deeply, then eased me to my back and climbed on top of me. We didn't talk. We didn't need to. We both knew what the other wanted.

That was a very special brand of knowledge—when words become extraneous. I closed my eyes and pulled his smell into my nose—salt and soap and sunshine. There was no other way to describe it or just how easily that perfect smell took me back to our other time. When I had found hope and joy in the simplest things. When I knew what it was like to be happy.

But I wouldn't live in the past. Not today. Thinking like that did a lot of damage to a person, and it ruined the present. I opened my eyes and kissed his forehead. I studied every line, every new, tiny crease around his eyes. This was exactly what I'd wanted so badly the other morning. To have him weigh me down and make me remember that this was the here-and-now.

He thrust inside exactly as he'd done so many times, but now was different. I felt both whole and vulnerable. We were one again. Something I'd thought would never happen. I'd been convinced the Eamon chapter of my life was over, that he and I were never meant to be.

And now it felt as though my once-hidden second act with Eamon was just beginning.

———

On Monday morning, I called Summer and took a personal day. In nearly eight years at NACI, I hadn't taken a single day off. I was the person who scheduled a dentist appointment at lunch so I wouldn't miss work. But Eamon was already making me do things I would never do. We'd spent all day Sunday naked or half-dressed, in bed or in the shower. I'd even gone to bed with wet hair.

Summer was as shocked as I was when I called. "I hope everything's okay."

"Everything's great." Eamon was in the bathroom, so I could contain my enthusiasm without worrying that he might think I wasn't ridiculously happy right now. I didn't want to gush to my boss or give any details about how I might be having sex all day long. Not professional. "I have some things I'd like to get done around the apartment. Stuff I've been putting off."

Eamon was standing in the doorway now, completely naked, leaning against the jamb and listening. Good God, my sister was right. I was a lucky bitch. I patted his spot on the bed next to me.

"You have more than enough days, so I'm not worried about it," Summer said.

"And everything will be okay with you-know-who?"

"Oh, Miles? Don't worry about him. I'll take care of him. We'll miss you, of course, but enjoy your day. I'll see you tomorrow."

"Yes. Absolutely. See you then."

Eamon climbed into bed while I ended my call and rolled to my side, placing my phone on the bedside table. "Your hair's a very sexy bird's nest," he said, kissing my neck and pressing his long body up against my back.

Would I ever grow immune to Eamon's touch? Would I ever get to the point where this wasn't pure bliss? "So you're telling me you like things that are a complete disaster."

"The more disastrous the better."

"And you're happy with the sheets the way they are right now?" I kicked at the covers. Everything was twisted up—the duvet, the top sheet. Even the fitted sheet kept popping off the corner closest to my head, which was driving me crazy.

"Hadn't even noticed there was a problem." He pressed a single kiss to my cheek. "That's how happy I am to be here."

I rolled to my back and peered up at him. If my hair was a disaster, his wasn't much better, but he pulled off the disheveled look perfectly. The man could've walked into a photo shoot at that very moment and he would've had no problem. "I'm happy you're here, too."

"It's amazing, isn't it? Being together again after all this time?"

I smiled, smoothing his hair back from his face. "It really is. I keep having to remind myself that this is really happening. I woke up in the middle of the night and I flipped on the lamp for a second just so I could make sure it was really you."

"Expecting someone else?"

I slapped his arm playfully. "No."

"You really did that?"

"I did."

The way his face lit up was so beautiful. It made it hard to breathe. "I must've been tired to sleep through that."

"You outdid yourself yesterday." Just saying it made me hungry for more of him. I had once thought this was a feeling you could only have in your teens or twenties. Now I knew I'd been wrong.

"The sex is even better now. How is that possible?"

I popped up on to my elbow. "Yes. I was just thinking the same thing."

Under the tangled covers, he trailed his fingers from my waist, up over my hip and down my thigh. It was like someone running their hands over every button inside an elevator—everything inside me was back on again. "You're much freer with your body now, Katherine. It's really very sexy."

I laughed quietly. He wasn't wrong, but boy howdy had Eamon and I made a solid run at being free with our bodies the first time we'd been together. "I'm sort of over worrying about the parts of me that pudge out. I'll never be as skinny as you, anyway."

"I love every square inch of you, especially the wobbly bits." He pushed me onto my back and started kissing my neck again, lazily blazing a trail with his mouth that led across my chest and ended at my breasts. He pressed soft kisses in a circle, which was heavenly on its own, but I nearly shot off into space when he drew my nipple into his mouth.

I arched into him. He knew exactly how to make me weak. I reached over to my bedside table and grabbed the box of condoms sitting there. "Last one," I said, handing him the packet.

"Better make it count." He rolled to his side then he had me at his mercy again. He went as deep as he could, pressing into my hips with his, nuzzling my neck with his scratchy beard. I wrapped my legs around him, digging my heels into his ass and running my hands all over his back. It didn't take long before we were both gasping for breath.

I curled into him, kissing his chest. "We should probably think about food at some point."

He drew circles on my back with his hand. "We never ate dinner last night."

"I know. What sounds good? I could make eggs. Maybe French toast?" I started to get out of bed, but he stopped me with a tug of his arm. "Eamon. We just finished. I'd like to return to work without a limp."

He laughed. "Well done, keeping your head in the gutter."

"If anyone has their brain in the gutter, it's you." I relented and sat down on the bed.

"I need to say something. And I don't think it's a good idea to wait on it." There was a sharp edge to his voice that made my stomach sink. There was something wrong, or at the very least something bothering him, and it didn't seem fair that we should have to face anything hard or difficult right now. We were just getting started.

"What is it?"

"We never talked about this when you were in Ireland.

Everything snuck up on us so fast." He held my hand, playing with my fingers, looking down and avoiding my eyes.

"What is it?" I couldn't begin to imagine what it was that we hadn't talked about. We'd talked about so much—dreams and beauty and aspirations.

When he looked up, his steely gray eyes nearly made the earth stop spinning. "Love. We never talked about love. All that time together and we never said 'I love you'." He reached up and it was his turn to push the hair back from my face. "Truth is, I love you. I think I have always loved you. Even all this time. I think I've loved you since before we even knew each other."

Tears wobbled in my eyes. I felt that, too. I'd put it in my letter. The one that was never read. I'd put *I love you* out into the universe and it disappeared. "I love you, too, Eamon. I feel like I have this second chance at life right now. Just because you're back in it."

We kissed, and my wet cheeks rubbed against his. We were both half laughing, half serious. This was a kiss we would both remember.

"I actually said I love you in the letter I wrote. The one you never got."

His eyes grew sad again. "You did?" He shook his head and collapsed on his back, staring up at the ceiling. "I hate that I never saw it. I hate thinking that you said that and you never got a response from me." Rolling onto his side, he looked at me with all earnestness. "If I'd seen that, I would've written you back. I would've called you. I would've flown to see you or bought you a plane ticket. I want you to know that."

Somehow, that wasn't what I wanted to hear, even though at the time, I would've done anything for those things to have happened. "But you didn't see it. And those things didn't happen. And I can't live with any more regrets. So let's just not talk about it anymore." I had too many regrets living in my heart already.

He kissed me tenderly. "We have today and I love you. That's all that matters."

"We have tomorrow and the day after that, too."

"If we're lucky, yes."

I settled my head against his chest and he pulled me closer. "I love you, Eamon. That never went away."

And I meant it. Every syllable.

CHAPTER TWELVE

I WASN'T DOING A PARTICULARLY good job at achieving a work-Eamon balance. In fact, I was failing spectacularly.

"I really, really, really have to go into work today. I'll get fired if I don't. It's been three days. I'm sure I have a million things to catch up on." I shuffled backwards across the floor of my bedroom wearing only my underwear, headed for the closet to grab some clothes.

Eamon was in hot pursuit wearing only his boxers, which hung super low on his hips. "I know. You have things to do. So do I."

I stepped into my gray wool trousers and zipped them up, then pulled a black silk blouse from its hanger. "That's right. You need to get some writing done. This will be a good thing for both of us." I only got one button done before Eamon was standing right in front of me, drawing a finger down my chest and popping it out of its hole. "Hey..." My voice faded as he stole a kiss, pressing his bare belly against mine. Trying to dress yourself while a super hot rock star, one who could start a fire with his voice, was kissing you, was exactly as difficult as it sounded.

"Sorry. I'm distracting you."

"Honestly, you're just feeding my ego right now, which under normal circumstances would be great, but my new boss is an asshole and I don't want to piss him off any more than I probably already have."

A bit dejected, he puttered over to the chair and grabbed his jeans. "I understand."

I managed to get my blouse buttoned and even tucked it in. "I'll be home by six. I promise." I grabbed my black pumps from the bottom of the closet and worked my feet into them. "The extra key is on the kitchen counter in case you decide to go out. There's a ton of food in the fridge."

"I'm a big boy. I can figure it out. Just go. The sooner you leave, the sooner you can come back."

I smiled and kissed him one more time. "I love you."

"I love you, too." He swatted me on the ass as I walked out of the room.

I made the subway with zero seconds to spare, having to stand for the ride to my office, which was always a challenge in heels. Part of me almost wished Eamon had been successful at keeping me home, which said a lot considering how much I loved my job. Perhaps it was just the Miles effect—everything had been great until he arrived.

As expected, I had about five million emails waiting for me, and people lining up at my office door almost as soon as I got in.

"We missed you, Katherine. What were you up to?" Maria from the marketing team wanted me to troubleshoot the typography for ads for a new meal delivery company.

"I have an old friend in town and we haven't seen each other in a long time. It just seemed like a good idea to spend some quality time together."

"Sounds fun. The office doesn't run the same without you though. I hope you know that."

"Thank you so much. I really, truly appreciate it."

She smiled. "I wouldn't say it if it wasn't the truth. Thanks for your help on this."

I craned my neck to see if anyone else was lurking at my doorstep, but I'd worked through the queue, so I returned to the endless job of answering email. A few minutes later, another knock came at my door, I looked up and my stomach sank. "Hello, Miles. How are you today?"

He waltzed into my office and sat in the chair opposite my desk. Sure, being the boss affords you certain privileges, but it would've been nice if he'd asked if he could have a seat. "I see that you're back. You'll forgive me for not quite knowing the landscape of the office yet, but is it a habit of yours to miss three days of work with no notice?"

"Actually, aside from when I had food poisoning two years ago, I've missed exactly zero days of work since I've been here."

He nodded, but in no way seemed satisfied. "I see." He crossed his giraffe-ish legs, bright striped socks peeking out between the hem of his pants and his walnut brown wingtips. How clever of him to pair a rainbow with his dull gray suit.

"You can ask Summer. She'll tell you." I hated that I sounded like a teenager making excuses, but this was what he was bringing out in me—the worst.

"I'll have a look at your file as soon as I leave." He pulled his phone out of his pocket. "Siri, remind me to check Katherine Fuller's personnel file in an hour."

I sat there listening to the automated voice repeat his request back to him. Miles was a certifiable jerk. At least he'd given me permission to think that of him.

"Summer adores you, you know," he went on. "She's convinced that you are one of the most crucial people on the team."

He was just waiting for me to ask what he thought of me,

which I already knew, so I wasn't about to take the bait. Still, I was trembling with a mix of fear and anger I couldn't quite wrap my head around. "Summer is the best boss anyone could ever want."

"Yes. Well, now that I've been here a good month or so, I think we're going to do some restructuring."

"What does that mean?"

"Shifting of personnel. A few changes."

From out in the hall, came the sound of a woman squealing. *Oh my God.* Then another. *Oh my God.* And another. *It's you.*

"What in bloody hell is going on out there?" Miles shot out of his seat and bolted into the hall.

I followed him to the door, but hung back, clutching my phone. If someone was out there with a gun, somebody was going to need to call 911. A steady stream of my coworkers were filing out into the central space that led to reception. The chatter was non-stop, the volume building. At that point, it was clear that whatever was going on, no one was getting shot, so I ventured out to see for myself.

The walkway was packed with people now, everyone shuffling forward. Phillip from accounting asked, "Who is it?"

One of the college interns answered, "I don't know. Some old guy wearing sunglasses."

The previous squealing was still going on, there was only more of it, now accompanied by the flash of camera phones. I squeezed past Phillip and that's when I saw what was going on. Eamon was here, signing autographs and posing for photos. Several of my female coworkers were practically hanging on him, taking selfies.

"Everyone, back to your desks!" Miles shouted above the din.

Nobody listened.

"Excuse me, sir. Do you have business here?" Miles asked Eamon.

Eamon propped his sunglasses up on his forehead and there was an audible gasp from the women working reception. "I'm here to see Katherine."

Miles whipped around and narrowed his beady eyes on me. "Ms. Fuller, it seems you have a guest."

I slinked ahead, giving Miles a wide berth and walking around several people to get directly to Eamon. "Hey. What are you doing here? I thought you were writing."

He took my hand and smiled, then pressed a kiss to my cheek, which prompted more gasping from the peanut gallery. You'd have thought he was Elvis on the Ed Sullivan show. I wasn't exactly upset about it. I was aware of how spectacular a prize he was. "I thought I'd take you to lunch."

I glanced up at the clock above reception. It was already past one. Lunch was a reasonable request. "Oh. Okay. Sure." The crowd had dissipated, but I could feel Miles's looming presence behind me.

As if he knew what I was thinking, Eamon reached past me and held out his hand. "Hello there. Eamon MacWard. You must be Miles." Eamon slyly slid me a wink. He *had* been paying attention all those times I'd bitched about Miles.

Miles obliged the handshake, but his spine was stiff as a board. "I'm Mr. Ashby. You'll have to excuse me if I don't know why our staff is so enamored of you."

"Ah, well, I'm a musician."

"Unless you play Chopin, I'm afraid I've never heard of you." Miles chuckled dismissively and I truly wanted to punch him.

"Eamon just finished a sold-out U.S. Tour." I had to stick up for my guy.

"The New York show was amazing." Janice from HR

chimed in as she walked past, stealing a head-to-toe eyeful of Eamon.

Miles huffed. "Ms. Fuller, I wasn't aware you had a so-called famous husband."

"I don't." I was then stuck with the task of slapping a label on Eamon when we'd discussed nothing of the sort. "Eamon is my..." I winced, but took the leap anyway. "Boyfriend."

The smile on his face was my reward for bravery. "That's right. Old flames. Reunited."

"I see. Well, Ms. Fuller, I'm sure you're aware that this is a place of business and not social hour. Spouses are welcome for a moment or two if they are not a disruption. Otherwise, this is highly unusual."

It took every ounce of self-control I had not to stomp on Miles's wingtips and tell him he was an asshole. "I'm sorry."

"Don't let it happen again." He straightened his tie. "Mr. MacWard. Good day." With that, he stalked off.

I stepped closer to Eamon. "I'm so sorry."

"Weren't kidding when you said he was a jerk."

"He's such a pain in the butt," I whispered. "Everyone else who works here is so nice."

"So? Lunch? You game?"

I hesitated, knowing Miles would use any excuse right now to rake me over the coals. Still, I wasn't sure I cared. "Yes. I'd love it. Come to my office and I'll grab my purse and coat."

Eamon followed me to my modest work abode. "This is where the magic happens?" He gestured to the stacks of files on my desk, mostly projects that needed a final pass from me before they moved forward. "Looks like you have a lot of magic to do."

Miles strolled by and cleared his throat.

"The fucking gall of that guy..." I muttered under my breath as I put on my coat.

"Got the impression that boyfriends and girlfriends and loved ones in general are frowned upon around here."

"He just doesn't like me."

Eamon's eyebrows drew together. "How is that possible?"

"Not everyone likes me."

He pressed a soft kiss against my lips. "I adore you. That's got to count for more than whatever that British prick thinks."

I closed my eyes and drew in his beguiling smell. "I'd much rather have you. That's for sure."

"It's an argument for marriage, y'know. Your jerky boss won't be able to give you such a hard time."

Just like that, Eamon was moving too fast for me. "You don't really mean that."

"Maybe I do."

"You just got back. We're just starting to get to know each other again."

He took my hand. "Yeah. You're right. Speaking of which, Rachel is bringing Fiona to the city in a few days. I already told her we'd meet them."

The Eamon train was officially a runaway now. He had a toe in every square inch of my life. It mostly made me happy, but these were all big steps forward, when for me even the tiny ones were scary.

CHAPTER THIRTEEN

A FEW DAYS LATER, Eamon and I walked to the park in my neighborhood to meet up with Rachel and Fiona. It felt a bit as if I was marching toward my fate. I'd never been good at confronting the past. Now I was going to meet Eamon's. The leaves rustled in the cool November wind, some letting go of the branches that had been their home for months and fluttering to the ground.

"Last chance to tell me what happened between you and Rachel." I didn't want to be so basic with the question, but we were closing in on the park and I wanted to know what we were walking into. I'd already asked him about it several times since he told me they were coming to town, and he'd dodged the topic at every turn.

Eamon cleared his throat and distanced himself from me—it was only inches, but it felt like a chasm. "It's complicated. And not terribly fun to talk about."

I slipped my hand under his biceps and snugged him closer. I wasn't about to let him get away. "Sometimes it helps to talk about it."

"I usually write a song if I need to do that."

"Humor me. Now. Before we get to the park."

He sucked in a deep breath and stuffed his hands into his pants pockets. It was chilly, but the way he had his shoulders up around his ears made it seem like we were out here in the depths of winter. "I was a terrible husband. That's all you need to know."

"That's it?"

"I don't want to talk about it, okay? It's the biggest failure of my life." He came to a stop in the middle of the sidewalk and grabbed my hand. "If I have any chance of getting you to think about us as something long-term, I'm not helping my case by telling you how badly I fucked up the first time."

"It only makes you human to fail. And it takes two people to end a marriage. There's no way it was all you."

"Believe me, I was no help. No help at all." He pulled back the sleeve of his coat and looked at his watch. "Come on. I don't want to be late."

When we came up on the tall iron fencing surrounding the park, the sounds of children playing rang out between the other sounds of the city—impatient taxi drivers laying on the horn while unwitting pedestrians passed too close to cars and set off the alarms. A boy chased a ball past the park entrance. His mother yelled after him. That was when I saw Rachel. She was sitting on a bench, but the instant she looked up and spotted Eamon, a flicker of recognition crossed her face that was impossible to miss. She was still in love with him. I could see it.

She played it cool though, uncrossing her legs and rising from her perch. She took a few steps toward the play structure, cupped her hands around her mouth, and called for Fiona. From behind a slide, a shock of auburn hair popped up. There she was—the real light of Eamon's life.

Fiona turned and saw Eamon, then took off after him. He did the same, letting go of my hand and rushing up to her. He scooped her up into his arms and held her for a few heartbeats. Fiona was going to be like her dad—tall.

Rachel and I converged on them at the same time and I tried to ignore the way it felt like I was intruding in their lives. Yes, Eamon wanted me there, and I was going to have to meet them both at some point, but it felt as though I was treading on the sanctity of their history.

Eamon leaned down and kissed Fiona's forehead. "I want you to meet Katherine."

Fiona walked right up to me and stuck out her hand. "Hello. I'm Fiona. I'm his daughter. I'm eight, but really, I'm practically nine. Only thirty-seven more days until my birthday."

I shook her small cold hand, a bit mesmerized. Fiona was not only a beautiful girl, with bright pink cheeks, shocking blue-gray eyes, and a thick head of wavy hair. I could see her Dad in there. It was plain as day. And it made me love her from the very first minute. "I'm Katherine. I'm nearly thirty-three, but I don't like to talk about it too much."

Fiona waved it off. "That's nothing. Dad's forty."

"So I've heard."

Eamon cleared his throat. "Katherine, Rachel. Rachel, this is Katherine."

"I finally meet the famous Katherine." Rachel pulled off a fluffy mitten and shook my hand. She was much more petite than I'd imagined. Probably only an inch or two above five feet. She was also more beautiful in person than I'd bargained on—gorgeous dark brown hair and striking blue eyes. No wonder Eamon had wanted her for his wife.

"You must have me confused with someone else. I'm definitely not famous. That'd be your husband." *Shit.* I shook my head. "I mean your ex-husband. That would be Eamon." I was officially bungling this. I hoped to God that Eamon wasn't embarrassed by me. "Really I'm more infamous than anything."

"He's talked about you forever," Rachel said.

I glanced over at Eamon and his eyebrows popped up, but he didn't say anything. I still couldn't comprehend that Eamon had ever spoken a single word about me to anyone. "It's very nice to meet you."

"And you as well."

Fiona grabbed my hand. "Katherine, come play."

I shuffled along, looking back at Eamon. "I'll be over here, playing."

"Have fun!"

Fiona was a whirlwind, climbing ladders and swooping down slides, spinning and skipping and twirling in constant motion. I was determined to keep up with her. All those hours at the gym had to be worth something. She led and I followed, like Alice shadowing the white rabbit down the hole into Wonderland. She giggled at nearly everything. It was contagious. Once I started laughing, I couldn't stop, cold air rushing in and out of my lungs. She did outrun me eventually.

"Fiona. I need a sec." I leaned against the play structure, gasping. "And I keep hitting my head on that bar above the slide."

She stopped dead in her tracks, standing straight as a pin. "Let's go on the swings. It's practically like having a rest."

Practically. We wound our way over and found two at the far end, giving us a straight view of Rachel and Eamon. They were sitting on the same bench, but each at their respective end. Rachel had her legs and arms crossed. Eamon was on the edge of his seat, leaning forward, resting his elbows on his knees. There was some conversation going back and forth between them, but it wasn't much. There were certainly long stretches when no words were uttered. That was when I sensed the void between them—the place where whatever love they'd shared must have died.

"Do you like my dad?" Fiona whizzed past me on the swing.

"I do. I like him a lot." I was taking a more leisurely approach to this pursuit. My legs and face were freezing.

"My mam says you've known each other a long time. Since before she knew him."

"That's true. But we've been apart for a long time, too."

Fiona suddenly dragged her feet across the playground blacktop. "Why were you apart? If you liked each other?"

I came to a stop, too. "Bad timing, I suppose. Plus, you should be happy I left. You might not have been born otherwise."

Fiona tilted her head and stared at me much in the way her father could, making me feel like she could see right inside my head. "I would've found a way to be born. I can't imagine not being here."

I found myself marveling at her, even after only a half hour. What an amazing way to look at the world. She was nearly nine, halfway between my age and Amy's when we lost our mom. Had we been like her? So precocious and comfortable in our own skin? Somehow, I doubted it, especially of myself.

"Fiona, come here. I want to see you," Eamon called.

She ran right to him, but I took my time, wanting to give them their space. Right away, she climbed up onto his lap and starting talking a million miles a minute. That reminded me of Amy.

"Did you and Katherine have fun?" Eamon asked.

"I did. I like her, Dad." Fiona's forehead crinkled. "I hope that's okay with you, Mam."

Rachel laughed. "Yeah. Perfectly okay with me." Her answer had a definite undertone of *He's yours. You can have him.*

"Good. I'm glad you got to meet each other," Eamon said.

Rachel pressed her lips together. "Eamon, have you had a

chance to think about taking Fiona for a few weeks? I really want to go on this trip."

"I haven't talked to Katherine about it yet."

"Seriously, Eamon? I asked you more than two weeks ago. James and I haven't been able to get away on our own at all. Now that you have a bit of a break, it's time for you to spend time with your daughter." Rachel's voice was about as irritated as a person's could be.

Eamon turned to me. "I hate to put you on the spot, and you don't have to answer right now, but would it be alright if Fiona stayed with us at your place for a few weeks while Rachel goes to Mexico?" He'd said he didn't want to put me on the spot, but he looked at me like his whole life was riding on this moment.

"You really don't have to answer right now," Rachel interjected. "He should have asked you earlier."

Eamon looked away, seeming annoyed. Fiona was leaning back, practically threatening to break his arm. How could I ever say no to that sweet face? There was no way I could.

"Of course Fiona can stay with us. As long as you like."

Fiona bounced up and down and squealed. "Yay!"

Now I was truly happy I'd agreed, albeit also a bit surprised. I was not the person who dealt well with spur-of-the-minute, seat-of-my-pants decisions. "Amy left her bed, so Fiona can have her own room. We have plenty of space." I couldn't ignore the way I'd said "we". It had just come out. Like I was totally comfortable with so much change. Maybe this was the perfect time for it. I was already on a bit of a roll.

Rachel and I were both cold, so the four of us walked to the coffee shop on the corner and wedged ourselves around a small bistro table, Fiona sipping hot cocoa, Eamon and I going for coffee, and Rachel opting for tea.

"What does your husband do?" I asked Rachel, desperate to make small talk. Eamon had told me so little.

"He's an art dealer. Owns a gallery in Philadelphia. I work there, too, when I'm not home-schooling Fiona."

I was a bit surprised they'd opted to home-school Fiona. "What will she do for school when she comes to stay with us?"

"She can Skype with her tutor. Otherwise, you've got Thanksgiving in there. She doesn't need to be studying every day."

Thanksgiving. I hadn't even considered that. My first big holiday with Eamon and his daughter would be there, too. Talk about a giant leap into domesticity for me. "Sounds good."

"I'm hoping I can drop her off the Monday before Thanksgiving, if that works."

Eamon looked to me for an answer. "Of course. Any day is fine."

Rachel smiled. "Grand. Thanks."

We said our goodbyes out on the street, Fiona and Eamon taking the longest to part.

"I love you, Fi. You know that, don't you?"

She brushed her hair off her face. "Of course, Daddy. I love you, too."

I was fairly certain my heart was about to explode.

Eamon and I walked back to my apartment, only talking about little things like what to have for dinner. The minute we walked through the door, clothes started to come off. Sex was this thing we were driven to pursue with each other, any chance we had, especially if we'd gone several hours without it.

As we settled in under the covers, I had to ask Eamon about his marriage again. I had to know what went wrong.

"Why do you want to know, exactly?"

"It's just, I looked at the three of you together in the park and I was trying to piece it all together. Rachel seems like a great mom and she's clearly smart and beautiful. I'm wondering why it didn't work."

He sighed and sat up in bed, scooting back and leaning against the headboard. I followed and clicked on the bedside lamp. "Rachel and I care about each other, and we love each other as people, but we were never in love. We were never desperate to be together. We got married because I went and got her pregnant and her parents are as Catholic as they come. Her mam was dying and Rachel couldn't stand to upset her, but there was no hiding her belly. We had to do it."

I listened, taking in the details and fitting them in with the parts I already knew. When Eamon had gotten married all those years ago, the news had thrown me for such a loop. The fact that I'd found out while I was standing in line at CVS to buy tampons and toothpaste only made it worse. Sharing someone you love with the world was incredibly hard. Sharing someone you loved and lost is impossible.

The headline on the wedding issue had made it difficult to ignore. *Irish Rocker Eamon MacWard Ties the Knot.* Inside was a spread of beautiful professional pictures. Eamon looking so dashing in a gray coat and tails, holding hands with a truly stunning Rachel. They were smiling. Their hands were intertwined. At the time, it was a dagger to my heart.

"What happened after you got married? You must've been happy for at least a little while."

"The second record blew up and I went on the road. I wasn't there when Fiona was born. And I wasn't there when Rachel's mam passed. She was understandably pissed when I came home from tour. She had a six week-old and was trying to mourn. It was terrible. I tried to be a help, but it was like a wall had gone up between us. Turns out there was another fella in the picture at that point. Can't blame her. She'd gotten nothing but a ring and a house out of me."

"Is that the man she's married to now?"

Eamon nodded. "Yeah. She's very happy. There's a lot to be

said for listening to your heart. I should've done it a long time ago." The saddest smile I'd ever seen rolled across his face. He reached for my hand and pulled it flat against his bare chest. His warmth, the fine hair, the thump of his heart—it all put a tiny mark on me. "I'm pissed at myself for waiting for you to come back into my life. It was stupid. I should've gone after you the minute my marriage was over."

"Maybe that's the way it was supposed to happen. And I wasn't in the best place either. I was struggling to find the right job. My dad was drinking too much. Amy was finishing law school and was a miserable pain in my butt."

"I could've been there for you. We could've been there for each other."

"But you were touring like a madman, weren't you? I wouldn't have wanted to deal with that. That would've been too hard. Saying goodbye all the time."

"I hate goodbye."

"I do, too."

"Let's never say goodbye again. I know you don't want to talk about marriage, but could you promise me that much?"

Good God the man had a way of putting me in a corner, but it wasn't difficult to answer. "I promise, Eamon. I promise."

After all, it was the last thing I ever wanted to say to anyone.

CHAPTER FOURTEEN

THE PROCESS of folding my world into Eamon's, and vice versa, had officially begun. A few days after I met Fiona and Rachel, Eamon and I went over to Luke and Amy's place in Brooklyn for dinner.

"I'm so excited you're here," Amy exclaimed as soon as she flung open the door. Her face was lit up like a Christmas tree. Who knew she was going to be so thrilled about our arrival? Of course, she went in for a hug from Eamon before she got one from me. It was hard to blame her.

"Thanks for the invitation. You must be Luke. I've heard a lot about you," Eamon held out his hand.

"Oh, man. It is so great to meet you. I'm a big fan," Luke said.

Eamon glanced over at me and smiled. This was uncomfortable for him. As much as he was forced to be in the spotlight, he didn't like it. "Thanks. I appreciate it."

"Come on in. I just bought a new turntable. Maybe you can tell me what you think." Luke led Eamon into the other room, leaving Amy and me by ourselves.

"Help me in the kitchen?" Amy asked. "I'm still working on dinner."

I took off my coat and hung it on the rack next to the front door. The air was perfumed with wine and the homey fragrance of something that had been cooking all day long. "It smells amazing in here. I hope you didn't go to much trouble."

Amy and Luke's kitchen was small, typical for New York, except it was completely updated—stainless steel appliances and stone countertops and basically perfect, nothing like my set-up in the city. "Just *Beef Bourguignon*." Amy lifted the lid off a Le Creuset French Dutch oven, in amethyst purple, one of the newer colors. NACI and I worked on the account. "I hope it tastes half as good as it smells." She replaced the lid and poured us each a glass of red wine. "Cheers. Here's to handsome men who like us."

I clinked my glass with hers. "Fingers crossed it stays that way." I took a long sip, thinking *so far, so good.*

"How are things with Eamon?" Amy whispered, leaning back against the counter.

"It's a little weird getting used to having someone in my space who isn't their own autonomous human being."

Amy laughed. "I'm not exactly sure what that means."

I took a glance down the hall to make sure Eamon and Luke weren't within earshot. "It's just that I have to think about him in addition to me. What we're going to eat for dinner. What we're going to do on the weekend. Stuff like that. I never had to bother with that with you."

"That's what you get with a roommate who you are also fucking."

My face went white hot. How Amy still managed to embarrass me was a mystery, but she did. "True."

"And that's commitment. Living together. Becoming a part of each other's lives."

My younger sister was now the mature, seasoned one. The one who knew exactly what she was doing. I was the one lagging behind and flailing. "It's not bad. I love having him here. It's just different."

"You have a rosy glow. That's all that matters." Amy elbowed me in the ribcage and I laughed again.

"I missed you." I had to admit it.

"We talk almost every day. And we got together to do all the wedding stuff."

"I know. It's not the same though. Just hanging out. Talking. It's nice."

"Speaking of the wedding, I heard from the florist and her quote was quite reasonable, so that's all set."

I couldn't help but notice how she'd just whizzed past the moment I'd been trying to have with her. "Sounds like you have it all figured out. Anything I can do?"

She shook her head and glanced at the kitchen timer. "Nope. But I'll let you know if that changes. Let's get the guys so we can eat."

Eamon and Luke were sitting on the living room couch, intently listening to the vinyl spinning on the turntable.

"It's John Martyn," Eamon shouted above the music.

"I have no clue who that is." My musical naiveté aside, Eamon was awfully adorable right now. He was so excited. Like a little kid.

"Basically the James Taylor of England. Huge influence on me."

I sat down on the couch next to him. How awesome to learn something new. "Very cool."

Luke was beaming at Eamon. They grinned at each other, apparently now bonded over this piece of music synergy between them.

"I'm going to need you to turn that down though." Amy

placed her hand on Luke's shoulder.

He lunged for the volume knob. "Absolutely. Sorry."

"No worries. We're ready to eat and I'd like to be able to speak during our meal if that's okay with you."

Eamon and I had a seat at the small table for four, which straddled the space between the living room and kitchen. Amy had set out some familiar cloth napkins with tiny embroidered roses on them—very girly for her, but something our neighbor Mrs. Abelman gave to our family after she learned of Grandma Price's thievery, which included several tablecloths and napkin sets. I could've suggested Amy carry one of these on her wedding day if the necklace didn't pan out, but that would have to be my backup plan. The pearls were my top priority.

Amy brought her culinary masterpiece to the table, setting it right in the center. Luke followed with a basket of bread.

"Looks grand, Amy. Thank you," Eamon said.

Judging by the blush on her face, you'd have thought he'd told her she was the most beautiful woman in the world. "Aren't you sweet?"

"He is," I said. "It's absolutely true."

"Don't tell anyone. It will interfere with my brooding poet image." Eamon laughed. He was fantastic at poking fun at himself.

The dinner progressed as we roamed from topic to topic—the wedding (of course), music (ditto), and our jobs. I wasn't eager to talk about work, since Miles was making me miserable, but somehow it didn't even matter tonight. The wine was flowing, music playing, and most notably, there wasn't a single instant of tension. As I watched my sister laugh so hard that she was clutching her stomach, I had to wonder if this was what contentment felt like. I couldn't think of anything more I wanted at that moment—my favorite people, good conversation, and a lovely meal. It felt perfect.

"I have a *Tarte Tatin* for dessert," Amy announced when it was clear that no one could possibly eat another bite of her magnificent Julia Child moment. "The apples are almost ready. I just need to put on the puff pastry."

Eamon leaned back and rubbed his flat belly. "Good thing I don't need to do anything tomorrow. Except maybe try to write some songs." *Try* being the operative word. By his own admission, he'd been anything but prolific since he'd come to New York.

"Okay, Eamon. I'm glad you brought this up. Is it true that Katherine is *Sunny Girl?*" Amy asked.

Eamon put his arm around me and kissed my temple. "One hundred percent true."

I was filled with a stupid sense of pride. "Told you so."

Amy did not seem convinced. "Huh."

"That surprise you?" Eamon asked. "I love your sister very much. I loved her all those years ago, too. I had to write a song about her."

"It only surprises me because she was anything but sunny when we were growing up."

"Can I help with dessert?" I asked, wanting to change the subject.

"Yeah. That'd be great. We'll let the guys get back to their music."

Luke bussed the dishes first, then Amy and I went to work, unfolding the thawed pastry dough and cutting it into a circle for the baking dish. We were interrupted by her cellphone ringing and buzzing across the counter. Amy wiped her hands clean and picked it up. "Oh, crap. It's Dad." She looked over at the work-in-progress. "I'll let it go to voicemail."

"What if there's something wrong?"

"Shit."

I took the phone from her. "I'll talk to him. You get that thing in the oven."

Whenever my dad called, I went through a bizarre progression of feelings—excitement and dread, guilt and love. Amy and I adored our dad, but things had not been easy over the years. It wasn't that we felt like he owed us anything for the many times we'd swept in to help him. It was more that it bothered us when he acted as if none of it had ever happened.

"Dad, hi, it's Katherine. Amy can't talk right now. She's cooking."

"Oh, okay. It's nice to hear your voice, Katie-boo." My Dad was the only person who'd ever called me by that name. My mother had thought it was idiotic. I liked it purely for sentimentality's sake. "Are you over at her apartment? What's she making?"

I gave him the rundown of the evening and the menu, adding in as many Food Network descriptors as I could.

"Great," he said. "How's work?"

This was starting to feel like small talk, but that was typical for Dad. "Work is great. I have a new boss and he's kind of a handful, but I'm dealing with it. Otherwise, I'm just busy. Getting used to life at home without Amy. That's taken some adjustment, but I'm getting there."

She glanced over at me and rolled her eyes.

"You two have always been so close. You had to know it would take some getting used to."

"Of course. It's just the little things. Like how quiet the apartment can be." I made the chatterbox gesture with my hands. Amy nodded in agreement and started digging around in the fridge.

"When someone's gone, it's the little things that you'll miss the most." Dad was being sentimental. I could hear it in his voice. "With your mom, it was the way she used to hum when she was cooking dinner. It got faster and more intense depending on how elaborate the meal was. Thanksgiving, you'd have thought she was conducting a Philharmonic orchestra in there."

I laughed, which felt good. I couldn't count the number of phone conversations that ended up with one of us crying or at least in a dour mood. "That's cute."

"Remember when we learned to cook after she passed away?"

"Mrs. Abelman came over and taught us."

"She offered to bring us meals every day, but I knew we had to learn for ourselves."

In truth, I learned to cook and Dad watched. He was an old-fashioned guy—his dad had never cooked, so it was a foreign concept to him. I was prepared to help in any way I could. There was a lot of responsibility on my shoulders, but more than anything, I was desperate to find a way to redeem myself. Was I really that evil, awful girl that Grandma Price thought I was? Being a hard worker seemed like the best way to prove I wasn't.

"I don't think I ever want to eat baked chicken again," I said.

Dad chuckled. "True, true." He cleared his throat. "Well, I called to talk to Amy about something, but I need to tell you something, too. There's a new lady in my life, Katherine. I've been waiting to tell you because I wasn't sure whether it was serious or not, but it is."

"Oh, my gosh, Dad. That's wonderful." I clapped my hand over the phone and whispered to Amy, "He has a girlfriend." To my knowledge, Dad hadn't dated anyone in the last twenty years.

Amy's eyes got shifty. "You didn't know that?"

"What? You did?"

"Well, yeah."

I choked back a grumble. "Dad, you told Amy?"

"Just this morning. She called me on her way to the gym. Just to chat. I was going to call you next."

"Okay. Well, who's your girlfriend?"

"Her name's Julia. We met at the post office of all places. She moved to Connecticut three years ago, but her husband was diagnosed with cancer right after that, and he passed away. So we're both widowers, which is nice."

"Sure." I wandered away from the kitchen now that Amy had turned on her stand mixer to make whipped cream.

"There was a long line at the post office that day. And we got to talking. The next thing I knew, I was asking her to coffee."

So sweet. I smiled wide and leaned against the corner of the wall in the living room as Luke breezed past me, apparently on his way to help Amy in the kitchen. Eamon looked up from an album cover he was studying and gazed at me with his adorable appreciative stare.

"Good for you, Dad."

"It's been six months now. I thought it was time to tell you girls."

"I have someone new in my life, too. Well, it's someone I knew before. From when I lived in Ireland." Now I really had Eamon's attention. He set aside the album cover on the table then took a long draw of his wine, not taking his eyes off me.

"Is this the musician Amy was telling me about?" Dad asked.

"She told you?"

"You know your sister. She has a mouth like a sieve. Everything comes out eventually."

Eamon rose from the sofa and wound his way over, placing a kiss on my cheek then pointing down the hall toward the bathroom. Being near him still brought about that flutter in my chest. Would that feeling ever go away?

"So, tell me about your guy," Dad said. "I don't think I can pronounce his name."

"It's Aim-un, but spelled with an E-A. He's staying with me right now. He just finished a tour of the US and he's busy working on material for a new album."

"Do you love him?"

My dad was not beating around the bush. "I do love him. Very much."

"Does that mean I'll be marrying off both daughters soon?"

"We're taking it one step at a time right now. We spent a lot of time away from each other. We're still getting reacquainted."

Eamon emerged from the bathroom, and sauntered over to me. He brushed my arm with the back of his hand, looking into my eyes. I could hardly stand up straight and it wasn't even like he'd touched my skin—this was all through a wool cardigan.

"Do you think he'd like to come for Thanksgiving? Up here? To Connecticut?"

"Really? We haven't done Thanksgiving at home in years." For a long time, it was easier for Dad to come into the city and for Amy and I to host at our apartment. She and I shared the cooking duties, I'd sleep on the couch, and let Dad have my bed. We celebrated the holiday without feeling like the ghost of my mother was in attendance. It wasn't that we didn't want Mom there. We merely wanted to keep things light.

"I know, I know. And I would otherwise say that would be fine, but Julia has dogs and it's very hard for her to leave them. She doesn't like to put them in a kennel."

I pulled the phone away from my ear and muted it. "My Dad wants to know if you want to come to Connecticut for Thanksgiving."

"Yeah. Absolutely." Eamon answered with zero deliberation, his face lighting up, which made me infinitely happy. "Fiona will be with us though," he added.

I took Amy's phone off mute. "Dad, can Eamon bring his daughter? We could put a blow-up mattress on the floor in my room." Thinking about going home and bringing Eamon made me both excited and unsettled. He was going to know that things were weird the instant he walked into that house. I was going to have to tell him everything and pray that he didn't think less of me.

"Does that mean you'll come?" Dad asked.

"Yes, Dad. We'll come." I smiled at Eamon, overcome with how much this meant to me.

"I thought it'd be nice to have everyone here. Amy and Luke. You and Eamon."

"You already asked Amy?"

"This morning. I thought I'd ask her first. You're a tougher nut to crack."

"Dad, don't say that." Although why I didn't want him to say that was a mystery. He wasn't wrong. "I always want to spend Thanksgiving with you."

"You also don't like change. I know that, too."

"Well, we're looking forward to coming up. We'll take the train. It'll be a big adventure."

Amy walked by. "Dessert's ready. Tell Dad I'll call him back."

"Gotta go, Dad. Duty calls."

He laughed. "Love you, honey."

"Love you, too." I hung up Amy's phone, making a mental note to give her crap about Dad later. She'd had plenty of opportunity to tell me about his new girlfriend and Thanksgiving. I joined everyone at the table and we all dug in. One bite of the gooey apple and caramel concoction and my resentment over the phone call evaporated. "Ames. This is phenomenal."

"It is," Eamon agreed, going in for another bite.

The wine started to flow again, especially after dessert,

when we chatted about Thanksgiving. Eamon said he'd book the train tickets for everyone—his treat, and Luke said he'd book a car to pick us up at the station. It was all sewn up then. Ready or not, I was not only headed home, I was bringing Eamon with me.

He rubbed his belly for what must've been the twentieth time. "Amy, fantastic meal. Well done."

I took that as our cue to head out. It was late anyway, nearly eleven. Eamon requested an Uber and we said our goodbyes. In the car back into the city, Eamon and I held hands, both of us staring out the window in a food-induced stupor.

"My dad's excited to meet you and Fiona," I said.

"Can't wait to meet him." He squeezed my hand. "It means a lot that you'll take me there, Katherine. It means a great deal."

I smiled at him. "It means a lot to me that you'll come. You'll love my dad. He's the sweetest guy."

I turned back and rested my head against the window. My dad really was incredibly kind and generous. Even with his occasional flakiness, we never questioned that he loved us. He never got mad. His temperament was almost always even. He'd even been that way when ten year-old me finally worked up the nerve to tell him about Mom and Gordon.

"Daddy, do you know Gordon from the flower shop? The delivery man?" I asked when Dad came into my room to check on me. I'd been deathly ill all day, Sunday. I swallowed hard, which hurt. My throat was dry and felt like an oven.

"I suppose I do. I think I met him once."

"Mom sometimes has him stay over at our house. When you're out of town. Or sometimes she takes us to his house and we sit in the living room and watch TV while she goes into the bedroom with him."

That was the moment when I truly saw just how lovely my

dad's eyes were—the most beautiful pale shade of blue. "Has this been going on for a long time?"

"He's been coming over since you got the job from Apex Hardware. But Amy and I saw her kiss him at the flower shop way before that."

"I see."

"You aren't going to get a divorce are you? Please don't get a divorce. Maybe you can talk to Mom and tell her to stop? Amy and I don't like him. He's not funny and he's not even that nice to us, either."

He held his finger to his lips and glanced over his shoulder at my bedroom door. Mom had gone to church by herself that day, but he knew she'd be home soon. "It's okay, honey. I don't want you to give this another thought, okay? Everything will be just fine. I'll take care of it. I promise."

"Really?" Dad had always been a softie, wanting to eradicate any problem that arose. Still, that had seemed a little too perfect an answer.

"Yes, really. You just concentrate on getting better, okay?" He leaned forward and kissed me on the forehead. "Everything will be just fine."

Little did I know that fewer than twenty-four hours later, my mother would be dead.

CHAPTER FIFTEEN

WE TOOK the train from Penn Station to Old Saybrook. Eamon had booked the five of us in business class, and paid for the tickets. An early wedding gift, he'd said, with a smile and a shrug of his skinny shoulders. I wasn't sure he could be any sweeter.

He and I held hands and watched out the windows as the snowy landscape chugged past. It was not common to have any snow this early in the winter, but the weather had been all kinds of wonky and much of the Northeast had been hit hard. Some parts of Connecticut and Massachusetts had more than eight inches. Normally this time of year, you got nothing more than mud.

Fiona, who had been living with us for two days, sat across from Eamon and me, riding backwards. She'd occasionally pop up onto her knees and look out the window, especially if Eamon told her there was something special to see like birds or water. Otherwise, she drew pictures of horses and sang to herself. Her voice was already nearly as beautiful as her dad's. Someday, it might be even more so. Luke and Amy napped in the row behind us, fingers twined.

We transferred at Old Saybrook, lugging our suitcases behind us, and we rode to the end of the line, Hoop Hole Hill Road, where Luke had a driver with a minivan pick us up. Between the five of us and our luggage it would've been too much for Dad's car. He'd bought a Prius a few years back, after Amy and I expressed concern about him not having reliable transportation in the winter. He'd gone for years not using his car at all. After Mom had died, we were the excuse. He refused to drive us anywhere. He was too worried it would traumatize us. On the rare occasion we were invited to a sleepover at another girl's house, we had to ask for a ride.

But Amy and I were not invited to many sleepovers. Right after Mom's death, we became the poor Fuller girls, worthy of pity and sorry looks, not parties or celebrations. We made people uncomfortable. Amy and I saw it on faces everywhere we went and we didn't fully understand it, but we could feel it. Months after Mom's death, the rumors started. She'd been drunk. She was on drugs. She'd been trying to kill all three of us. Most of it was lies, but there were only so many times you could deny something so ugly before people started to think you were covering it up. And of course, Amy and I both knew there was some ugliness in there. We just didn't want to talk about it. If anyone ever wondered why we'd both been so desperate to get the hell out of Chester when we got older, that was the biggest reason.

Fiona sat between Eamon and me in the last row of the van. He put his arm around her, and around me at the same time, rubbing my shoulder gently. He seemed to know when things were weighing on me, which was both a blessing and a curse. He was so quick to comfort. I never had to ask. But he was equally fast with the questions.

"You okay?" he asked.

Do you have about a million years for me to explain? "I'm good. I just want us to have a nice Thanksgiving."

"I've never had an American Thanksgiving," Fiona said, kicking her legs. "And I don't feel right about us killing a turkey. They're lovely birds. They have nice feathers."

Eamon laughed and leaned down to press a kiss to Fiona's head. "We won't be killing the turkey ourselves. And I promise you, however lovely turkeys are, you'll find them equally delicious."

She gazed up at him. "I don't know, Dad. I might just live on mashed potatoes."

"I'd expect nothing less of a good Irish girl."

The driver took the turn onto our road. The houses in this part of town were farther apart, set off the road, all just as old and modest as ours—shutters and windows like soldiers lined up in a row. Amy and I had always loved these generous yards when we were kids. We could roam for days. The summers here had been especially lovely, especially before we'd lost Mom, running across the mossy lawn in bare feet and playing tag. Even when you got an acorn to the arch of your foot, you didn't care. You were free. Of course, our lemonade stands never saw much business, too little traffic in our corner of the world, but we sat there anyway, baking in the sun in folding chairs, drinking up our wares and bemoaning our lack of profits.

Despite the good memories, pulling up to the old house made my stomach churn, a clear indication of how much my past was not my past. It was as much a part of my minute-to-minute life as breathing. It didn't take much to remind me of it. It was deeply woven into what and who I was.

Dad came bounding outside and the screen door smacked loudly against the frame when he let go of it. He had a smile so wide on his face that I nearly questioned whether it was really him. The new girlfriend, Julia, was right behind him, along with her two dogs—a yellow Lab and a Huskie. Julia wasn't moving particularly fast, but Dad had mentioned her hip bothered her, so hopefully that was the problem, not us.

"My girls are home." His voice was bursting with relieved and happy notes. Yes, it was hard for Amy and me to come back. But maybe we had put it off for too long. It hadn't been fair of us to leave him here by himself just because he was doing better, because he wasn't drinking.

"Mr. Fuller." Eamon held out his hand for my dad.

"Dad, this is Eamon. And his daughter, Fiona." I watched as my dad shook Eamon's hand, overcome with a feeling that was hard to describe—a mix of pride and surprise and happiness. How do you feel when you see something you thought would never happen?

Dad bent at the waist to greet Fiona face-to-face. I knew in that moment that my dad needed to be a grandparent, STAT. I'd have to talk to Amy about that. "Hello, my dear. You've come a long way. You must be hungry."

"Starving. There was nothing to eat on the train."

"Fiona, you never said a thing about being hungry." Eamon sounded more than a bit annoyed. He did pride himself on being an attentive dad.

"I didn't really realize it until just now when Mr. Fuller asked me."

"Maybe we should go inside and fix that," I said. "It's freezing."

"Luke and I will get the bags," Eamon said. Luke was already unloading suitcases from the back of the minivan.

Amy, Fiona, and I followed Dad and Julia inside. Why certain places always smelled the same was beyond me, but that was certainly true of our childhood home. It never changed. It was spent firewood and a bit of a dusty, old smell, like dried flowers or the yellowed pages of a book. We stomped the snow from our shoes out on the three-season porch and I showed Fiona where to leave them, in the old tin tray right next to the door. In her stocking feet, she tore off into the house with my dad.

I held the front door open as Luke and Eamon came up the front stairs toting our luggage.

"Thank you for doing that. Taking care of the bags," I said to Eamon as he took off his boots. Amy and Luke had already stepped inside.

"Of course." His eyebrows drew together. "I like your dad. What I met of him. Hoping I get some time with him over the next few days. It might help me decipher the puzzle of Katherine Fuller."

"There's no puzzle. I'm an open book. It just happens to be a very dull book."

He pulled me into a hug and kissed the top of my head. "Nice try. I don't believe that for a second."

"I'm serious." What I really wanted to say is that he shouldn't try to decipher me. Whatever he'd already figured out about me was more than enough. He made me happy and I appeared to do the same for him. Why did we need anything more than that? I really didn't think we did.

"Let's go inside. I want to warm up."

"Of course."

The fire was in full roar. The TV was off, which had never been the case when Amy and I were young. Dad was always watching TV, even if it was just in the background while he did a crossword puzzle or was reading the newspaper. From the living room, with its wide-plank wood floors and braided rag rugs, I could hear Dad and Fiona laughing. All I could think was that sound—my dad and a child, laughing—had been missing from these walls for too long.

I took Eamon's hand and we stepped into the kitchen.

Everything was as it had always been. In the far corner was the same retro kitchen table that Dad had bought for Mom from a yard sale, the only thing Grandma Price didn't bother to take. Dad had three or four packages of cookies spread out on it, and he and Fiona were discussing the pros and cons of each kind. The copper teakettle rattled on the stovetop, not quite at a full boil.

"Are you a tea drinker, Eamon?" Julia asked, getting up from the table. She had a young face with very few wrinkles, but her hair was gray and pulled back in a high ponytail.

"From time to time, but I'd take something stronger if you have it."

My shoulders stiffened. There was no telling how dad would react. For his many struggles with alcohol, he'd never gone to Alcoholics Anonymous. He'd never admitted he had a problem. We'd only had varying degrees of success with getting him to stop self-medicating.

"I've got some beer," Dad answered. "I don't have much else in the house, but we can always make a run to the liquor store in the morning."

"Beer is perfect. Katherine? You want one?" Eamon asked.

"Definitely."

With Julia's help, Eamon got us our drinks and we leaned against the kitchen counter, watching as Dad explored the joys of a sugar high with Fiona. The dogs were curled up under the table. Eamon put his arm around me and kissed my temple. "I'm glad to be here. Thank you for sharing this with me."

I looked up into his handsome face, his cheeks a bit ruddy from the cold. "I'm glad you came. I'm not sure I could've done this without you."

"Really? Your dad seems wonderful."

Dad laughed, throwing his head back. "He is," I said. That

was part of what always made it so hard. Not that any of us deserved what had happened, but he certainly hadn't.

"Luke asked me to be a groomsman while we were unloading the luggage." Eamon offered this tidbit as if he were commenting that it might rain tomorrow.

"He did?"

He took another drink of his beer, keeping his eyes on me and nodding. "He did. I practically feel like part of the family." His eyebrows jumped and he smiled.

"That's awesome. And I'm glad I'll have someone else to help me deal with the craziness of that day. As much as those two claim to want something low-key, something tells me it's going to end up being a nightmare."

"It'll be fun. Don't worry so much. Personally, I love weddings."

"You do?"

"What's not to love? Free food and liquor, dancing if it's a good one. Everyone's happy and feeling romantic."

"Let's hope for that next month."

Eamon surveyed the kitchen. "I'm trying to envision your childhood in this house."

"Yeah, me too."

"Come on. Show me around and you can explain to me what the hell that means."

I started the tour with the living room. "This is where Dad spent most of our childhood, sitting in this chair, watching TV or doing the crossword puzzle."

"Same chair?"

"Same exact chair. Amy and I bought him a new one for Christmas a few years ago, but he refused delivery. He wanted no part of it. He says that this one knows his butt."

"An important quality in a chair."

"Or so I'm told." We walked past the couch and the fireplace, flanked by built-in bookcases filled to the brim with books my dad had mostly bought at the thrift store.

"Has the house changed much since you were a kid?"

"Not really. There's mostly just more junk. Dad likes to collect things. He's incapable of turning down a good deal. Even if it's something he doesn't need."

Eamon pointed to the dozens of fishing lures adorning the wall near the bottom of the stairs. "Is he a big fisherman?"

"Unless something has changed in the last few years, nope. I actually don't know if he's ever been fishing. He just likes the way they look, I think."

On the other side of the staircase, still on the front of the house, was the alcove where Dad kept his desk and piles of old magazines and newspaper clippings. He'd been talking for years about getting it organized or turning it into a hobby room, but that never quite happened. He was always getting distracted by new ideas, new projects, new things to collect and acquire.

Eamon wandered ahead, looking at pictures Dad had of Amy and me on the wall—high school graduation, college graduation, a Christmas from when we were teenagers, me with a mouth full of metal.

"Nice braces," Eamon said.

"Thanks. My dad's room is through there." I pointed to the closed door on the far side of the office. "The rest of the bedrooms are upstairs. We can take our stuff up and get settled if you want."

"Sounds like a plan." Eamon grabbed our suitcase and Fiona's duffel from the bottom of the stairs and lugged it up while I followed.

"First door on the right." He stepped inside and I flipped on the light. Dad had already set up the air mattress for Fiona and made up her bed. How very domesticated of him.

"So this is where the magic happened," Eamon said, half laughing.

"You already made that joke about my office. And not quite, but you're funny."

"You and Amy really shared this room?"

"Yep. From right after our mom passed away. We were sad and I think it helped us to be together." Dad had moved Amy's bed back into her room about six years ago, when she'd brought several college friends up for a long weekend. The other furniture, like her old bookcase, was either living at my house or at Luke's.

"I noticed there aren't any pictures of your mom up in the house. Is that just because your dad moved on eventually?"

This was the danger of bringing Eamon here—questions about my mom. They were inevitable. And I had to answer them. I wouldn't keep anything from him anymore. At least not intentionally. "My grandmother took all of them when she died. She was really traumatized and I think she kind of freaked out. But she never gave them back, either."

"Bloody awful."

On a long list of awful things, that one wasn't actually at the top of the list. "It was."

"How did she die? If your grandmother was traumatized. I mean, if you don't mind me asking?"

"A car accident. I was ten. Amy was eight. And we were in the car." I waited to feel better after sharing these details I hadn't yet told him, but I knew very well that this was the sanitized version of what had happened. Not even a fraction of the real events.

Eamon pulled me into a hug and stroked my back. "That's so terrible, love. I'm very sorry."

"Yeah. It's sad."

"I don't know how you can live without any pictures of her. That must feel so strange."

I couldn't have held back my sigh if I'd wanted to. I sank deeper into his embrace. "I don't need a picture, Eamon. I see my mother every time I look in the mirror."

"What?" He grasped my shoulders and looked me square in the eye.

"My mother. Aside from not quite getting her amazing cheekbones, I look exactly like her. Exactly."

CHAPTER SIXTEEN

I DIDN'T SLEEP WELL that first night back in the house. There were too many memories around me, the kind you not only can't avoid if you shut your eyes, the kind that get worse when you do. I kept hearing my mother's voice in snippets from real life conversations more than twenty years ago—talk of flowers and weddings, true love and fate. How could she have ever betrayed our sweet, adorable dad? Or had she been in love with Gordon and I was simply too young and stupid to understand? Was their romance meant to be? Or was it a case of cruel timing?

I woke in the morning feeling on edge, although a kiss from Eamon on my forehead before he went downstairs to fetch coffee, and a smile from Fiona as she scrambled to go play with Julia's dogs, Tilly and Sadie, helped me shake it off. The nights had always been the worst in this house. I don't know why I'd expected that to be different.

My phone beeped with a notification—a returned message from Aunt Lucy.

Katherine,

If you want something from my mother, I can't be of much

*help. She stopped speaking to me when I put her in the home. I
doubt she'll want to hear from you, but she might be willing to do
something for Amy. She always liked Amy. She's at Shady Pines
in Haddam, Room 204, if you want to try.*

Lucy

A grumble rose from my throat and I fought the desire to
chuck my phone out the window, but I didn't want to go dig
through the snow for it, so I tossed it onto the air mattress Fiona
had slept on. It bounced twice and hit the floor.

"Everything okay?" Eamon strolled into the room, looking like
heaven in a gray, cabled sweater. He handed me a cup of coffee.

"I wanted to contact my grandmother about getting a necklace that belonged to my mom for Amy to wear at her wedding."

He sat next to me on the bed and put his arm around my
waist. "And?"

"And I had to contact my Aunt Lucy first because she's a
good intermediary, but she said she can't help me."

Eamon leaned away from me and a crease formed between
his eyes. "Why would you need an intermediary to speak to
your own grandmother? Just because of the pictures?"

"It's a long story."

"I'm starting to feel like that's your answer any time I ask
about your family."

I drew in a deep breath through my nose. I needed to be
more open with him about these things. I knew that. "My grandmother took more than my mother's photos after she died. She
took everything that belonged to her. Jewelry. Clothes. Everything. She also stopped speaking to us. Every now and then we'd
get a card for a birthday, but that was it."

"Losing a child has to be horrible. I can't begin to think of it.
But I hate that she took it out on you. Was it because you were
too much a reminder of her daughter?"

"I guess."

"What are you going to do about the necklace?"

"I really want Amy to have it. She's given me so little responsibility for the wedding, This is the one thing I should be able to do."

"Worth a phone call, isn't it? I can't believe a woman would say no to her own granddaughters, especially when one is getting married."

"You haven't met my grandmother."

Fiona stumbled into the room, nearly out of breath. Eamon caught her in his arms. "Slow down there, love. You're going to hurt yourself."

"Dad, Amy and Luke are going into town to the grocery store. Can I go?"

"Well, sure." He smoothed back Fiona's untamed curls then glanced over at me. "Would you like me to clear out? So you can make your phone call?"

No time like the present, right? "Actually, that would be great. Then I can just get it over with and I don't need to think about it anymore."

"It's settled then. I'm going to the grocery, too."

"But Dad..."

"What?"

"Luke said he would buy me candy. Are you going to ruin that? Because if you are, you are not invited."

Eamon cracked the adoring grin he reserved just for his daughter. "We're on holiday. You can have your candy."

Fiona jumped up and down, making the old wood floors creak. "Grand!"

Eamon patted my knee and kissed my temple. "Be back in a bit. Good luck."

"Thanks." I loved him, but he had no idea how much luck I

was going to need. I stood a better chance of finding a pot of gold than convincing my grandmother to do anything.

A moment later, the glass in the front door rattled and their voices came from outside, followed by the slams of car doors. I shuffled across the room to get my phone, and pulled up the web browser to search for the nursing home. The Shady Pines website came right up. From the looks of it, it was quite nice. Leave it to Grandma to blow everything out of proportion.

I sat down on the bed again and scooted back up against the wall. My call was quickly answered by an automated system instructing me to dial nine and the resident's room number, and also to have a blessed day. I dialed for 204. The phone rang and rang. And rang. I was about to hang up when an unfamiliar woman's voice came over the line.

"Ms. Price's room. This is Beverly speaking." She spoke with a kind and patient manner, almost as if she was living on a different speed than the modern world.

"Hello. My name is Katherine Fuller. I'm Ms. Price's granddaughter. I was hoping to speak to her."

"Oh. I see. She's just finishing up in the bathroom. Shouldn't be more than a few minutes." It sounded as though she placed the receiver on a hard surface and I could hear muffled voices and a fair bit of arguing, most of it coming from my grandmother.

"Hello." Her greeting showed zero affection. It was merely the way a person answers the phone.

"Grandma. Hi. It's Katherine." Just like that, I was ten years old again. My voice was small. I was tiny. Insignificant. Being in my childhood room was only making the feeling more powerful. All around me were reminders of what I used to be, of what had happened.

"So you waited until I was nearly dead to call me."

"What? No. Not at all."

"There is no inheritance. Everything is going to the Fraternal Order of Police. They're the only people who gave a crap when your grandfather died."

Amy and I would've given a crap if she'd actually informed us that he'd passed. We'd found out about it from our dad, who read it in the newspaper. The obituary ran the day *after* the funeral. "I'm not calling about money." I kneaded my forehead. I didn't want to come out and just ask for the necklace. We had a lot of catching up to do. "How are you? I looked at the website for the place you're staying. It looks nice."

"It's not home. I'd rather be living with your aunt. Apparently I'm too much of a pain in the ass for that to happen."

"But you're doing okay?"

"What's the reason for the social call, Katherine? We haven't talked in twenty years and you up and decide to find my phone number? I know you want something, so just tell me." Her voice sliced right through me. There would be no reconciliation with Grandma Price. That was pretty clear now. It wasn't that I'd believed it could happen, but I'd been holding out a sliver of hope. If only for my sister.

"I'm calling because Amy is getting married."

"Good for her."

It was a good thing we weren't meeting face-to-face. She was really starting to push my buttons. "And I think she should be able to wear something of our mother's for her wedding. You have everything." *You stole everything.*

"Like what?"

I froze for a moment. That was an actual clear and rational answer from her. "The pearl necklace our mom wore on her wedding day."

"No. Absolutely not."

"What? Why?"

"Because it's mine and I don't have to part with it if I don't want to."

"But your granddaughter is getting married and she has nothing of her own mother's for her wedding day because you took everything."

"I had to preserve the memory of my own daughter. I wasn't about to trust any of you to do it. Knowing you all, you'd probably just sell everything."

"Grandma, that's not true and you know it. It wasn't fair, what you did. Amy and I deserve to have a small reminder of our mother. It's not too much to ask."

"No, Katherine, it *is* too much to ask. I lost my daughter. She shouldn't have died that day. Nobody seems to think about what I went through. Nobody cared then, and nobody cares now."

I drew a deep breath through my nose. Of course she'd suffered a horrible loss, but was I supposed to compare her pain to what Amy and I went through? "I cared. I cared a lot. I tried to hug you in the hospital the day after she died and you wouldn't even hug me back."

"I was in mourning!" she snapped.

I nearly dropped the phone. Her voice was like a razor blade. I was stuck in that place where your brain is telling you to be sensible and walk away from an argument but your gut is telling you to fight. I didn't want to take crap from someone who had no business serving it. But again, the necklace—I had to focus on that. "Okay. I'm sorry."

"Nobody should be held responsible for what they did that day."

That's very convenient for you. I wanted to ask if it was possible for her to say that no one should be held responsible for what they'd done the day before, or the day before that, but I knew better than to open my mouth on that subject. "Again. I'm sorry."

"Do you know how old your mother would be right now if she were still alive?"

That was a dagger straight to the center of my heart. "Of course I do. Fifty-five." I didn't like to think about what-ifs very often, mostly because it was hard for me to imagine things that hadn't happened. Too much of my brain was taken up by real events. But I did wonder every now and then what our mom would be like now.

"That's right. Fifty-five. Prime of her life. She should be here right now. If she was, I might not be living here. But she's not here and I'll never get over it. Never."

The guilt was pressing down on me, threatening to crush me right there, sitting on my old squeaky bed. Of course Mom should've been here right now. If I could take back everything I did, I would. But I couldn't. It had taken years to learn to live with that fact, and it was only to varying degrees of success. Some days it was much harder to accept.

"Do you think about that, Katherine? Because I do." Her voice started to fall apart at the seams. "My little girl should be here and she isn't. That's why I'm not giving you a damn thing. It's all I have left."

The line went dead, leaving me in silence. I ended the call and put the phone facedown on the bed. My face felt numb. There was an unsettling calmness to my thoughts. It was like everything had slowed down, stuck in the cold, creating too much quiet. One of the few ties I still had to my mother still blamed me. All these years later and she hadn't forgiven me for any of it. In some ways, I felt sorry for her. How could she walk the earth holding onto that much pain and misery? Did she think that was the only way to keep my mother's memory alive?

More questions came, dribbling into my brain like a slow

leak. Was I coping any better? Tamping everything down and hiding it, although a legitimate strategy, didn't help me move forward. So what would? Because the plain reality was that my heart and conscience were as heavy today as they'd been the day she died. I was simply used to the weight. Nothing could make the load lighter. No amount of doing good would ever change my part in what happened.

The rattle of the door downstairs pierced the silence, the sound of happy voices wound up the stairs. That was when the tears came. I loved hearing Eamon's voice alongside my dad's and my sister's. I loved hearing Fiona's bubbly giggle. It made me laugh, even when I didn't know the joke.

Eamon was coming up the stairs. I could tell by the pace of his footsteps. I wiped my cheeks dry with my hands. I didn't want him to see me crying.

"Howya." He appeared in the doorway. In this old house, especially on the second floor, his head came close to scraping the top of the doorframe. "We're back."

"Did you have fun?"

"I've never seen anyone shop like your father." He sat next to me on the bed and I instantly felt better. It was amazing how his presence calmed me. "It's a bloody tactical operation. Very fast. Very organized. No extra time allowed." He made chopping motions with his hand.

A breathy laugh burst from my lips. For as laid back as my dad could be, he didn't like being around a lot of people, and that meant most outings were swift affairs. "You should've seen Amy and I trying to keep up when we were kids. Now we don't even bother. We just hang back and let him gripe at us about dawdling."

He inched back and sat against the wall, pulling his leg up onto the bed. "Fiona was the only one he'd stop for. She had a lot of questions. It's the first time she's been in a proper American grocery store."

"Those two are totally hitting it off. It's adorable." My dad was having the fun with Fiona that he'd missed out on with me and Amy. It was so lovely to see that I couldn't even be melancholy about it. It only made me happy.

There were more footfalls on the stairs and Amy turned up. "Hey. Fiona wants to go for a walk in the woods. Just us girls. And Julia's dogs, of course. She said they could use some wearing out."

"Sounds good. I need some fresh air." I reached over and placed my hand on Eamon's knee. "You won't be bored if we leave you at home? It sounds like no boys allowed."

He shook his head. "It'll give me some time with your dad."

"Dad!" Fiona called up the stairs. "Come here! Grandpa Mark is doing magic!"

"The fun around here is non-stop," Eamon said.

"It was one of his many hobbies when we were little," Amy said. "It's been years since he's done any of that." She looked right at me, a bit horror-stricken. "I hope he doesn't try to do the one where he lights the dollar bill on fire."

"I'd better go down and supervise, huh?" Eamon got up from the bed.

"Yes. Please." A fire was the absolute last thing we needed.

Eamon left and Amy leaned against the doorway. "You okay? You seem down."

"I talked to Grandma Price. I called about Mom's necklace."

"You did? What did she say?"

I wanted so badly to spill my guts to my sister. She was the one person in the world who could understand what I was feeling. Plus, she'd experienced our grandmother's ire up close. She knew exactly how ugly it could be. But I couldn't do that to her. I'd promised her the necklace and I would deliver it. Maybe not on this trip. Maybe I'd have to bring in Aunt Lucy. But somehow I would get that damn necklace. Even if it killed me.

"She was her normal grumpy self. She's pissed at Aunt Lucy. She doesn't want to be living in that home."

Amy sat next to me and crossed her legs. "Can you blame her? I wouldn't want to live somewhere like that either."

"I'm sure it's not fun."

"What did she say about the necklace?"

I glanced over at Amy and saw more hope in her face than I could wrap my head around. I couldn't saddle her with this. I'd figure it out. Somehow. "She's looking for it. She told me to call her next week."

"But we'll be gone by then."

"I know. She said she would mail it to us. Made a big deal about me paying for the postage." I hoped that somewhere God would be okay with me lying like this. I was just protecting her.

"I hope she can find it."

I wrapped my arm around Amy and pulled her closer. "Don't worry. She will. I talked to her nurse. Beverly. She seemed nice. And reasonable. I can always talk to her if we need help."

"Oh. Okay."

"I'll get it. I promise." *Even if I have to put on a catsuit and sneak into a nursing home in the middle of the night and nab it.*

"Thanks." Amy dropped her head and started picking at her nails. "So, something sort of terrible happened at the grocery store."

"Did Dad do that thing where he argues with the butcher? It's so embarrassing."

Amy laughed quietly. "No. Not that. I, uh..." She looked over at me, her blue eyes wide. "I thought I saw him, Katherine. Gordon. And he looked at me. I don't think it was him, but damn, it really looked like him."

My heart wound up into a tiny ball. I slapped my hand against my chest to see if it was still beating. "You're sure it wasn't him? What did he look like? Did he say anything to you?"

"I can't really explain what he looked like. I only know that I don't think it was him. Didn't he say something once about a brother who lived here? Maybe that's who it was. Honestly, I'm glad it wasn't him. I don't know what I would've said or done. I probably would've punched him in the face."

"I forgot about the brother, but I think you're right. I'm pretty sure Gordon moved away. The last time we saw him was in high school. Remember? The football game?"

Amy nodded. "How could I forget?"

She'd been a freshman and I was a junior, the first home game of Amy's high school life. As much as my few friends and I had been outcasts, we still went to the football games. It was fun to sit in the stands in the crisp fall air, drinking soda and making fun of our classmates under our breath. We always sat in the same seats, off to the side and about ten rows up. A few minutes into the first quarter, we spotted Gordon marching up the concrete stadium steps. He looked at us as we walked by, both Amy and I in shock. He sat six or seven rows behind us. It made Amy and me deeply uncomfortable and nervous. We left at halftime and treated our friends to sundaes at McDonald's as a bribe for taking off early. We had to get out of there. We were too freaked out.

"Even if it wasn't him, I'm sorry you had to go through that. It must've been awful."

Amy shuddered. "Ugh. The thought of him is so creepy. I hope I never see him for real."

I might have been pretty traumatized by my phone conversation with Grandma Price, but at least I hadn't had to go through the shock of thinking I'd seen Gordon. "Me neither."

"I'm glad Luke was there. I told him who the guy looked

like. He was a little fascinated, but the whole cheating thing is a mystery to him. His family is so...what's the word?"

"Committed?"

"Yes. Exactly."

"So you told Luke? About everything?"

"Well, yeah. As soon as I knew we were coming for Thanksgiving, I sort of had to. I just didn't want it to be weird."

"What did he say?"

"What everyone says. That he was so sorry and that it must have been so hard for us. It was sweet, but you know what it's like. You just sort of want the conversation to end."

I never talked about it to anyone, not since high school, but I knew exactly what she was saying. That pitiful look on people's faces—it only made you wish that much harder that the bad stuff had never happened.

"You told Eamon, right?"

Slow as molasses, I shook my head. "Nope."

She sighed. "I say just get it over with. You'll feel so much better."

"Like ripping off a bandage?"

"More like ripping a fifty-foot long dressing off a gaping head wound, but yeah. It's better to get on with your life. You can't live under the shadow of it forever. It'll bring you closer together. I promise."

I drew in a deep breath. I hoped she was right, especially since I wasn't convinced at all about that last part. As madly in love as Eamon and I were with each other, I knew our dynamic would change when I told him. I had no reason to think otherwise. It had gone that way with everyone I'd ever told, which was why I'd simply stopped talking about it.

"Of course, it's probably easy for me to say that," she went on. "I was unconscious after the accident. You were awake. Sitting in the car for hours, waiting for someone to rescue us.

And you were the one with mom before she came to get me at school."

Once again I felt like my whole body had been dipped in ice water. My brain was moving at half speed, dragging me back again, like it wanted to torture me and force me to remember every last detail.

As if I could ever forget.

CHAPTER SEVENTEEN

AMY and I headed downstairs to pry Fiona from Magic Hour with Grandpa Mark so we could go on our hike. The days were so short now. Mid-day was really the best time to go. We didn't want to risk getting stuck in the woods in the dark. Amy and I knew our way very well, but anyone could get confused.

"Fiona's going to need boots," I said, walking into the kitchen. "Maybe I can run into town and find her some that will fit."

"I think I've got a box of your old winter stuff in the attic," Dad said. "I'll get it down."

"You kept that stuff? For what?"

"I keep everything, Katherine. You know that." He got up from the table, but I stopped him before he could leave the kitchen.

"I don't want you going up into the attic and digging around. Eamon and I will do it."

"You realize I'm perfectly fine when you're not here," Dad said.

"No, no," Eamon said. "Katherine and I are happy to do it. Fiona wants to be with you anyway."

Eamon really did have a knack for smoothing things over. We headed back upstairs to the pull-down for the attic, in the hall between my room and Amy's. Eamon did the honors and went up first, but I got the benefit of watching his perfect behind in motion. The man's butt was made for jeans.

I'd forgotten how huge our attic was, with ceilings high enough for Eamon to nearly stand up straight. "I have no clue where to start," I admitted. There were cardboard boxes everywhere, none of them stacked neatly. "I guess I should've asked him. Maybe we should start over by the Christmas stuff. Maybe he put things in here seasonally."

"I like the way your mind works."

Eamon kneeled down in front of a stack and began shifting crates. It only took a few minutes before he found it. "Here we go. Winter coats and boots."

"Hopefully there's only one of these. I still don't know why he wouldn't donate this crap to the thrift store. Or throw it out. Who wants twenty year-old coats and boots?"

"Mam never threw anything out either. Had a devil of a time going through everything after she passed." Eamon's mom had died a few years after I left Ireland, another detail of his life I'd had to learn from a magazine.

"Perils of being an only child, huh?"

"One of many."

"Did it take you a long time to sort through her things?"

"Months. Rachel came and helped a few times. She and my mam were close. They liked each other quite a bit. Of course, my mam knew the truth of our marriage and our divorce. Rachel's mam never did. I think it was a big relief for Rachel. She didn't have to come clean about anything."

I crouched down next to him. "I really wish I could've met her. Your mom."

"I feel the same way about yours."

A vision popped into my head, of me as an adult with my mom. My conversation with Grandma Price had planted a seed in my brain. Would we have been close? The sort of mom and daughter who talk on the phone every day? Who tell each other everything?

These were questions with only hypothetical answers. Any closeness I'd had with my mom, or lack thereof, was framed by the trappings of childhood—the times we baked cookies together or the times she sent me to my room with no dinner. Wasn't closeness with a parent measured in the later years? When bigger, more life-changing issues were at stakes? And anyone, at any time, could decide that they wanted out?

Maybe she and Dad would've patched things up. Maybe she would have changed her behavior because of the things I said. I might have grown up a far less hardened person. I might have said yes on that night when Eamon first proposed to me. I might not have thought he was making a joke. I might have stayed in Ireland and never left Eamon at all.

"I know about the photos and why they're gone, but nobody talks about your mom, either," Eamon said. "What was she like?"

Another question with no easy answer. "I guess she was a regular mom. She did normal mom stuff like make us school lunches and helped with our homework. She worked at the flower shop in town." *And she tried to fold us into the life she wanted with a man who wasn't our dad.*

"Nice." Eamon began fishing things out of the box, coats and old ratty mittens. At the bottom was a pair of pink fleece-lined rubber boots that had once belonged to me. "These?"

"Oh. Wow. These were mine." I took one of them in my hand. They were a lighter color than I'd remembered, but perhaps the years had faded them. I should've been wearing them the day of the accident. If I'd gone to school that morning, they would've been on my feet. But I was home sick with a high fever, half delirious. When Mom made me get in the car so we could get Amy from school, I couldn't find my boots, and she told me there was no time to look for them. She'd told me to wear sneakers, with my pajamas no less, because she didn't want to wait for me to get dressed in proper clothes. If I'd had those boots on, I wouldn't have come so perilously close to getting frostbite on my toes from all those hours in the car, stuck at the bottom of an embankment, begging God to let Amy and me live. Why Dad had kept these boots was beyond me. But at least they hadn't been with us in the car that day. I would've been sick to my stomach right now.

"Sure," I said. "I was ten when I wore them, but Fiona's much taller than I was at her age. Her feet might be bigger."

"The MacWards are known for their big feet." Eamon chuckled and tossed the box back into place. "That's settled then."

We climbed down the rickety wood ladder and he closed up the hatch. Amy and Fiona were downstairs already bundled up, Fiona standing there in her socks.

"These are Katherine's. Take good care of them." Eamon handed over the boots.

"Don't be silly. Get them as dirty and wet as you like. You can trash them for all I care."

Fiona worked her feet into the boots while I grabbed my coat, mittens, hat and scarf. Amy headed out into the front yard with the dogs, which were starting to get hyper.

Eamon pecked Fiona on the cheek, but saved a real kiss for me, right on the lips. "You lasses have fun. Be safe."

"We will. Don't let my dad drive you crazy. Maybe you and Luke can watch TV or something."

"No way. This is my chance to pepper your dad with questions you never want to answer."

Great. "Try to keep things light. He doesn't do well with serious."

Eamon nodded and shoved his hands into his pockets. "Something tells me we'll be fine."

If only I could be so certain. Out Fiona and I went into the cold. It was a beautiful day—clear and bright with not much wind, but this was not typical Thanksgiving weather. "God, it's freezing," I said.

Fiona grabbed my hand. "That's why we need to go exploring. It'll keep us warm. Come on." She let go of me and ran ahead, Tilly and Sadie following her and leaving paw prints in the snow.

Amy and I brought up the rear, keeping tabs on Fiona. "Stay on the path," Amy shouted.

Fiona tossed back her head and yelled, "Okay!"

"She's so great," Amy said. "She makes me want to have kids. Like right away. That wasn't even on my radar, to be honest. Marriage seemed like enough for right now, but she's so sweet and fun."

"I know. She makes me want to have kids, too. Or maybe just spend more time with her."

"How are things with her mom? Is it awkward?"

"Surprisingly, it's not that weird. I mean, I'm pretty sure Rachel still has a thing for Eamon, but maybe that's me being paranoid. And it's not like it's a problem. She seems happily married."

"It'd be hard not to carry a torch for a guy like Eamon. I don't know how you walk around without your tongue dragging on the floor."

"Very funny. I manage." Fiona was into the woods now, but was doing a good job staying on the path. The snow we rarely had at Thanksgiving was ankle-deep, and with the sun on its afternoon fall, the shadows of the thousands of trees around us began to shift and swell. It was like being in a carnival fun house. Your eyes could deceive you. The dogs were bounding, nipping at each other, darting off into the trees and rolling in the snow.

"Just stay on the path," I called to Fiona.

She turned and flashed her bright blue eyes at me. "I'll be fine."

And your father will kill me if anything happens to you. "Let's catch up to her," I said to Amy. "It makes me nervous when she's so far ahead."

Amy agreed and we walked double-time to close the gap. "What do you think, Fiona? Is this anything like Ireland?"

"There are woods next to Dad's house. I like to explore them, but he doesn't let me go by myself and we don't have any dogs." Tilly stopped and rounded back to her, endeavoring to stick her nose right in Fiona's face. "I wish Dad would let me get a dog."

"I always wanted one when I was your age, Fiona, but Grandpa Mark wouldn't let us get one, either," I said. "Too much work, apparently."

The path narrowed, and Fiona led the way, the dogs flanking her on each side and trudging through the snow-covered underbrush. "How could a dog be too much work? That makes no sense," she proclaimed.

"I agree." I was next in line in our little parade through the woods. The cold was getting to my face so that I could hardly feel my cheeks, but the rest of my body was warming up.

"What were you like as a girl, Katherine? When you were my age?"

I wasn't quite sure how to answer that question. If any adult had spent too much time analyzing their childhood self, it was me.

"Katherine was bossy." Amy had apparently decided to chime in.

"I can see that." Fiona came to a stop where the path forked. "Which way?"

"Left!" Amy and I answered in unison. We never went right. Not any more.

"No one ever says that boys are bossy." I was desperate to redirect our conversation. Luckily, Fiona hadn't seemed to take issue with us barking orders at her.

Fiona turned around and planted her hands on her hips. "Why is that?"

The dogs stopped and looked at her. Apparently they didn't know the reason either.

"Because men don't like to think of women as leaders," Amy said.

"Well, I don't like them being so stupid. Well, not all men. Dad isn't stupid. Or Luke. Or Grandpa Mark." Fiona returned to the trail, matter-of-fact.

"I really wasn't that bossy, anyway. The oldest child always seems like that, but it's only because they're older and know more." I had to stick up for myself.

"What in the world are you talking about?" Amy asked from behind me. "You always set the rules if we were playing a game. You always overruled me when it came to TV. You were always blaming me for things if we got in trouble."

That brought Fiona to a dead stop. She whipped around, her hair splaying out from under her hat. "What sort of trouble?"

"We broke a neighbor's birdbath once." Amy was once again lightning fast with her response. She loved telling this story. "We were goofing around in their backyard and we weren't supposed to be back there. Katherine told our mom that we were both responsible, when the truth is that it was all her idea."

"Now who can't remember things right? It was not my idea. You were obsessed with that red squirrel that used to sit in her back yard. That's why we went over there. So you could try to catch it. I was just the dummy who agreed to it."

Fiona stood there, looking back and forth at us as we argued about quite literally the stupidest thing ever, something that had happened twenty-five years ago. "Did you ever do anything really bad?" she asked.

Amy and I both gawked at her then we stared at each other, neither of us coming forth with an answer. Had it been really bad? What we did? Our intentions had been good. We were trying to keep our family together.

"Every kid does bad things." Amy didn't take her eyes off me. There was so much forgiveness on her face every time we talked about this. That was undoubtedly a huge part of why I was attached to her. She understood I'd never meant for things to go so wrong. "It's all about whether or not you're willing to own up to it later. And apologize if necessary."

"I always say I'm sorry," Fiona said.

"That's a very good idea," I said.

"Now let's talk about something fun," Amy added. I was so relieved. "Fiona, do you know about Katherine's special eyesight?" She pointed down at the snow.

"What kind of special?" Fiona's eyes were wide with wonder. I loved that about her. She was so open to any idea, no prejudice or prejudgment. Just curiosity.

I crouched down and scooped up a small handful. "Snow comes in all different colors, not just white. There's red and green and orange. Even black. Most people see some slight color variation, especially later in the winter, but I can see it right away."

"She can see something like a million more colors than you or I can," Amy added.

Fiona took some of the snow in her hand and held it right in front of her face, seeming perplexed. "Did something happen to you to make your eyes like that?"

I'd wondered that same thing a few times, but I shook my head. "It's the way I was born. Most people have three cones in their eyes for seeing colors. I have four."

"Pretty cool, huh?" Amy asked.

"It is. But how do I know you aren't fibbing us?"

She sounded a bit like Miles. "A doctor had me tested. He told me that."

"I can see special things, too."

"You can?" I asked.

"Yeah. Dad says so. He says I can see hearts."

I crouched down and looked into her sweet eyes. "You mean people's hearts?"

She pushed aside a strand of her red hair that had peeked out from beneath her hat. "He says I can see when people are bad and people are good. I once told my mum that the gardener had an ugly heart and then they found him peeping in people's windows a few weeks later."

I looked up at Amy, who bugged her eyes at me. "Huh. Well, maybe you really can see hearts."

"I can see Amy's. It's purple with yellow and white swirls." She patted Amy's jacket and then turned to me. "Daddy's is dark red with black stripes."

"Oh, my. That sounds very colorful. What about mine? What does mine look like?"

Fiona's eyebrows drew together tightly and she stared right into the center of my chest. Her lips were pursed, like she was trying very hard at something. "I can't see yours. I've looked for it, but I can't see it."

I glanced over at Amy again, who now seemed bewildered. "Katherine sent her heart to the shop for some mending," she said.

"My heart ran off to the circus. To train lions and elephants."

"Or maybe it's hiding." Fiona cupped her hands around her mouth. "Hello! Katherine's heart, are you in there?"

I laughed. Fiona was being clever and cute, after all. But on the inside, I felt so helpless, like being here was always going to drag me back into the past. I wanted to look ahead, but everything around me—the house, the cold, the woods—was telling me that it didn't matter how hard I tried to ignore history. It was always going to be here. Whether I could accept it or not.

CHAPTER EIGHTEEN

MY INVISIBLE, quite possibly non-existent heart and I were the last ones inside the house after our hike through the woods. I was doing my best to dig in my heels and prevent a downward spiral, but when a sweet, adorable kid tells you she isn't sure you have a heart, it sticks to you like glue. It wasn't that I believed Fiona could truly see hearts, but she was an intuitive kid, an old soul. Maybe she saw things in me that no one else could see. The things no one else *wanted* to see. The parts I'd been desperate to hide. The parts that made it so unbelievable to my sister that Eamon ever saw me as *Sunny Girl*.

"I'm bloody freezing," Fiona said, working her spindly legs out of her boots.

Amy hung Fiona's jacket on the hook. "How about some hot cocoa?"

"Yes, please." Fiona bounced on her toes in her many layers of socks.

I followed them into the kitchen. Eamon and Dad were sitting at the table, talking and laughing. "What'd I miss?" I asked.

Eamon practically sprang out of his chair and pulled me into his arms. "I missed you."

"We weren't gone too long, were we?" I wanted to ask him exactly how certain he was about Fiona's ability to see the good and bad in a person, but I knew how ridiculous it would sound the instant I said the words.

Eamon shook his head and pressed the back of his warm hand against my icy cheek. "Nah."

I leaned into his touch, drinking in his body heat. "That feels so good."

"Cocoa coming up." Amy ripped open a paper packet and dumped it into a mug.

"Did you and Dad have fun?" I asked Eamon.

"We talked about you the whole time." He turned and cast my father a conspiratorial look, which made me all kinds of nervous. Once you got my dad talking, he didn't tend to stop.

"You've got quite a guy here, Katie-boo. Hold on to him."

"I'll do my best." I looked into Eamon's eyes, trying to decipher what in the heck was going on. He and my dad were so happy it was like they'd been huffing helium while Amy, Fiona, and I were gone. But maybe I was seeing things, too stuck on Fiona's appraisal of the state of my heart.

"Amy, we'll be a few minutes late for cocoa if that's alright." Eamon was speaking to my sister, but looked at me the whole time. "Katherine and I have something to talk about."

"We do?"

He took my hand. "Yes. Come on. It won't take long."

I nearly stumbled out of the kitchen as Eamon led me through the living room and up the stairs to my room. He ushered me inside and closed the door behind us.

"Eamon, we can't have sex in the middle of the day when everyone is downstairs. The walls are paper-thin and the floors creak like crazy. Everyone will hear us."

He grinned and took both of my hands. "Had a wonderful talk with your father." His voice was soft, with a leading inflection. When he spoke to me like that, he could have anything he wanted. Anything.

"Good. I'm glad." I could only assume they hadn't talked about anything of consequence. He was being so goofy.

"And now that I've asked *him* a very important question, it's time for me to ask you. Properly." Eamon dropped to one knee and gazed up at me, still holding on to my hands. "Katherine, I love you. I love you with every bone in my body. Every thought I have is of you. Will you marry me?"

Oh no no no no no. This was *not* the time for this. Marriage? I wasn't even sure I had a heart. Plus, I hadn't told him everything. Not just the details about my mom and the accident, either. That had to come first. If I was going to marry him and spend the rest of my life with him, he needed to know everything. He needed to know the things I hadn't told Amy. The thing that haunted me every time I looked at my sister, the possible explanation for why my heart was in hiding.

"Oh, Eamon. This really isn't the right time for this. Not here. Not in this house. Not now." What I really wanted to say was that this wasn't the way this should be going. He was supposed to wait for me to find the perfect time to spill my guts.

"You're doing this to me twice? You're turning me down a second time?" His face fell and that made me sink down onto the bed, if only to bridge the gap between us. Every minute he spent kneeling was sheer torture.

"That's not fair. I didn't know you were serious the first time. We've talked about this."

"Well, I'm absolutely serious right now. There's no pub. No drinking. I asked your father for your hand, Katherine. I've never been more serious in my entire life."

I sucked in a breath, feeling like I would never get enough

oxygen. "Eamon, there are things you don't know. Things I need to tell you. About my past. I won't feel right about us moving forward if I don't tell you first."

He shook his head. "No. Nothing in anyone's past matters. Either you love me and want to be with me or you don't."

"It's not as simple as that. I do love you. And I do want to be with you." I couldn't take my eyes off him, no matter how hard it was to see his face with such pain across it. Still, I was hyper aware of where I was, and the way my mother's presence made me feel like everything was closing in on me. It was if she was glowering over my shoulder, shaking her head at me.

"I'm starting to think *I'm* the reason you're so bloody terrified of marriage. That it's not marriage, but it's marriage to me."

"No. No. That's not true."

"Then what is true, Katherine? Help me understand."

"I need to tell you something first. About my mom and me."

"Katherine, your mother is gone. Nothing you say to me will change my mind. I love you. You are the sweetest, most generous, kindest woman in the world and my life isn't going to be right without you."

Tears started to leak from the corners of my eyes. "Don't put me on a pedestal, Eamon. I don't belong there."

"Enough." He ran his hands through his hair. The instant he looked at the door, I knew he was leaving. "I have to get some air." He rose to his feet, turned the squeaky knob and stormed out. I'd never seen him so hurt. Not even the day we first parted.

Fiona flew into the room. "Where's Dad going? Are we going with him?" She bounced on the edge of the bed.

I crouched down in front of her and took her two tiny hands in mine. "You know I love you, Fiona. Don't you?"

She nodded eagerly, blowing her curly hair from her forehead. "I love you, too."

"Good. I love your dad, too. I love him a lot. But he and I

have to talk. And it might take a while. Are you okay to stay with Aunt Amy?"

"Yeah. Sure."

I straightened and sucked in a deep breath. "Okay, great. We'll be back as quick as we can."

Fiona flopped back on the bed in dramatic fashion. "I'll be fine."

I thundered down the stairs, nearly going sideways in the narrow stairwell. Out on the porch, Eamon's motorcycle boots were missing from the line of shoes. Cold hung in the air from his departure. I needed to hustle up. I worked my feet into my boots and grabbed my coat from the old wood tree. "Ames, I need to run out for a bit. Keep an eye on Fiona for me, okay?" I called.

"Got it," Amy yelled in response.

I hardly had both arms in the sleeves when I burst through the door and slammed it behind me. The cold pinched my cheeks as I zipped up my jacket and coiled a scarf around my neck. I'd just started to warm up and now I was back out in the cold. I followed Eamon's tracks around and behind the house. His strides were ridiculously long. Of course, he was mad, so that might have been part of it. As I looked ahead, I could see that his trail disappeared into the woods. Of course he'd gone that way. Nothing about this could be easy.

I walked double-time hoping to catch a glimpse of him. The sun was dropping down so fast it was like we were having a race. The deep evening chill was settling in. The sky overhead was still clear, but steadily darkening. What was left of the day's rays took the trees in the woods and turned them into spindly blue shadows on the snow. I had such a love/hate relationship with these woods. Amy and I had played for a million hours in them. But the farthest reaches held our darkest memory.

"Eamon," I called. "Where are you? Wait for me." My

breath came in gasping puffs of white, such a shock to the cold that it hung in the air, not disappearing. No answer from Eamon. He was angry, and I couldn't blame him.

I headed between the trees, now nearly running on the path. My mind had too much to process, so it all came in a deluge. *I love him. Of course I love him. But are we ready for marriage? What if it didn't work? It would kill Fiona. It would kill me. It might kill Eamon. He knows there's something big between us and he doesn't care, but I have to tell him. I'll feel so much better when I do.*

I reached the point where the path split and of course, Eamon had taken the path I hadn't wanted him to. He'd gone right. This one was not well traveled and had tons of rocks, as well as downed trees across it and tangles of dead poison ivy. But at least there were only his tracks in the snow to follow. I would take what I could get right now.

"Eamon!" The cold was snapping at my ears like an angry dog. Why hadn't I worn a hat? "Eamon! Please stop!" I was half-running now, dodging suspicious lumps in the snow, bracing myself on trees, my hand-knit mittens catching on the bark and doing nothing to keep out the cold.

Just then I saw a shadow move between the trees ahead. He was probably a good quarter mile ahead of me, but his legs were ridiculously long. No wonder he'd gained so much time on me.

"Eamon!" I yelled again. Snow started to fall—tiny, wispy flakes floating to Earth.

"Go back to the house!" Eamon's voice echoed between the trees, but knowing how mad he was only kept me going. Plus, I had to stop him before he got too far. Another half mile or so and he'd be through the woods and out to the road. The road where my mother hit a patch of ice and the car spun out, hitting a tree and killing her instantly.

I couldn't let Eamon get that far. I couldn't let him go. I

couldn't let him get away from me. The desperation hung heavy in my chest, while every shade of gray and blue and white in the snowflakes was a reminder of that day with my mom. Every shadow in the trees was bringing back the hours Amy and I spent in the back seat, waiting for someone to rescue us.

I felt sick to my stomach, and desperately wanted to stop, but did Eamon have any survival skills at all? He was a rock star, for God's sake. Up ahead, I saw a dark blip of a shadow that had to be him, winding between the trees. I ran faster. I had to get to him. He was my salvation. I knew that now. My steps became desperate lurches. My foot hooked on a branch under the snow. I landed with a thud, my knee squarely meeting a rock. Pain sizzled up my thigh. I rolled to my back for a second then forced myself to my feet, running even faster. "Eamon! Please stop! I'm begging you!"

Like magic, he did what I asked. In profile, I saw him place his hands on his hips and look skyward. I kept going. I was gasping when I got to him.

"You never should've come after me." He turned and looked down at my leg. "What happened?"

Sure enough, I had a gash in my favorite jeans. "I fell." I reached down and touched my knee with my mitten. The blood soaked right through it.

"You're bleeding." He crouched down, his hands on my thighs. His presence was so powerful it made me want to weep. How could I be so desperate to hold on to someone while feeling so destined to push him away?

"You're right. I am terrified of marriage. I haven't told you everything about me. My parents. My family." He looked up at me with his penetrating gray eyes and I had to start. I had to let it go. I had to unravel everything with five little words. "It was all my fault."

Something about finally saying it was so overwhelming that

I had to sit. I didn't bother thinking about it. I sank to the ground. Right on my butt. The cold shot straight through me like an arrow. The melting snow soaked my pants. My knee throbbed, but I ignored it. I needed the strength for the words that were now spilling from my lips...

"I told my dad that my mom had been cheating on him. I told him that she made us spend time with her boyfriend, like she was trying to pretend he was our father. Dad was crushed when I told him, but he said everything would be okay, but I was sick and had a fever, and I don't know. I think he was just telling me what I wanted to hear. He confronted her the next morning. Amy was at school, but I was at home. As soon as Dad left for work, Mom let me have it. She barged into my room and started screaming about how I didn't understand. She and Gordon were in love. I was so sick, half delirious from my fever. She told me that I had ruined everything. I had destroyed our family and things would never be the same."

As the words rolled from my mouth, I could see the cold swirling around me. Blue. Black. Silver. The colors came at me like I'd climbed inside a dark kaleidoscope, and the images from the day were whizzing by me so fast I couldn't keep up. This was like that day in the car. It felt so real, like it was right in front of me. Like I could reach out and touch Amy. Like I could touch my mom. If only for a second.

I sensed that Eamon was still by my side, but I had to keep talking. I came out here to tell him everything. "She started packing our suitcases. She said she was taking me and Amy to live with him. I yelled no and tried to run away, but she slapped me and told me to obey her. When I screamed that he wasn't even our family, she told me that I didn't understand. She made me pack my bag. She made me get in the car, in my pajamas, so we could get Amy at school. She made me go inside the building and stand there while my classmates walked past, staring at my tear-stained, fever-filled face. I listened to her lie to the school secretary about where we were going. I couldn't say a thing. I was so terrified of what she would do. As soon as we had Amy, Mom practically dragged us through the parking lot. In the car, the screaming started again. If I had just kept my mouth shut, everything would've been fine. She kept saying it over and over again."

I could see every frame of it in my head—my mother gaining speed, the dark stands of trees lining the road, flying past us too fast, sending choppy flashes of light into the car. I could feel the rumble of the tires over chunky ice and snow. I could hear her screaming at both of us, her voice raw and savage. Fury and rage. Amy cried. She sobbed, gasping for air. *Stop it, Mommy. Stop it.*

"I couldn't take it anymore. Amy was so upset. I started yelling back at my mom, telling her she had to stop and take us home. Dad would come looking for us. He would know where we went. I was so desperate. I remember hearing that in my voice. I couldn't get her to listen. She just kept saying no. Over and over again."

No. No. No.

"I was wrong. She was right. Amy screamed."

Do something, Katherine. Do something.

"So I did. I said the worst thing ever. I asked her the worst question a ten-year-old kid could ever ask her mom. I shrieked it at the top of my lungs. *Why are you such a fucking bitch? Why are you such a whore?*"

Something wrapped itself around me. Eamon? I couldn't see him. In my head, the movie kept playing. It rolled on. It didn't care to stop.

"She turned around. She was so mad. So mad. And then the car skated across ice. Impossibly fast. It slammed into a tree. It ricocheted and slid backward. Down an embankment. My mother was still staring at me when the car stopped. Her neck had snapped. She was staring right at me. Bright blue eyes. Golden hair. Crimson blood leaking from her lips. The same face I see when I brush my teeth or put on my makeup. The same face I can never escape. I thought Amy was dead, too. She was unconscious. All I could do was pray that she would live. It was too late for my mom."

Sitting in the snow was only a fraction of what it had been like in the back seat of that car. I was there for hours, crying, whimpering, and wondering if anyone would ever find us or if this was the fate we were destined for. Or even worse, the fate I had set in motion. I didn't know what to think. So much of what I loved was gone. And it felt like the cold was coming for everything that was left.

"Katherine. Katherine. Stop for a minute. Listen to me."

I heard Eamon's voice, but it was like I was drowning or someone had their hands over my ears. If I hadn't had his accent to guide me, I wouldn't have known it was him. My breaths shuddered out of my throat, and I gulped it back in, but I was desperate for air. More air. The trees, the snow and ground were tilting and pitching and coming at me. The cold clawed my lungs. It seeped into my legs and pulled on my body like an angry sea.

Something else was pulling on me, tugging me away, but I couldn't see where it was. I was nearly blind, everything around me a million shades of black and shadows now. But then there was heat on my cheek. Then my forehead. And finally my back. I keeled into it. I clung to it. I had to have more.

"Katherine. Talk to me, darling."

The way his words hit my ears, it felt like my head popped up out of the ocean. Eamon was the warmth. He was the one saving me from the snow and cold. He was saving me from myself. "I'm sorry. I'm so sorry." Tears had nearly frozen my eyes shut. "That's why I am the way I am. And I didn't tell you because I thought it would mean I wasn't *Sunny Girl*. I'm not some happy-go-lucky person. I don't know that I can give you what Amy and Luke have. I'm terrified I'm going to mess it up."

"Shh. Shh. Take a deep breath. You need to calm down. You were a kid, Katherine. You can't blame yourself for what happened. And I don't want what Amy and Luke have. I want what we have."

"I ruined everyone's lives that day. I ended my mother's. If I hadn't said anything, this wouldn't have happened."

He pulled me tighter against him. He was not about to let me go. He wasn't about to let the cold take me. "Things happen. Accidents happen. You did what you thought was right. It was a tragic event, but you can't blame yourself. You just can't."

A blip of clarity dropped into my head, an instant where the tears stopped. "Why?" I muttered. "Why can't I blame myself? And don't say it's because I was a kid. It's somebody's fault. I knew that what I was doing was serious. Amy and I talked about it for weeks and weeks. But me and my fucked up sense of right and wrong just couldn't let it go. I couldn't let her drag us to his house anymore. I couldn't let her invite him over and pretend like everything was normal. It was so not normal." I sobbed again and curled into him.

"It wasn't normal. And it wasn't right. You did the right thing. It just didn't turn out the way you thought it would."

I was shaking again, even with the steadying force of Eamon's arms around me. "I was such a dumb kid. I thought she and Dad would stay together and work everything out. There was no way that was going to happen."

Eamon blew out an exasperated breath. "Katherine, let me just tell you one more time. You can't judge yourself by what happened when you were ten. It's not fair. No one should be measured by their actions at that age. It's craziness."

"Fiona could be measured by her actions at this age. She'd do great. She's so perfect."

Eamon laughed, which had a profound effect on me. It began to lift me out of the bizarre fog I'd talked myself into. "She does seem pretty bloody perfect, doesn't she? I worry that means we're really in for it when she becomes a teenager."

"She can't see my heart. She told me that today."

"What?"

"My heart. She said she can see everybody's heart, but she couldn't see mine. Do you think that means I'm a bad person?"

Eamon shook his head. "Come on. It's freezing out here. Let's got back to the house and talk about this." He picked himself up off the ground and helped me to standing.

"Oh, man. My knee. I really fucked it up."

"All the more reason to get back." He put my arm around his shoulders and we started walking. The sun had set. All you could see were tiny glowing squares ahead, the windows of our house and the neighbors'.

"You didn't answer my question about Fiona seeing my heart." We trudged along the narrow path, through the snow that was more compact now. I held on to Eamon with everything I had. I didn't want to let him go.

"It's a game she plays. I told her when she was little that she could see people's hearts because she was always a good judge of people."

"She told me the story about the gardener."

"Exactly. It doesn't mean she can really see them."

"But she's still a good judge of character. Was that her way of telling me I'm a bad person?"

Eamon came to a stop and turned to me, pulling me into a firm embrace. "I don't know why she told you that, but I can tell you that she adores you. She's drawn to you. She wants to play with you and talk to you as much as she possibly can. She doesn't feel that way about bad people."

I sucked in a deep breath. The icy air that had punished my lungs earlier was cleansing now. I'd told Eamon the gruesome tale and unlike every other person who'd heard it before him, he reined me in after it was said and done. He didn't push me away. He held me closer.

"Thank you. Thank you for listening to me and putting up with my erratic behavior. I'm so sorry about this afternoon. It's not that I don't want to get married to you. I love you. I really, really do. And I don't want you to go anywhere. I'm just not ready. That's all. And I can't get engaged here, anyway. I don't want that moment to be tainted by old memories. Now you know why. Exactly why."

He pressed a kiss to my forehead. "Do you feel better now? Now that you've told me everything?"

I reared my head back and peered into his eyes, now only barely visible in the pitch dark. Luckily, we could see the house and its gleaming gold windows. "I feel so much better. A million times better."

"Good. I'm glad. You know you can tell me anything, darling. You can't make me fall out of love with you because of something that happened in the past. It's all just part of you and I love you. You can't scare me."

"Promise?"

"I promise."

"Good. Because there's one more thing I didn't tell you."

"We'll freeze to death out here if it's another story like the one you just told me."

I took his hand again and resumed our hike, with me leading the way. I still knew every subtle turn in this path. It was carved into my memory, just like the thing I was about to say. "It's not an actual story. It's the one detail I didn't tell you."

We stopped when we cleared the woods and stood at the back of my dad's property. The warm glow from the house was brighter now. Eamon was so unbelievably handsome in the light. "Why did you leave something out?"

"Because it's something Amy doesn't know, something my dad doesn't know, either."

"Can you tell me?"

I looked to the house again. I could see my dad in the kitchen with Fiona. My heart ached for the words that were about to come out of my mouth, but I knew I had to let them out. Then we could go back inside and be a family again. "The man my mom had an affair with? I'm pretty sure he's Amy's real dad."

CHAPTER NINETEEN

DESPITE THE CANON of terrible memories contained in my childhood home, it felt so good to step across the threshold after being in the woods with Eamon for so long. Waves of laughter filtered out onto the porch. Dad, Julia, Amy, Luke, and Fiona were playing charades in the living room in front of a roaring fire. This was what coming home had once felt like, a lifetime ago.

Amy sprang up from the sofa when she spotted us. "We were about to send out a search party. Everything okay?" She grimaced when she saw my current state up close. I didn't need to look in a mirror to know that I looked like hell.

"Everything's good. I just need to go upstairs and change. I fell and banged up my knee."

"Oh, shit," Amy said. "The First Aid kit should be in Dad's room. I'll get it."

She scampered off and Eamon helped me with my coat, then let me lean on him as I hobbled inside. We waited for Amy at the bottom of the stairs and resumed our previous conversation, without words, just disbelieving looks from him and my agreement.

Holy shit.

I know.

If it hadn't been so cold outside, we could have stayed out there for hours debating the bomb I'd dropped about Amy.

She emerged from Dad's room. "Do you need help?"

"I think I can handle it." Eamon took the kit from her and tucked it under his arm.

"Come down when you're done," Amy said, bubbly as a can of shaken soda. "Fiona is hilarious at charades. You should've seen her act out *Gone with the Wind*. I nearly died laughing."

A smile crossed Eamon's face. "We will. We won't be long." A step at a time, he helped me up the stairs and into my bedroom. "We need to get you out of those pants."

"I'm usually way more excited to hear you say that." I peeled off my jeans, wincing when the ragged edges of the torn fabric stuck to my knee. I settled on the edge of the bed and grabbed a throw blanket to drape across my still-frozen thighs.

"You can't tell her. You know that, right?" Eamon carefully dabbed at my skin with antiseptic on a gauze pad.

I let loose a heavy sigh. "I know I can't tell her. I don't even know if it's true. My mom was so furious that morning and I was so scared. I'm not even sure I remember it right." Except that there was something in my gut telling me that I had perfect recall of that day. My brain could screw up plenty, but not this. "She was throwing our clothes into suitcases and telling me that all three of us were going to live with him. I was panicked. It was the last thing I saw coming. I tried to argue my way out of it by saying that we couldn't live with him because her boyfriend wasn't part of our family. She snapped at me and said she was pretty sure he was part of Amy's."

"My God, Katherine. She made a holy show of herself that day, didn't she?" He shook his head in dismay and squeezed some antibiotic cream onto my knee. "I think she was just angry.

No good comes out of saying anything after all this time. You were right to keep the secret."

Funny how he could so simply answer a question I'd asked myself for more than twenty years. "You think so?"

"I would've done the same thing."

My heart, visible or not, felt so much lighter. "I don't want to look back anymore. I don't even want to think about it anymore."

"Then don't. You've unburdened yourself. Let it go."

"I feel better after telling you everything."

"Ya do?" The sweetest look came over his face as he peeled off the backing of a bandage.

"I do. So much better. I think I just needed to get it all of my chest."

He placed a gentle kiss on my leg right above my knee and helped me pour myself into a pair of yoga pants. "I love you, Katherine. Please don't ever feel like you can't tell me something. Our relationship needs to be an open book for it to work."

"I know. You're right. Thank you for understanding." It felt a little bit like my heart might explode. If I'd known I would feel this way after coming clean, I would've done it much sooner.

An especially loud cacophony of laughter found its way upstairs. "Sounds like we're missing out on the fun."

"We'd better get down there or we'll never hear the end of it."

———

EVEN AFTER STAYING up too late playing charades, I woke on Thanksgiving morning just before seven. Maybe it was my conscience that decided to shake me from my sleep, like a child impossibly excited for Christmas morning. I couldn't remember ever feeling like this, aside from the time I spent in Ireland. My heart was so unburdened it was like being a new person.

I snuggled closer to Eamon, taking his arm and draping it around my waist. "Good morning," I whispered into his neck.

He hitched a leg over mine and tugged me even closer. "Morning."

"Did you sleep well?"

"So well that I still am. Sleeping." He kept his eyes closed.

"Sorry." I smiled and rolled to my back, looking around my room. Most vestiges of the old me had disappeared. Amy's kitten posters had been taken down long ago. The aquarium we never took great care of was probably residing in the attic, knowing my dad. Still, there were little things that would always be familiar—the smudge of pink nail polish on the light switch plate or the worn spot on the floor where Amy used to dance while singing into a hairbrush. Those could be my reminders of childhood now. I could reframe it all. Life had gone on after that terrible day. And it hadn't all been terrible. Eamon came after that.

And now Fiona, who flopped over on her bed, her eyes popping open. As I often did with her dad, we had a wordless conversation with eyebrows and mouths. She hated that air mattress. I could see it on her face. I patted my leg and she took my cue, scrambling out of bed. Her bare feet across the wood floors made another familiar sound. She climbed up on our bed and began the process of wedging herself between her father and me.

"Fiona. What in the world are you doing?" Eamon rolled to his back and rubbed his eyes.

She and I laughed conspiratorially. "I'm getting into this big comfy bed with you and Katherine. Now scoot over. Please."

Eamon grumbled while I relinquished the biggest swath of

territory and pulled back the covers so Fiona could climb underneath.

"It's so cozy." She wiggled like a worm under the blankets.

"Your feet are freezing," Eamon said.

"Let me move them, then."

Next thing I knew, her icy toes brushed my calf. "Hey. Why do I get the ice cube feet?"

"Dad complained first."

"Are these the rules of snuggling?"

She cozied up next to me. "I never thought about the rules. I think we should devise them."

"We wouldn't want any confusion later."

"Precisely. There *are* three of us in this bed. Things could definitely get confusing."

I looked into her eyes, the blue-gray of a stormy summer sky. I'd fallen so in love with her that my chest got tight every time I looked at her. "Where do we start?"

"Everyone must keep their freezing feet to themselves," Eamon chimed in.

Fiona turned back to her dad. "That's impossible. You're too tall. My feet will naturally run into your knees."

"Especially since he has such knobby ones," I added.

Eamon popped up on to his elbow. "I feel attacked."

"You're outnumbered. Two girls, one boy." Fiona was lightning fast with her answers.

"Even if the numbers were in my favor, I would never pick on someone's knees."

"Katherine, I think Dad wants you to say you're sorry."

He slid me one of his cocky half-grins. "An apology would be appreciated, yes."

"I'm very sorry. It was not my intention to body shame your bony knees."

"No more goofing around. What are some *real* rules?" Fiona

asked. "I think that you get to have as much of the bed as you can cover with your body. Like King of the Hill."

"That sounds cutthroat," I said. "What happens if I get pushed to the edge and roll out onto the floor?"

"You climb back up on the bed and claim the empty space, of course."

"My goodness, Katherine," Eamon said. "That should have been perfectly self-explanatory."

"It wasn't. It also doesn't sound particularly restful."

"Oh, it isn't," Fiona said. "But this is snuggling, not sleeping. They are two very different things."

"And what is this?" Eamon threw back the covers and tickled Fiona without mercy.

Her wiry legs and arms flailed as her giggles and yelps filled the room with happy noise. I recoiled to avoid the inventible smack of a wayward hand or elbow.

"Stop, Daddy, stop," Fiona gasped.

He obliged, but laughter kept tumbling out of her. Eamon had a permanent grin painted on his face.

"Tickling is *not* part of snuggling, Daddy. Someone could get hurt."

"Got it. I'll refrain from it until I've learned all the rules."

"Who's hungry?" I asked.

"I am,""Fiona answered. "But are we allowed to eat on Thanksgiving morning? Or do we wait until the big meal so we can stuff ourselves?"

"We have to eat now. We're going to need our strength to cook all that food."

"Will Amy and Luke come to breakfast?" she asked.

I shrugged. "Maybe you should go ask them."

Fiona scrabbled over the top of me and climbed out of bed.

"Knock quietly," Eamon said. "And don't open the door if there's no answer."

"Really. You act as though I have no manners." Fiona marched out of the room.

Eamon and I quickly drifted back together.

"How are you feeling this morning?" he asked. "Everything okay after yesterday? I know it was hard on you, but I'm so glad you told me. I don't like having secrets between us."

I nodded. "I know it's better this way. It was just hard. I was so worried it would change the way you see me. Knowing my past."

"It does change it, but not in a bad way. It only lets me see that we still have a lot to learn about each other. But that doesn't bother me. We have time. Right?"

"Yes. We do." I gazed into his eyes and brushed his hair from the side of his face. "I just need until the wedding is over. Then we can talk about our future. I don't want to overshadow Amy and you know how she is. She'll likely throw a temper tantrum if there's even the slightest rumbling of someone else trying to take her spotlight."

"We could get engaged and not tell anyone."

"Weren't you just saying you don't like secrets?"

Out in the hall, I could hear Luke's and Amy's voices. Fiona was, of course, talking a million miles a minute, even faster than Amy.

"But this would be different. It would be our secret."

I reached down and took his hand in mine. "The minute you and I decide to get married, I'm going to want to call Amy and tell her everything. If I wait, she'll know it the second I finally tell her. And she'd never forgive me."

Eamon drew in a deep breath through his nose and nodded. "Makes sense."

"Are you disappointed?"

He shrugged. "Well, yeah. Of course. But I can wait. I've

already waited plenty long. What's a few more weeks? I just have one stipulation though."

"What's that?"

"You'd better not expect a proposal from me the minute Amy and Luke exchange their vows. I still want to surprise you. You won't know when it's coming."

I smiled wide. "That sounds wonderful."

Fiona burst into our room. "Amy wants me to tell you that coffee is on and if you don't get your butts downstairs in five minutes, you'll have to wait for the second pot."

I laughed and shook my head. "On our way."

Eamon proceeded downstairs in his gray t-shirt and blue plaid pajama pants, but I grabbed an old sweatshirt and some slippers before catching up to him.

The kitchen was already full of the most amazing morning smells—coffee and bacon, which Luke was tending on the stove while Eamon sipped coffee and chatted with him. Amy had put cinnamon rolls in the oven. Dad and Julia were sitting at the table with Fiona, who was still working out the rules of snuggling.

Amy walked over to me. "We should probably make up a cooking schedule for today, don't you think?"

"Yes. That oven is so tiny. We're going to have to get creative."

Fiona, Dad, and Julia all burst out laughing. Fiona was keening so hard she nearly fell out of her chair.

"Let's go sort this out in Dad's office," Amy said.

"Perfect." I followed her through the living room, where Dad already had the TV on and tuned to the station that would be playing the Macy's Thanksgiving Day parade.

Amy began rifling through the stacks of newspapers on Dad's desk. "Lord only knows how long it will take me to find a pad of paper and a pen."

I held out my arms. "Here. Hand me a stack."

"Why does he keep all of this crap?"

"He swears he's only keeping the important stuff." I turned to put the papers on an old TV tray Dad was using as a table. I laid them on top of a pile of magazines, but half of them toppled over to the floor.

"Bingo. An actual notepad," Amy said.

For a second, I considered leaving the papers on the floor, but Dad liked his mess tidy. I crouched down and saw a face that stopped me dead in my tracks. "Oh my God. Amy." I couldn't pick it up. I didn't want to touch it.

"What?"

"He's dead."

"Who is?"

I straightened, leaving the paper on the floor. "Him. Oh my God, I can't even look at him." Except that I couldn't tear my eyes away from the black and white photograph of Gordon Stewart, the man who our mother had claimed to love. The man who our mother had said was family to Amy.

Ever brave, Amy plucked the newspaper from the floor and read, shaking her head slowly from side to side. "Wow. Lung cancer."

"I didn't know he still lived here."

Amy scanned the page. "It says that he moved back five years ago to be closer to his brother. He had no other family, apparently."

Just hearing the details of his life made me ill. Or maybe it was guilt. There was a part of me that wished the man had never existed, but how horrible was that? He was dead now. Gone. Just like Mom.

"Is it bad that it makes me sick to my stomach to think about how much time we spent around him?" Amy asked. "I love Mom, but that's one thing I can't forgive her for."

"No, it's not bad. I was thinking the same exact thing." Thank God I had Amy in all of this. I could explain the crap out of what had happened to us, but she'd had to live it, too. She understood how bizarre it all was. "It was weird. Most people sneak around when they have an affair, but not her."

"I will never forget the morning he wore Dad's robe. That was so messed up."

My stomach clenched as another unwelcome memory flooded my brain—it wasn't just the flecks of blue and black in the old stoneware plates my mom loved. It wasn't just the camel color of dad's velour robe. It was the smell of coffee and orange juice and maple syrup hanging in the air and the way it blended with that baked aroma of the furnace working too hard to heat the house. The sound of bacon sizzling and popping in fat in the cast iron pan. The soft nubby feel of my flannel nightgown against my thighs as I wrung my hands in my lap under the table and wished that I could close my eyes and make him disappear and never, ever come back. Ever. And worst of all, the knowledge that Amy was feeling the same exact thing I was. It hadn't merely radiated off her, it was like there was an invisible channel between us, with muddy sickening water that looked and smelled like death flowing back and forth. At that moment, I wanted more than anything to shield Amy from all of it. I was ten. I could take it. She was eight. She was innocent.

"So that's it then, huh?" Amy asked. "That chapter is really closed now." She folded the paper in half and then in half again.

"What are you doing with that? You aren't keeping it, are you?"

"Oh, hell no. I'm tossing it in the fireplace. Where it belongs."

"Smart. That's smart." I trailed her into the living room and after we scouted out the kitchen to make sure Dad wasn't about to walk in, I pulled back the old brass screen in front of the fireplace.

Amy grabbed one of those long matches from the mantle and kneeled down on the brick hearth. With a single strike, it sparked into flame. The newspaper caught fire right away and Amy tossed it on top of the ashes from last night. She put her arm around my shoulders as we watched the flames erase the memory of a man neither of us had ever wanted in our lives. It didn't take long for it to all be gone, and the fire snuffed itself out.

I put the screen back in place. "Feel better?"

Amy nodded. "Yeah. I do."

"What are you two doing?" Dad's voice came from behind us.

Amy looked at me and we both agreed without a word that he didn't need to know. "Just getting rid of some trash," she said. "Those cinnamon rolls ready yet?"

"You set the timer. I don't know how I should know," he answered.

"I'll go grab the notepad you found." "I traipsed back into Dad's office. Should I have stopped her from burning the obituary? Out of respect? How messed up was the idea of that? I wasn't sure what was going through my head—what was done was done. Gordon Stewart was gone now. Amy and I could get on with the rest of our lives with as clean a slate as the universe was ever going to give us.

CHAPTER TWENTY

MY FIRST DAY back at work after Thanksgiving was blissfully uneventful. Miles was taking a few extra days off, spending them at his villa in Anguilla with his kids, his new wife and his ex-wife. How very modern of him. Summer and I had rolled our eyes about it more than once. He was such a pretentious, pompous ass.

After work, I came home and made dinner for three. It was just spaghetti, but Fiona loved it and even helped me in the kitchen. Even if that was as close as I ever got to domesticity, it felt like a win. I loved taking care of her and Eamon. There was no bad history here—only happy days ahead.

Eamon and Fiona were watching TV and I was tidying up the kitchen when I got a call from Amy.

"Did you get a letter today? From Bill Stewart? In Connecticut?"

I cradled the phone between my shoulder and ear, wiping my hands dry on a towel. "No. Why? Is something wrong?" That name...Bill Stewart. Did I even know who that was?

"I don't know. I mean I'm not sure what it means." She was

distressed. I could hear it. Amy did not get this worked up about anything other than maybe wedding stuff.

"What does it say?"

"It's about *Gordon*." She whispered his name like she was daring to say *Voldemort* out loud. "Actually, it's *from* him."

The blood in my veins went cold. "I don't understand. He's dead. How can you get a letter from a dead person?"

"I guess he wrote it when he was sick and knew that he was dying? He, um... I don't even know how to say this." She was on the verge of tears. Paper rustled in the background. She must have had the letter right there, reading it.

I wanted to console her, but my mind was moving so fast I could hardly keep up. This was one thing I had not bargained on. A letter? What in the hell could he have said to her in a letter? And why was she getting it now? Weeks after his death?

"He says I was his only family other than his brother. He left me stuff in his will. What the hell does that mean, Katherine? His family?"

My mouth fell open, frozen. From beyond the grave, he was messing up our lives, again. I wanted to hide from it, but I couldn't. Amy needed me. "Take a deep breath. I'm coming over right now."

"Yes, please. Hurry."

I hung up the phone, still disbelieving what she'd just told me.

"What's wrong?" Eamon looked over from the TV. As soon as he saw my face, he got up from the couch and headed straight for me.

"Amy got a letter. From the man my mom had the affair with."

"Wait. I thought he was dead."

I explained the rest, the words sounding no better when I said them aloud. "She's really upset and I told her I would come over." I was about to walk into a buzz saw, but what choice did I have? "I had to. She's my sister. She needs me."

Eamon nodded and took my hand. "Yeah. Of course. We should call for a car. I don't want you taking the subway out to Brooklyn at night."

"It's fine. It might be good for me to have the time to think."

"Will you take a car back then?"

"I will."

"What are you going to say to her?"

That was the sixty-four thousand-dollar question. "I don't know what I can do other than tell her the truth."

I grabbed my coat and my purse, kissed Eamon and Fiona goodbye, and hurried down to the subway station. I'd always sort of liked riding the subway—the rocking back and forth was oddly soothing to me. Those carrot orange and goldenrod molded plastic seats let me know I was at home. Of course, taking the train tonight was only prolonging the inevitable. A car would've been much faster this time of day, but the truth was that I needed time to think.

Memories, mostly bad, began to rifle through my head again, the stuff I'd thought I could finally set aside. Things like the first time we were taken over to his house. I was six and Amy was only four, but I remembered it like it had been tattooed on my brain. We were parked on his couch in front of the television. Mom had brought a DVD with her, *The Little Mermaid*, a movie we'd watched one hundred times. The sound was turned up to what seemed like an unusual level, but neither of us said a thing. Amy and I had no clue what was going on, so we did as we were told and sat there while the adults disappeared down the hall.

I looked over at Amy during the first scene in Ursula's lair, watching her in profile, cast in blue from the light of the TV. She had the most adorable little nose, her eyes wide as she was transfixed by the story, mumbling the words to herself. Even then, it felt like I understood how innocent we were, and that something bad was happening. I tried to chalk it up to the movie. Ursula had always made me nervous anyway. I was always the kid who wanted to fast-forward over the bad parts.

We got thirsty after awhile and went into the kitchen to find some water. We had to open nearly every cabinet to find the glasses, and we were terrified of being found out, like we were tiny thieves in the night. I remember exactly how unsettling it felt like to be in that strange house, brought there by our own mother. It was no less surreal now. But Amy and I had lived it. Of that much I was sure.

I sucked in a deep breath and set my temple against the train window, letting the force of it knock my head. When would this feeling ever go away? This deeply-seated sense of damage, an open wound that refused to heal. Would it always stay with me? Would I never be free of it? I would've wished for amnesia if Amy and Eamon and Fiona and my dad didn't mean so much to me.

I reached the stop closest to Amy and Luke's new place and filed off with the other passengers, trudging up the stairs and out into the night air. It was cold tonight and it almost smelled like snow, but it was still early for that. Mother Nature playing tricks, or maybe I was just missing our time back at Dad's, a trip I had been so apprehensive about, but that turned out surprising and wonderful. I would've done anything to go back in time just a few days.

My walk was only four blocks, but I was freezing by the time I got there. I jabbed at the button for their unit and immediately put my mitten back on. I was buzzed up right away.

Amy was waiting at the top of the landing, wearing a fuzzy sky blue sweatshirt, leggings, and slippers. She looked like hell, even from a distance. "Thank God you're here. I'm freaking out."

I rushed up the stairs and into her arms. She'd been crying. I wanted to cry, but I wasn't there yet. All I could think at that moment was how unfair this was to both of us. We never asked for this. Not a single drop of it. And we couldn't shake it. It was starting to feel like a curse.

Luke was standing in the doorway to their apartment. "Thanks for coming over, Katherine. Amy has been really upset and I have to admit, I'm a bit out of my depth on this one. I've only known for a few weeks about your mom and everything that happened to you girls." He stood there like he was looking to us for guidance. "What can I do? Open another bottle of wine?"

Another bottle? At least that gave me a better sense of my sister's state of coherency.

Amy shook her head. "It's okay, hon. I just need to talk to Katherine. It'll be okay." She popped up onto her tiptoes and kissed his cheek. "Love you."

I swear to God, he gazed right into her eyes in the most romantic, loving way I could've imagined. "I love you, too." Luke flickered his attention at me then headed down the hall.

Amy and I settled on the sofa in the living room. The cleansing breaths I'd been taking since first coming up on her building were doing nothing to calm my heart or my head. The letter was sitting right there on the coffee table, like a death sentence or *FIN* at the end of a French film, and it struck me how impossibly simple this moment was...weeks and months and years of worry about this coming out, and what it would do to my relationship with my sister, and it all came down to a piece of paper stuffed into an envelope. I had to believe that she and I were stronger than whatever was in that letter. We'd weathered so much impossible shit and we always came out on the other side of it, stronger.

She handed it to me. "I've read it fifty times. I understand the words, but it doesn't make any sense. It has to be a sick joke or his brother is trying to get money out of me, but that doesn't make sense either."

My hands were shaking as I unfolded it, which was nothing more than cheap printer paper. For a moment, all I saw were marks of black on white, but then it came into focus.

Dear Amy,

By the time you receive this letter, I will be gone. I have late stage lung cancer and don't have long to live. I guess all those cigarettes I smoked when I was a teenager finally caught up to me. One thing you learn when you're facing death is that there are certain things you must say before you leave this world. You can't rest until you've said them. I need peace. That is the aim of my letter.

I want you to know that I loved your mother very much. No, it wasn't right for us to be together, but we couldn't stay apart. We tried many times over the years, but some bonds are simply unbreakable. They won't go away no matter how hard you try. I know I didn't lose as much as you and your sister did on that January day, but I lost the love of my life. She was my one bright spot. I could never marry anyone else. No one could hold a candle to your mom. Losing her left a void that was impossible to fill.

I don't have much family, Amy. In fact it's just you and my brother, who was instructed to mail this letter to you after my death. You will receive a more formal notification from the attorney about the terms of my will. I didn't have much to leave you, but there's some money, as well as a few of your mother's things. They're not much, just small things she'd left at my house:

Two lipsticks (one red, one pink)

One pair small gold hoop earrings

One bottle of perfume

The makeup is so old by now. I probably should've thrown it away. But I could never bring myself to do it. She meant that much to me.

I also saved the letters your mother wrote to me over the years. I don't know if it's appropriate for you to have them, as they contain a lot of romantic sentiments. But they are a piece of her, and I kept them, so I'll leave that decision up to you. You may contact my brother if you would like to have them. He's under instructions to dispose of them if he doesn't hear from you within a year.

I hope you live a long and happy life. I hope your sister does as well. You girls were the light of your mother's life and she loved you both very much. I hope you know that. I hope you felt it during the years you had with her, because I know first-hand that those years were not enough. She had a very generous heart. That is the thing I will remember about her most. It's impossible to forget.

I'm sorry we never got to have a traditional relationship. It never felt right to reach out to you after your mother passed away. I didn't want to intrude on the life you had with the family you had left. Your mother and I were never certain whether you are my biological daughter. All I can say is that every time I looked at you, I knew with my heart that you were mine.

With all my love,
Gordon Stewart

Tears ran down my face. It was as bad as I'd imagined, but somehow worse. As sad as my mother's story was, it was now even more tragic. He had adored her. Everything she had said to me that morning about how much she loved him was apparently returned, in equal measure. And had I been nothing more than a clueless kid who didn't get it? Absolutely. Had the feelings between them been stronger than what was between her and my dad?

How do you even measure the strength of love?

By seeing how long it lasts? Whether it can survive the tests life throws at it? All these years later, as recently as a few months ago, Gordon Stewart was still walking this earth and loving my mom.

But what if things had been different? What if we had gone to live with Gordon Stewart? Would she have been happy? What would have happened when the supposed drudgery of routine—school lunches and weeknight dinners and laundry and the same sex every Saturday night—took over? Would she have eventually become unhappy with him? Was there some gene in my mother's line that made hearts want to wander? She might have felt trapped in her marriage, but if she'd gone to be with Gordon, she could've very well been walking into another trap.

"Well?" Amy asked, with all the impatient agitation a rightfully freaked out person could muster.

"I don't even know where to start." It was the truth. There was a lot to unpack. Decades of an unproven secret, of a guess my mother let slip, left lurking in my brain.

"Do you think it's true? Do you think I'm really his daughter?" She sprang from her end of the couch and started pacing on the other side of the coffee table, flapping her hands and shaking her head. "What if it's really true? My dad isn't who I think he is?"

"It says that he wasn't certain about it."

"But he left me money. Nothing is more certain than money. Why do that?"

I shook my head and put the letter back where it belonged—in the damn envelope. "He said he had almost no family."

"Almost, Katherine. Almost. If you aren't sure, you just leave it all to your brother. You don't write the letter. You only write what he wrote and talk to a lawyer about putting someone in your will if you're really, really, really fucking sure about it." Her face was ruddy with frustration all while my heart was sinking to my stomach.

"I have to tell you something."

She froze for a heartbeat or two then turned to me. She was impossibly still, like a cat waiting for the perfect moment to pounce. "Why are you not more freaked out about this? You hated him just as much as I did. Maybe more."

As much as I wanted to, I could no longer shrink away from the thing that had been between us all these years. It had to come out. It was no longer my secret to keep. "I don't really know what to say other than I'm sorry, but I knew about this."

"The letter?"

I shook my head. "No. In fact, when we found his obituary, I thought this was all over, but apparently not. I knew, Amy. I knew that he and Mom suspected this."

She didn't blink. There was no realization crossing her face, not the tiniest twitch of a muscle. "You knew? How long have you known?" I got up from the couch and went to hug her, but she recoiled and stepped back. "Don't touch me right now. I need you to just answer the question. How long did you know?"

"Mom slipped and said something the morning of the accident. When she was packing the suitcases and I was in a panic, trying to figure out what in the hell she was doing. When she told me that we were going to live with him, I blurted out that he wasn't even family. That's when she said that he might be *your* family."

Her mouth went slack and she wrapped her arms around herself. The look she shot at me was both devastating and *devastated*, damaging in equal measure, scorching the world we shared, just the two of us. "Luke!" she yelled. "Come here, please. I need you to tell my sister to leave."

"What? Amy, no. Come on. Let's talk about this. Please. I never told you because I wasn't sure. What good was it going to do to tell you something that I wasn't even sure was true?"

Luke rushed into the room. "What's going on? Is everything okay?"

"Katherine needs to leave. And never come back."

"What?" He looked at me, then at her, and back again. "What happened?"

"She knew about the stuff that was in the letter. She's known for more than twenty fucking years and she never told me. We slept in the same bedroom every night and told each other every deep dark secret and she never fucking told me." Her voice was falling apart at the seams and my heart was breaking just as fast, but I didn't think it was a good idea to move closer to her, no matter how badly I needed to hug her. She would only push me away. "I should've known that I couldn't trust you when I found out about Eamon. No normal person keeps him a secret."

"Amy. Come on. I didn't keep him a total secret. I just didn't tell you the whole thing, and that was out of guilt. I was off having fun in Ireland and you were dealing with Dad. It wasn't right and I felt horrible about it."

"Eamon told Luke that he proposed to you and you said no. You don't want to be happy, do you, Katherine? You just want to be miserable and you want everyone else to be miserable, too. That's why you've been such a pain in the ass about our wedding. That's why all of the snide looks at the engagement party and clamming up at the florist."

My shoulders dropped in defeat. "I'm helping you the best I can. I don't know what else to say. Most of the time it feels like you don't want my help. I'm not going to force that. And I said no to Eamon because it didn't feel right to get engaged right before your wedding. It didn't feel right to get engaged in that house. It holds too many terrible memories for me."

"You have always held that over my head." She pointed at me and her jaw tightened. "That you had to endure the worst of it from Mom. Well, I'm sick of it. I suffered, too, dammit. It's not my fault you were sick that morning and had to stay home from school."

"I feel like I should probably go in the other room," Luke muttered.

Amy shot him a look. "No. Stay. I need you here." She then turned her attention back to me. "I listened to you when we were kids and you said we should tell Dad about what was going on. But I wish we hadn't. Our lives would've been totally different if you'd just shut your mouth, Katherine. Everyone's lives. Our entire family." Her eyes blazed with something so hurtful I couldn't put a name on it. I only knew that it was designed for me. "Not just my life or yours. Dad's, Mom's. Even Gordon Stewart's life would've been different. Do you have any idea what you stole from me? My childhood. My mother. And even after all of that was gone, you stole the only chance I had to possibly have a relationship with the man who might have been my real dad. He's dead now and I can't get him back, either." She bent over at the waist and rested her hands on her knees, completely out of breath. "Fuck. You just stood there and let me put his obituary in the fireplace. You didn't say a single thing. I think I'm going to be sick."

"We don't know that you're his daughter, Ames. And I'm still your sister. We've always had each other. Nothing will ever change that."

She straightened, but her head bobbed back and forth like she was drunk. "No. You're not my sister anymore. I don't see any way I can ever forgive you for this. You lied to me for twenty-two years."

"Lying and keeping a hurtful fact from someone are not the same thing."

"Don't get technical with me. You were the one person on the planet I felt I could always count on and now I realize that was all bullshit." She closed her eyes and pinched the bridge of her nose. "I can't talk to you anymore. I need you to leave."

I slowly picked up my purse from the couch. "I understand. You need time to think."

"No. I don't need time to think. You and I are done."

"What does that even mean? What about the wedding?"

"You'll still be my maid of honor. It will be weird if that changes. But I don't want you to be involved in any other way. I'll get Luke's mom or sister to do it. Show up for the shower. And the rehearsal. Please try to keep the sarcasm to a minimum that night if you would. I'm so fucking tired of it. Now if you don't mind, I need you to leave so that I can write a letter to the man who might be my uncle and see if I can get some shred of memories of my mother back."

With no other options, I skulked out of the apartment, closing the door behind me. As soon as I made it down the first flight of stairs, I heard Luke.

"Katherine," he whispered. "I'll talk to her. I'll try to find a way to fix this."

I knew exactly how horrible I'd been for doubting him for even a minute. "You're the best thing that ever happened to her." And I was convinced that I was the worst.

"It'll be okay. We'll figure it out."

I drew in a deep breath. Maybe Luke really was that magical. Maybe he could get Amy to see past the secret I kept from her. But it felt so unlikely right now. "Just love her and I'll try to figure out a way to fix the rest of it. I think this is a disaster only I can clean up."

He glanced back into their apartment, nodding, before returning his sights to me. "Call me at work."

"I will." I slinked down the stairs and opened the front door to their building. It was snowing. Big, fat silvery flakes floating to earth. It wasn't sticking, except to the patches of ground skirting the trees along the sidewalk. I trudged down the steps and sat on the bottom tread. It was freezing and I didn't care. I didn't even put on my mittens. Part of me wanted the cold to just take me.

I pulled out my phone and called Eamon.

"What happened?" he answered.

"It was bad. Really, really bad. She never wants to speak to me again."

"What? No."

"What, yes."

"She's in shock. Give her a few days to cool down. You two will patch things up. She loves you. I know that much for sure."

I rested my elbows on my knees and looked up at the black sky, letting the snow land on my cheeks and lips. I couldn't feel them melt when they hit my skin. I was already too frozen. "I'm not so sure."

"Where are you now?"

"Sitting on the steps outside her building, hoping to become part of an eventual snow bank. Maybe the borough of Brooklyn will just scoop me up in a plow."

"Do you need me to call you a car?"

"Yes, please. Thank you."

"I love you, Katherine. It will all work out. I'm positive."

"I love you, too," I said, understanding in that moment exactly how much I needed him.

CHAPTER TWENTY-ONE

IN THE DAYS following my cataclysmic visit to see Amy, I began subsisting on cheese-flavored crackers and wine. It wasn't like I cared that much about heart disease any more. If that ended up being the reason I croaked, at least I could first slip into a deliciously salty coma.

Eamon had been busy writing during the day while I was at work. Supposedly. He declined to play a single song for me, not even a few bars, insisting that nothing was ready yet. Frankly, he was being weird about the whole thing, avoiding the topic or getting testy when I brought it up. *"You can't force creativity, Katherine,"* he'd say. Who was I to debate him?

After another day of avoiding Miles at work and getting exactly zero phone calls from my sister, I'd settled in on the couch with a fresh red box of crackers, paired with a passable Cabernet. Eamon waltzed into the living room and sat next to me on the couch.

"I thought you were keeping off the carbs. Your bridesmaid's dress."

Cheeks packed like a hamster, I shot Eamon a look that said he'd better stop right there. "I'm self-medicating," I mumbled, hoping my breath didn't smell like a cheese shop. I washed it all down with a long slog of wine. "This is the only thing that feels good right now."

"If you want something to feel good, Fiona goes to bed in two hours. This isn't the healthiest approach to dealing with your sister."

"I know it's not healthy. It's horrible. It's dysfunctional and stupid. But I can't help myself."

"I see." He sat back and crossed his arms over his chest.

"Don't worry. I've got it all figured out. I'm going to buy a t-shirt that says 'Body by Cheez-Its' and then everyone will know what happened to me."

He cracked half of a smile. "I do love your wobbly bits. More of you to love."

Oh, great. More of me to love—exactly what I'd never wanted Eamon to say about me.

He grabbed the box and took a handful, while I tried to squash down my territorial feelings about the cheddar-parmesan duo. They were my favorite. And that was the only box in the apartment. "Now what?" he asked.

"I don't know. I have a hideous sparkly binder dedicated to her wedding, but she doesn't want my help. I have a million things I want to say to her running around in my head, but she doesn't want to talk to me. And to top it all off, we have to go to this stupid couple's bridal shower this weekend where I get to pretend that everything's fine when it isn't."

"You're the maid of honor. No getting around that."

"She's only keeping me in the wedding because she doesn't want Dad to know there's trouble between us."

"It's not sustainable. You two can't pretend forever."

"And I can't let on with Dad. It would kill him. So pretend, I must."

"Luke and I were talking about it today. We agreed it's not

fair to your father to tell him. You don't really have any way of knowing whether it's true or not, anyway."

"You talked to Luke about it?"

"We had lunch. I needed a break and we've been meaning to get together. Plus, he wanted my opinion on the groomsmen gifts he was looking at."

I reclaimed the box and started main-lining the crackers again. Amy hated me while Luke and Eamon were having the bromance of the century. None of this was fair. "I thought you were writing. You're supposed to be writing. It's December and you're supposed to go into the studio in January to record. Don't you have a meeting with your record label in a week?"

"Will you stop nagging me about my songs? We're not talking about me right now, anyway." He snatched the box of crackers from my clutches, closed it, and plunked it on the end table out of my reach. "You've got to stop being so self-destructive. You need to funnel this negativity into something positive."

"Like what? Honey mustard pretzel bites?" I waited for a laugh, but it never came.

"I was thinking your mother's necklace. Have you thought about what you're going to do to get it?"

Yet another damning detail in my life. "I left a message for my grandmother yesterday. She never called me back."

"Maybe call the nurse you spoke to? Maybe she can help."

On any other day, I would've admired his optimism, but it felt pointless. Still, I supposed I had to try. This was my best chance at redemption. "Do you think it's too late to call?"

Eamon shrugged. "Not sure. Most places would have nurses working around the clock. If nothing else, you could leave a message."

"Right. Good. I'll do that." I grabbed my phone from the coffee table and looked up the number for the nursing home, which I'd saved in my notes. When the automated system answered, I didn't know which extension to dial, so I hit 'O' instead.

"It's a beautiful day at Shady Pines. How may I direct your call?"

"Oh. Hello. I'm the granddaughter of one of your residents. I was hoping to speak to one of the nurses. Beverly?"

"I'm sorry, but Beverly has gone home for the day. Would you like to leave a message?"

I sighed. "Yes, please." I gave her my info, prayed that Beverly would care enough to call me back, and hung up. "Had to leave a message."

"So I heard."

Fiona flitted into the room. "Katherine, will you read to me tonight?"

Eamon pulled her into a hug. "Katherine's not having the best night, love. Will I do?"

"But Dad. You don't do the voices like she does."

"People love my voice. People pay money to hear my voice."

Fiona rolled her eyes and settled on his lap. I snuggled up next to him. This was one of my favorite things about having her stay at the apartment—when it was just the three of us, I could feel the love in the room. It was better than crackers or wine. That was for sure.

"I would love to read to you," I said, getting up from the couch. "It's one of the best parts of my day."

Eamon grinned and I knew what he was thinking. I needed to stop being such a pessimist. Some things, like reading bedtime stories to Fiona, were perfect. Everything else would get worked out. It had to.

———

A SHORT FORTY-EIGHT HOURS LATER, Beverly hadn't called

me back yet, and the day of Amy and Luke's couple's shower-slash-cocktail party had arrived. "I'm dreading this," I said to Eamon. It didn't matter how ridiculously handsome he looked wearing dark-as-midnight jeans, a charcoal suit coat with a subtle black windowpane, and a white dress shirt. That wasn't going to improve my mood.

"Maybe she'll see you and things will be okay. Hard to be angry with someone when they're in front of your face."

"She had no problem being angry to my face the other day." I stepped into my dress and turned my back to him so he could zip me up. He had this habit of standing super close to me when he did it, with his hips a whisper's distance from my ass and his breath warming my neck. I could admit it—I purposely picked clothes with zippers I couldn't do on my own. The experience was sublime.

"She's had time to cool down. I'm sure she'll be happy to see you." He placed his hands on my shoulders and kissed the top of my head, only reconfirming my gut feeling—we should just stay home and have sex instead.

That would really show my sister.

"You know, maybe I'm not going to be happy to see her. She's being so unfair. I was trying to protect her. I don't know why she can't see that. And what was I supposed to do? Just offhandedly tell her that while we were running around the yard one day?"

"I agree. It's an impossible situation. Which means at some point, somebody is going to have to break."

I'd already broken. I was just pissed off enough that I was starting to put myself back together, quite possibly at the very worst time. "Let's just go. God forbid we're late. I'll never hear the end of it."

Eamon and I held hands in the backseat on our way out to Luke's parents' house. Neither one of us said anything for a long stretch, and the quiet, in this particular vehicle, felt an awful lot like the drive to the cemetery after my mother's funeral. That was the first time I'd been in a fancy car. Amy, Dad, and I rode alone, which seemed fitting. It was just the three of us left. Amy and I each had new dresses, bought for us by Mrs. Abelman from next door. Amy's was pale pink and mine was a similar tone of lavender. Mrs. Abelman had said that black was too dour for children, and that the colors were subdued enough for the occasion. Dad agreed. He didn't want to see us in black. He couldn't bear such a blatant display of how dark that day was.

Amy and I had each been given a white rose to carry, and because the ladies from Mom's flower shop were kind and thoughtful, the thorns had been removed so we wouldn't hurt ourselves. Sitting in the back of the car, we each had them lying neatly across our lap. Nobody moved. Nobody said a thing. But then Amy started pulling the petals off hers. One by one. *Pop. Pop.*

"Amy, no," my father had said, placing his hand over hers. "Don't do that, sweetie. You're supposed to put the flower on Mommy's casket. You want it to be pretty for her, don't you?"

I sat in silence, but Amy jerked the flower away, turning it over and pulling the petals from the other side.

"She can't see it," Amy said, almost defiantly.

"But she'll be watching from heaven," Dad countered.

That made her stop. She thrust the rose into my lap and keeled forward, sobbing uncontrollably, her shoulders shaking. I started to cry so deeply that I couldn't even make any noise. My chin quivered, I gasped for breaths, but the tears were coming so fast out of my eyes that I could hardly see. Dad started to cry, too, and he reached across the back of the seat until he got my shoulder and he pulled both of us closer. He was trying to comfort us, but the truth was that it only felt like permission to fall apart, and Amy and I both gave into it. It was a full and complete surrender. How does it feel to drown in sadness? To be at the bottom of the deepest, darkest water, looking in the direction that you think is up, eyes wide open, and you still can't see any light? No sun?

That was the way I felt that day.

Much like my dad had done more than twenty years ago Eamon put his arm around my shoulders and tugged me closer. "You sure you're okay?" he asked.

"I don't really have a choice, do I? Either this turns out great or it's a disaster. I still have to be here. She's my sister and she's getting married. These are facts."

"Hopefully it'll end up somewhere between great and a disaster."

"Thanks for the vote of confidence."

He looked down at me with his comforting eyes. "Just a guess. Maybe I'll be wrong. Either way, I'll be there. If you're feeling out of sorts, give me a high sign and we'll make our escape."

"We should have a code word." The driver turned into Luke's parents' neighborhood. Cars were already lined up along the street. Ahead a massive cluster of white and silver balloons were tied to the lamppost next to the gate, bobbing in the night breeze.

"Any ideas?"

"Tequila?"

"As a code word?"

"Or a coping mechanism."

Eamon laughed. "How about Fiona? If you need to leave, remind me to call Fiona."

How did he manage to be so damn sweet and sexy at the same time? "You're so much more sensible than I am."

We climbed out of the car and scaled the massive stone stairs to the front door. Luke greeted us with a smile that could only be described as perfectly normal and genuine. Maybe this wasn't going to be as bad as I'd thought.

"I'm so glad you two are here." He shook hands with Eamon and then gave me a hug. He held on to me for an extra second or two, patting my back. That was when I knew that things were not going to go well. Those pats seemed to say *I'm so sorry, but your sister is still royally pissed at you.*

A waiter greeted us with a silver tray of champagne flutes. Eamon and I both took one and all I could think was *God bless Eamon*. He hated champagne. He'd taken two so we could trade when I was done drinking mine.

"Everyone's in the living room," Luke said. "We have cock-tails. Beer. All sorts of food."

Since I was familiar with the lay of the land, I led the way. This time, men and women were socializing together. How truly twenty-first century of the Mayhew family. Shelly had obviously been in charge of the flow of this event.

Amy was holding court on the sofa, flanked by two of her bridesmaids on one side and the notorious Aunt Jan on the other. At least I had an easy entree into chitchat with Jan. I could simply ask her how Justin Timberlake was doing. She seemed like the kind of person who lived for that moment, if only to have some eavesdropping bystander ask, "Do you know Justin Timberlake?"

Eamon offered me his still-full glass of champagne after I dispatched mine. "What next?"

"Just a glass of white wine," I said. "I should probably take it easy, huh?"

"You can always go hard later if you feel like it." He bobbed his eyebrows at me, smug as ever, and made his way to the bar in the corner.

"Crab cake?" a young woman in a black turtleneck and black pants offered.

I took one and popped it into my mouth, which I instantly regretted as I discovered a shard of shell with my teeth. I spit it out as demurely as possible into my napkin and went in search of the trash. Shelly was standing off to the side out in the hall, speaking with one of the servers. A tall silver trashcan was right next to her.

"Thanks so much for hosting," I said to Shelly as I slyly disposed of my treacherous canapé.

She narrowed her eyes to tiny slits. "You do know my mother did everything. She quite literally wouldn't let me make a single decision. She told everyone I was hosting to make it look like she's less of a control freak."

"And how's that going? You and your mom?"

"I still haven't told her. I'm thinking about waiting for Christmas morning. The wedding will be over, everyone will be drunk on eggnog, and most importantly, my dad's buying her a car."

"A car for Christmas. Must've been a good year."

Shelly shrugged, looking out over the party. "I'd say a normal year. He loves to buy her extravagant gifts so we can all be reminded how much they love each other."

It seemed to me like it would be a lot simpler and far less expensive if they just focused on the love part and worried about the cars when they needed a new one. "How's your love life?" I was careful not to say girlfriend. I was not going to out her at the shower she wasn't hosting.

"Great, actually." She smiled and a beautiful blush crossed her cheeks. It went wonderfully with her magenta hair. "How about you? Is that the guy you told me about?"

"It is, indeed. Eamon." He was on the far side of the room talking to Luke and Luke's dad, Tom. There were definitely a few women eyeing Eamon, but he seemed oblivious, smiling and laughing. It was so unfair how Eamon was at ease in pretty much any setting, but then again, part of that was simply being comfortable in his own skin. And what lovely skin it was.

Shelly clapped her hand over her mouth. "Holy crap. That's Eamon MacWard."

I laughed and nodded. "The same."

Shelly elbowed me in the ribs. "You didn't tell me your boyfriend was famous."

"Isn't that rude? Walking around talking about that?" I shrugged. "I don't know. Maybe I'm wrong."

"Aunt Jane would take out a full page ad in *The Times* and talk about it every chance she had."

"Well, we knew each other far before he was famous. I think that makes a difference. I look at him and just see Eamon. He leaves his socks on the floor like any other man."

A chorus of laughter rang out from the vicinity of the couch, reminding me that as much as I enjoyed talking to Shelly, I was only putting off the inevitable. I still hadn't spoken to Amy. We hadn't even made eye contact yet, but surely she had to know I was here. Eamon was, and he was impossible to miss.

"How's Amy holding up?" Shelly asked, clearly referring to the wedding and not the sisterly strife.

"Oh, uh, I haven't spoken to her yet. I didn't want to monopolize her." More like I didn't want her to lop off my head in front of her future in-laws. If anything ruined a bridal shower, it was blood spatter on the carpet.

"You should go talk to her. I need to check on the next wave of food to come out. My mother did give me a few menial tasks to handle."

"Okay. See you later." I blew out a breath through my nose, feeling as though I was headed for the executioner as I began my walk to the sofa.

Eamon intercepted me with my glass of wine. "Going in?"

"I gotta do it at some time," I said out of the corner of my mouth.

"I'll be your wing man."

Another step closer and Amy saw me. Our eyes connected and I struggled to decipher what in the hell she was trying to tell me with that look on her face—it was so strange. Was that joy? Excitement? Plain old happiness?

"There's my sister," Amy exclaimed, rising from the sofa. She stepped out from behind the coffee table and gave me a huge hug. "I'm so glad you're here."

I hesitated to give in to the embrace, but after a few seconds I realized that this must be her way of apologizing or at least telling me that I'd been forgiven. I was going to demand the words at a later date, but for now, this was fine. "We wouldn't miss it for the world."

She squeezed my upper arms when she let go, and I immediately began an appraisal of how much pressure she'd used. Was it an *I love you* squeeze? Or an *I will murder you in your sleep* squeeze?

"And there's handsome Eamon." Amy gave him a hug that didn't last nearly as long. That made me think there was something fishy going on. Any woman with half a brain would've hugged Eamon for way longer.

"I think you've got this," Eamon said to me. "I'm going back to talk to Luke and his father. Tom's a great guy, actually. Near encyclopedic knowledge of music. Fascinating to talk to."

I smiled thinly. "Okay. I'll see you in a bit."

I sat down and joined the other bridesmaids. There was a lot of chatter about the wedding and the honeymoon.

"You finally decided?" I asked. "I feel like you and Luke have been arguing about this for two months."

"We booked it last week. We're going to Peru in March.

We'll be living in a hut in the mountains so we can experience what it's like to be Peruvian."

I burst out laughing, but it was immediately clear that Amy was not making a joke. The other bridesmaids all had abject horror painted on their faces, but they didn't know my sister like I did. "Wait. You're serious?"

The look Amy directed at me gave me all the clues I needed as to where I stood with her. She hadn't forgiven me for a thing. This was all for show. "Of course I'm serious. Why would I joke about that?"

I had no answer for her question, or at least not one I was willing to say out loud. Amy was the queen of pedicures and pampering. Peru must have been Luke's idea. "You're just always so funny. Sometimes it's hard to know if you're trying to pull a fast one." I hated myself for covering up like that, but it was done.

Luckily, everyone else seemed ready to move on to other topics and I kept my mouth shut. After about an hour of excruciating chitchat, when everyone was pretty well hammered, Shelly announced that the happy couple would be opening gifts. Eamon came and sat on the arm of my chair while we all watched. There were Panini presses and Vitamix blenders, 800 thread-count Egyptian cotton sheets and silver place settings. Aunt Jan gave them eight crystal goblets, but she wrapped each one separately, so that one came from her and the remaining seven from the dogs. Nick Carter tucked a five hundred-dollar gift card to Nordstrom in his.

When it came time for Amy to open our gift, I was more than a little nervous. Ours had not come from a fancy department store, or even from their registry. Eamon and I found it at a flea market in the city, albeit from a reputable antiques dealer. I had to hope that the uniqueness of the gift, plus the fact that it was something they wanted and needed, would make it appreciated.

"Wow. It's heavy." Luke had no problem lifting the box, but the thing easily weighed far more than a crystal goblet.

Amy tore open the paper and opened the cardboard carton. Luke pulled the ornately scrolled fireplace screen from its container. Everyone let out a collective "ooh" and "ahh" like we were watching fireworks on the 4th of July. That made me feel one hundred percent better.

"You remembered. From the night you came over for dinner," Luke said. Indeed, he'd made a comment that night about wanting to light the fireplace, but needing a new screen.

Amy smiled and cocked her head. "Thanks, guys. I love it. This will be perfect for those times I need to burn things. Like newspapers."

Eamon looked down at me, seeming confused. I'd have to tell him later that my sister wasn't going to drop her vendetta against me anytime soon. "You're welcome. Katherine picked it out after we had dinner at your house. She polished it herself and everything."

Luke smiled wide, seeming genuinely appreciative. "We love it. We'll think of you every time we look at it."

I was now officially sick to my stomach.

I gripped Eamon's knee and looked up at him. "I think you should check in on Fiona."

"Really? Now?"

I squeezed a little harder, fighting back tears. "Yes. Now."

CHAPTER TWENTY-TWO

IT TOOK me a few days to recover from the bridal shower, especially since nothing else seemed to be going right. Eamon had his meeting today with his manager and record label so they could talk about the new record.

"Logic says I wear a suit to this meeting, but I don't want to. It all seems so pointless." Eamon was sitting on the end of the bed, staring into the void of the closet.

"Rock stars wear suits to meetings? Isn't getting to wear jeans or leather pants half of the point?"

"A suit says I'm serious. And for the record, I own exactly zero pairs of leather pants."

"You're Eamon MacWard. Aren't you going into this meeting with a presumption of seriousness?"

He let out an unsubtle grumble. I sat next to him on the bed and put on a pair of boots. Fiona was coming with me to work today, which I'd okayed with Summer as soon as Eamon booked the meeting and we realized she'd still be staying with us. Fiona was incredibly well behaved, but Eamon didn't want to take her to what might end up being a very tense meeting. I figured it was good for her to spend a day seeing what it was like being a woman in the modern workplace.

"Have you thought at all about what you're going to say about the new songs not being ready?"

His entire body stiffened, and not in a good way. "Of course I've thought about it. And I don't want to talk about it."

I would've been upset if that hadn't been the response I'd gotten for the last several weeks. "Okay, then. Fiona and I are headed to the office." I leaned over and kissed him on the cheek. "You'll do great."

"Thanks. I'll text you when I'm done. I can swing by and pick up Fiona."

Mittened hand-in-mittened hand, Fiona and I headed out into the cold and hiked to the subway to ride uptown.

"Hello, sir," she said to the pudgy young businessman in a skinny suit sitting across from us. He'd had only one earbud in, but was now putting in the second. "Lovely day today," she chirped to the teenaged girl standing in the aisle, who promptly stepped ahead to the next metal pole. It wasn't that Fiona was clueless as to the expected behavior on a subway. She'd done this before. It made Eamon a little crazy. "I like seeing what people will do to avoid talking to me," she explained for anyone to hear.

"You, Fiona, are officially one of my favorite people."

When we arrived at NACI, I got her set up at a small table in the corner of my office. She unpacked her drawing paper, colored pencils, and an iPad loaded with movies. "What should I draw first?"

I settled in behind my desk. "How about our subway ride?"

"Perfect. Then I can tell Daddy how awkward I made things."

"He'll love it."

I got to work, reviewing the January production schedule

and reading up on a potential new client Summer was bringing in tomorrow. It was like any other day at the office until I heard Miles's voice booming out in the hall.

"Ms. Fuller!"

Fiona turned to me and made a face. "What was that?"

"That would be my boss."

"He sounds terrible."

"He is," I whispered.

Miles appeared in my doorway. "Katherine, we have a massive problem. The Anthem Apparel catalog is quite honestly the most atrocious thing I have ever seen and you approved the final proof." He slammed the catalog down on my desk. "It has already gone out. To thousands and thousands of customers. Anthem is furious and this is your fault. We might lose one of our biggest clients because of you."

My stomach sank, but not so much because of Anthem. I hated the way he was acting in front of Fiona. She could handle plenty, but she was still only nine. "Do you mind lowering your voice? My boyfriend's daughter has come into work with me today. Fiona, this is Mr. Ashby."

Fiona got up from her chair and shook his hand. "Hello, Mr. Assby."

I have never in all my life had to try so hard not to laugh. "Uh, Fiona. It's Ashby. With an h."

She nodded in a condescending way, making it plain to me that she'd done it on purpose. She was very much her father's child, after all. "I'm so sorry."

"This is not a daycare center, Ms. Fuller."

I stepped out from behind my desk. "I'm aware of that. But Eamon and I had extenuating circumstances today. He had a business meeting and we couldn't leave Fiona at home. Summer okayed it weeks ago."

As if her ears had been burning, Summer poked her head into my office. "Is there a problem?"

Miles whipped around. "Your pet employee has made a massive mistake with the Anthem Apparel account and now they're threatening to drop us."

"First off, she's not my pet employee. She just happens to be very good at her job." Summer held out her hand. "Here. Let me see the catalog."

Miles handed it over. "It's all wrong."

Summer walked it over to me and we flipped through it together. "You're right. It is all wrong. This isn't what Katherine approved or suggested. I was there."

"She's right," I said. "Summer and I talked about this weeks ago. The printer must have disregarded the changes after the second round of proofs and gone back to the original version. This is definitely the one we rejected. It's the wrong stock. It's all yellow-y."

"It is not yellow-y, whatever that's supposed to mean. It's the saturation that's off. Any fool can see that."

I shook my head. "Sorry, but it's not that. It's the paper."

Miles snapped the catalog out of Summer's hand. "Don't get insubordinate with me, Ms. Fuller."

"And don't talk to me like that in front of my kid." The words popped out of my mouth before I'd had a chance to think about it, but it was exactly how I felt. I saw Fiona as my daughter, even when she wasn't really mine.

"I will speak however I like. I run this office if you haven't forgotten that."

"How could any of us possibly forget?"

Flames practically shot out of Miles's nose, and steam out of his ears. "I'm tired of you, Fuller. I simply can't tolerate this anymore. You're a phony and a fraud and no one will admit it.

Your so-called special eyesight is a sham. The emperor has no clothes."

"Even if it was a lie, and it's not, the truth is that everything that crosses Katherine's desk looks better. Clients are happier. This was one goof-up out of hundreds of projects she's worked on, and we don't know for certain that it was her fault in the first place." Summer crossed her arms. I was so lucky to have her on my side.

"All I hear is Katherine this and Katherine that. She's the secret weapon. She's the one who can do no wrong. But if we lose this account, it's her fault." Miles was never going to listen to reason. He'd been gunning for me since day one.

I turned to Summer. "I'm sorry, but I can't listen to him talk about me like that anymore, especially not in front of Fiona. Can you call the printer and work this out? I'm certain they made a mistake." I glanced over at Fiona and she had a look of shock on her face that never should've been there. For the kid who didn't have a problem with awkward, this was too much. "Fiona, honey, pack up your things. We're going to get some lunch and head home, okay?"

"Need I remind you it's the middle of the work day, Ms. Fuller?"

If Fiona hadn't been there, I would've taken Miles to the mat. But standing in that office, even knowing how much I loved my job and couldn't imagine doing anything else, the only thing I cared about was protecting Fiona from Miles and his ugliness. I would've fallen on a grenade for her. And the reality was that I didn't need Miles to believe me or trust me. I simply didn't care.

I took Fiona's hand and led her to the door. "Summer, I'll talk to you later, okay?"

"I'm so sorry about this." She shot Miles a look.

"If you leave Ms. Fuller, you're out of a damn job."

That was it. That was all I could take. "Now you're

swearing in front of a child? What is wrong with you?" Never mind that Eamon had a terribly foul mouth. It was the principle of the thing.

"A child who shouldn't even be here."

"That's it. I quit. I'm sorry, Summer, but I quit."

"You quit?" Miles's tone read as irate, but his face showed nothing but smug self-satisfaction. I wanted to knock that look off his face so bad.

Instead, I just patted him on the lapel. "Yep. Have fun figuring this stuff out without me."

With that, I took Fiona's hand, and we went in search of pizza. My heart was pounding as we walked down the street. As if my own sister hadn't made me feel useless enough, now Miles had done the same. How was I supposed to explain my eyesight to anyone? How was I to describe things that Miles could never see? It would be like trying to paint a picture of thin air or trying to explain what rain smelled like. Words would never be enough.

I sent Eamon a text from the pizza place. *Left work. Huge fight with Miles. Pizza with Fiona, then home.* Fiona was slowly munching away, but I didn't have an appetite, so I had them pack up my slice to go.

"Are you mad I called him Mr. Assby? It just sort of came out."

"No, honey. I'm not mad."

She put down her pizza and sat back in her seat. "I don't feel well."

"What's wrong? Is it your tummy?"

"I have a headache."

"Maybe it's because of the excitement at the office. I vote we skip the subway and take a cab."

I got us home as fast as I could. Fiona only wanted to snuggle on the couch, and I was fine with that. I didn't think I could handle anything more taxing. When Eamon came in through the door about an hour later, I could tell right away that his meeting had not gone well. Eamon never wore such a pained expression. Ever.

"Heya." He bent over to kiss me on top of the head, then did the same for Fiona. He stuffed his hands into his pockets, but had that expectant look on his face. He needed to talk.

I pulled Fiona's bangs from her forehead. "Hey kiddo, your dad and I are going to go have a chat. You okay to hang out here and watch TV?"

"You aren't going to be having sex, are you?"

"Fiona, where in the world did you get that idea from?" Eamon seemed genuinely annoyed, which only confirmed my worries. He had endless amounts of patience with Fiona.

"On the internet."

"I'll change the wifi password," I offered.

Fiona stretched out on the couch, letting her head hang halfway off the cushion. "I think I'll just lie here."

I crouched down. "Come and get us if you need anything."

"I will."

I took Eamon's hand. "Come on. Let's talk." I led him back to my bedroom and closed the door part way. "Before you tell me what happened, I just need to tell you that I quit my job today."

Eamon sank onto the bed and flopped back in frustration. "Are you kidding me?"

"I had a huge fight with Miles. He hates me and I hate him. It's not worth it anymore. Plus, he was being a royal asshole around Fiona and I guess he pushed me too far."

He sat back up. "Are you okay?"

"Yeah. I'm fine. I'll get another job somewhere. Don't worry. I have plenty of money saved."

He leaned forward and planted his elbows on his knees,

turning his head to look at me. "Money is the last thing I'm worried about. Married or not, you and I will be just fine."

"Oh. Okay." Eamon and I didn't talk about money, but he had insisted on paying the rent soon after he essentially moved in.

"Well, we'll be fine for at least a few years if I can't manage to write a new album. Assuming you want to stay together."

"Eamon. Of course I want to stay together. And you'll get the album written. I know it."

"The label's not only pissed I'm not ready to go into the studio next month, they hate the songs I finished. Every last one of them."

"What? No."

"It's true. They want me to collaborate with another song-writer." He ran his hands through his hair. "They do it in pop music all the time. And in Nashville. But that's just not me."

"Did you tell them you'd think about it?"

"I refused. I'm not singing somebody else's songs. I'm not going to turn into their puppet."

I wished I understood more about what he was going through. His process already mystified me, but one thing was clear—he was frustrated as all get out. "Why do you think you're having such a hard time writing?"

He pressed his lips together tightly and shrugged. Something about it made me think he had an inkling of the problem, but didn't want to admit it.

"Maybe nothing is inspiring you?" That idea was more than a little disappointing. I'd hoped our reunion would make him want to write another *Sunny Girl*.

He shook his head. "It's not that."

"Then what? Even if you're guessing, just tell me, so I can at least understand what you're going through."

He looked off into space and shook his head. I'd never seen him look so lost. "I'm too happy."

It took me a minute to absorb what he'd said. "Is there such a thing?"

"There is. There definitely is such a thing as too happy."

"I had no idea."

He sat a little straighter. "I need to tell you something, Katherine. And it might hurt your feelings. I might hurt you a lot. It's something I'm not proud of. At all. But I have to tell you."

My heart was pounding. What in the world could he be talking about? Did he want me to make him miserable? Because I was pretty sure I could do that if he really wanted me to. "Whatever is bothering you, just tell me."

He pulled me into a hug and held the side of my head against his chest, rocking me back and forth. It was both reassuring and unsettling. It felt as though he was preparing me not merely for bad news, but for the worst news ever. "Think about it. I wrote my best songs when you and I were apart. All those years I was out there in the world missing you or running in circles, thinking that we would never be together. The first album was good, but everything after that, everything I wrote after you left, was my best work."

I pushed back and peered into those gray eyes I loved so much. It all made sense now. And it had been in front of me the whole time. "That's why you never came looking for me."

"I'm not proud of it. I hate it. I feel like a selfish asshole, but every time I seriously considered looking for you, a new song would spill out of me, and that started this sick cycle of longing for you and depriving myself. That helped me write the songs that people seem to love."

"Are you saying you want to break up?"

He laughed and forced me to give in to his hug again. "No. I'm saying my career might not be much to brag about soon."

"Daddy." Fiona pushed open the door. "I think I'm sick."

That made two of us. Eamon touched her forehead with the back of his hand. "She's burning up."

"She wasn't feeling well at lunch." I took her small hand in mine. Her skin was hot and dry. "I think she might have a fever." I ran into the kitchen and grabbed some Tylenol and a glass of water.

Eamon brought her into the living room and sat her down on the couch. "Take these, darling."

Fiona closed her mouth and turned her head away. "No."

"Why not?" Eamon seemed both exhausted and still frustrated.

I kneeled next to Fiona. "I need you to take these for me. They'll make you feel better."

"I hate pills. It feels like I'm going to choke."

Eamon shrugged, telling me without words that I was on my own.

"I'll make Daddy get ice cream. Whatever flavor you want."

"Ice cream sounds disgusting." She made a terrible face, her eyes half open.

Eamon pulled his phone out of his pocket. "That's it. She's really sick. We're going to have to call a doctor."

———

It was absolutely true that in New York, you could get anything delivered, especially if you were willing to pay for it. Case in point, the doctor Eamon was able to get to come to the apartment on very short notice. Her fever had gone down a bit after the Tylenol, but it was still above one hundred. The doctor was sure whatever she had was viral. For now, we were to watch her, keep her hydrated, and let her rest.

The doctor's orders were no problem. I couldn't bear to leave her side, so I curled up next to her in bed. My need to be with her came with an even stronger feeling than I'd had earlier that day in the office. I wanted to shield her from everything. I wanted to build a bubble around her and keep everything and everyone else out.

"Rachel wants to talk to you." In the darkness of Fiona's room, Eamon handed me his phone and sat on the edge of the bed. "Go on. I'll watch her."

I handed him the washcloth I'd been holding on Fiona's forehead and took the call, ducking out into the hall. "Rachel. Hi."

"I didn't want to bother you, but I had to get your take on things. Eamon can get a bit freaked out by things like this. He doesn't do well with illness, especially not since his mam passed."

I tiptoed farther down the hall. "Oh, he's been wonderful with her. No freaking out at all. Or at least not as much as me. But the doctor assured us everything will be fine. And don't worry. I won't leave her side. I'll stay with her all night." I knew very well that this was not a life-or-death situation, but for the first time, I felt like I understood what it must mean to be a parent. To want to switch places with someone. To want more than anything to take away their suffering. As difficult as it was to endure, something about it felt so right. Like I was where I belonged.

"Thank you. I'm so glad you're there. And not just for Fiona. I know Eamon needs you, too."

If only Rachel had a few dozen hours for me to explain how much it meant to be needed, especially right now. "I wouldn't want to be anywhere else." With everything as fucked up as it was, with my own sister hating my guts and making me persona non grata at the wedding I'd helped her plan, it gave me immense inner peace to be able to say that to Rachel and to know in my heart that it was absolutely true.

"He loves you, ya know. It's killing him a bit that you won't marry him."

"He talked to you about it?"

"He did. Just now."

"I never said I wouldn't marry him. Things have just been crazy." As horrible as I felt at turning down Eamon's proposal, it had been the right thing to do. If we were going to spend our lives together, we had time to do that right. It wasn't that I'd wanted the perfect moment. I'd only wanted to go into it with a clean slate. Or as clean a slate as I could get. And the issue of his writing was going to weigh on us both until it got better. What if he never wrote another song again and it was all because of me? I didn't want to rob the world of Eamon MacWard.

"Katherine, I'm the last person to pressure anyone into marriage. I only know that I've seen in his eyes how much he loves you. He never had one-tenth of that for me. And it's not his fault. We were reckless. Except for Fiona, he and I were a mistake. But you two aren't. I know that."

My worry over making mistakes had been inescapable since the day my mom died. When you botched something so royally, you'd do anything to make sure you never messed up again. You'd even play it inexplicably safe. "Did he write songs when you two were together?"

"All the time, but I think it was his escape."

I wasn't sure how I was supposed to feel about this. I didn't want him to need an escape from me, but I wanted him to be able to find a way to write again. "He hasn't played me a single new song since coming to live with me. Anything he's written hasn't been good enough to share with me. Or so he says. The label and his manager are all over him about it."

"That lot needs to shove off. All they care about is money. Maybe he's not writing because he's happy."

Rachel clearly knew how Eamon worked, something I was only beginning to understand. I wanted him to be happy. I couldn't make him miserable. Not on purpose. "I love him, too. More than anything. I think he knows that."

"If there's any chance he doesn't, be sure to tell him."

I had one question perched on my lips. "You love him, don't you?"

Rachel laughed quietly into the phone. "I do. He and I will always be tied together. I just want him to have what he wanted when we were married."

"Love?"

She waited for a moment to answer and I felt like I was clinging to every second. "You, Katherine. You're all he's ever wanted. It's not easy for me to say that."

I could hardly believe that she had the guts to be so real with herself. I needed to be living my life more like Rachel. "Thank you for saying it. I appreciate it."

"Of course. I have to take care of you. You're taking care of the most important person in my life tonight."

"I'll do a good job. I promise."

"I know you will. I'm not worried about that."

Rachel and I said our goodbyes. I hung up the phone and padded back into Fiona's room. "You can go if you want," I said to Eamon. "I'll stay with her."

Eamon got up from the bed. "Maybe I'll go take a stab at writing."

"Only if you feel like it. I'm sorry if I pressured you."

"And I'm sorry I didn't tell you the real reason I didn't try to find you."

I popped up and kissed his cheek. "It's okay. I want to think this was the way things were supposed to happen."

"Are we calling it fate?"

"Something like that."

Eamon wandered out of the room and I stretched out next to Fiona. She stirred and coughed, then rolled on to her side facing me.

"You okay, sweetie? Can I get you anything? A drink of water?"

"No. Just stay with me. There's nothing worse than being lonely and sick." How true that was. "I forgot to tell you something today. When we were on the subway and you were watching me."

"What's that?"

"I saw your heart. I know what it looks like now."

"You do?" I didn't want to sound so surprised and excited, but I couldn't help it. That day in the woods, I'd been worried I didn't have one at all.

She nodded, her eyes half closed. She curled into a little ball. "It's purple and blue and pink. With some red and orange mixed in. It looks like a quilt. It's all patched up."

"It is?"

She coughed rather than answering. I rubbed her back and pressed the washcloth to her forehead again. Maybe it wasn't fate that brought Eamon back to me. Maybe it was something more. Maybe it was magic.

"I like your heart, Katherine. It's pretty. And it doesn't look like anyone else's."

CHAPTER TWENTY-THREE

ON THE THURSDAY before the wedding, I was in the throes of a scrape-me-from-the-ceiling panic. I'd been through my binder a million times, running down the minuscule tasks Amy had left for me. Yesterday, I called the florist and even stopped by her shop to double-check that the flowers were right. Delivery time and the country club address had been confirmed and reconfirmed. I checked in with the other bridesmaids to make sure they all knew where to be for the rehearsal and at what time. That was its own form of torture, since they'd all talked to Amy in recent weeks and I hadn't. They all thought everything was fine. Things were not fine, and it was the worst feeling in the world to hear other people talk about going out for drinks or dinner with her and Luke. Eamon and I should've been doing those things. Not anymore.

I'd asked for the time off from work months ago, right after Amy and Luke set the date for the wedding. I'd figured I would be aflutter with activity in the days leading up to the big day, stressed but happy from too much to do and lots of time with my sister. Instead, I was stressed out from doing nothing, which only gave me more time to stare down what the rest of my life might be like without her.

I couldn't take it anymore. I had to do something or I was going to lose it, and I knew very well that my last chance at making up with my sister revolved around the damn necklace. I'd talked to Beverly several times over the last ten days or so, but my grandmother had circled the wagons on my mother's pearls. She refused to give them up, and she wouldn't talk to me about it either. Even the front desk at Shady Pines was under orders not to put through a phone call from me. Which left me with no real alternative. I was going to have to storm the castle in person.

I marched into the bedroom to spring my plan on Eamon. Fiona was in Philadelphia with Rachel for a few days, but would return in time for the wedding. I missed her terribly. The apartment wasn't the same without her. "I'm going to Connecticut to get my mother's necklace." I'd been deliberate in not saying that I would *try* to get it. I had to succeed, and stating my intention to the universe felt like a necessary part of my endeavor.

Eamon looked up from his guitar, reading glasses perched on the end of his nose. A notebook and pencil were on the bed next to him. "Now. You're going to Connecticut right now."

"The clock is ticking and I can't sit around for another minute with nothing to do."

Eamon set his guitar aside and patted his lap. "I can always think of something to do."

"Very funny. I'm being serious."

"So am I." He smiled and did that thing where he makes his eyebrows bob up and down. His expression fell quickly though. Probably because he knew I was not happy. "I'll come with you. I'll keep you company on the train."

"You will?" My plan of attack was getting stronger by the

minute. If I was turned away at the door, I had backup. No retirement home receptionist stood a chance against Eamon's charms.

He clapped his hands and stood. "Yeah. Let's get to the train station."

I packed us a quick lunch and we retraced the route we'd taken at Thanksgiving, except we got off one stop earlier and took a car to Shady Pines. When we pulled up, I saw how much they'd airbrushed the photos on the website. The parking lot was an expanse of crumbling asphalt dotted with potholes full of watery muck. It was warmer now than at Thanksgiving, and whatever snow they'd gotten was in icy hunks refusing to melt, black like soot. A metal rain gutter had fallen from one corner of the roof, hanging perilously and bent in the middle. The brick façade was a jarring shade of rust, with stark white mortar along the joints. This wasn't the lovely picture I'd seen online. Or maybe I hadn't wanted to look closely enough.

Eamon didn't say a thing, bless his heart. He simply took my hand and led me up the walk to the front door. The lobby had a reception desk with wood-grain laminate, chipped and peeling at the corners. I was relieved that there wasn't a picture of me on the wall with a note about how I shouldn't be allowed in. A young woman with bright cheeks and a long red braid was busy hanging fluffy silvery garland around it. "Oh, hello!" She seemed genuinely pleased to see us. "Are you visiting someone today?" She scurried behind the desk and pulled out a clipboard with a yellow ribbon tied at the top and taped to the end of a pen. "Please fill in the resident's name and room number and I'll have one of the nurses bring them out. Or you can go to their room, whichever you prefer."

I surveyed the large common area beyond reception. Dozens of residents were parked in wheel chairs, some in front of a TV or at small tables playing games. Some were sitting by themselves, doing nothing more than staring out the window or into their own lap. "I, uh. Well, this is complicated. I'm here to see my grandmother, Marjorie Price, but she's not expecting me, and, um..." How exactly was I going to explain the part about how she didn't *want* to see me, either?

The receptionist cocked her head, pleasant hazel eyes blinking. And blinking. "Let me guess. Things are strained," she said, matter of fact.

Now it was my turn to blink. "Yes. Exactly."

"We get a lot of that. It's complicated when a loved one is placed in a permanent care facility. Would you like me to notify Ms. Price, or would you like me to page Beverly, the nurse who works on her wing?"

I nodded like a kid who'd been asked if she wanted ice cream for dinner. "Beverly. Please."

"It'll just be a moment." She picked up the phone and rested an elbow on the desk. "Mr. Stein, no changing the channel without everyone's okay," she called out.

An elderly man in a newsboy cap and high-water gray pants waved her off and sank down into a chair. Mr. Stein had apparently wanted to watch Wheel of Fortune.

"Beverly will be here in a moment."

"Thank you so much."

Eamon and I stood to the side and waited, not wanting to clog up the entrance, although no one was coming or going, which seemed so incredibly sad. The receptionist went back to her festive decorating and I decided that it was at least a good thing that pleasant people worked here.

"You must be Katherine," a warm, familiar voice came from behind me.

I turned to greet Beverly, who was quite the opposite of what I'd expected. I'd pictured round and jolly, but she was rail thin and nearly as tall as Eamon. She carried herself with a hunch, like she'd spent her life trying to keep people from noticing her height. "I'm so happy to meet you. This is my boyfriend, Eamon."

"Fiancé, actually. Katherine doesn't like to talk about it." Eamon had decided that he was going to start referring to us as engaged, even though we weren't.

Beverly looked him up and down and then shot me a pointed glance. "How are you not shouting about him from the rooftops?"

"It's not an official engagement."

"I've just asked her to marry me a few times."

Beverly laughed quietly and shook her head. "It's none of my business, but you might want to get this worked out, you two."

I'm trying.

"So what can I help you with today? Come to see Ms. Marjorie? Is this about the necklace?"

"Yes. My sister gets married on Saturday." The weight of it hit me hard. This was likely my only real shot at saving my relationship with my sister. "I had to try one last time, and she won't take my calls so I figured it would be best in person. I worried that if I called ahead of time, she'd just tell them not to let me in the front door."

"An ambush. I like it," Beverly said. "You must love your sister very much to endure a direct hit from Hurricane Marjorie. I hate to tell you this, but she's a Category 4 today."

I looked at Eamon, who actually appeared concerned. That made me feel one hundred times worse.

"Did something happen?" I asked.

"They ran out of biscuits at breakfast. Believe me, it doesn't take much to set her off." Beverly's eyes softened and she put her hand on my shoulder. "But all we can do is try. Come on. Let's see what we can do about getting that necklace."

Hand in hand, Eamon and I followed Beverly through a maze of halls. Every resident and worker we encountered greeted her. She seemed to be very popular. She stopped outside room 204. "I'll go in first, but I'll leave the door open so you can hear what's going on. I'll call for you when the moment seems right."

My heart felt as though it was going to stage a coup against the rest of my body, but Eamon squeezed my hand again and that helped my pulse settle.

"Hello, Marjorie," Beverly said from the other room. "I have a surprise for you. You have some visitors."

"If it's my daughter, you can tell her to go away unless she's brought my suitcase and is packing me up to go home."

Eamon and I looked at each other, half horrified, half stuck in this uncomfortable moment where my highly unreasonable grandmother held my fate in her hands.

"No. It's your granddaughter, Katherine. And her fiancé."

"Even Beverly calls me your fiancé," Eamon whispered into my ear.

"She's here to steal my Jennifer's things."

"No. No. That's not it at all. Your other granddaughter is about to get married. A girl needs something of her mother's when she gets married. Doesn't she?"

"In any normal family, yes. But our family is not normal."

I suddenly felt the closest I'd felt to Grandma Price in a very long time. She was so right. And I couldn't let Beverly continue to argue with her. I had to take the reins. If an old lady threw me out of a nursing home, it couldn't be any worse than anything else that had ever happened to me.

With a nod, I let Eamon know that I was going in, but I only got a pace or two into the room before I came to a stop. The far wall was covered in photographs of my mother.

Eamon grabbed my arm from behind. "Katherine. You *do*

look just like her." He stepped next to me, his eyes drawn to what was essentially a shrine to my mom.

"Hi, Grandma." She was perched on a small ice blue love seat, wearing the old lady version of a velour tracksuit in fuchsia pink. Every day of the twenty-plus years we hadn't seen each other was evident—wrinkles deeper, eyes sunken, and a full head of white hair. It was difficult to look at her when it felt as though my mother was peering over my shoulder from the pictures on the wall.

"My God. Katherine." Her voice made it sound like I was a ghost. Her eyes raked over me. I'd forgotten how difficult it was to fall under her appraisal. I was already flinching and wanting to shrink away.

But I had to stand up to her. I stepped closer, trying to focus on her and not the pictures I was both afraid of and eager to see, images I hadn't seen since before my mother died. My grandmother scrutinized me with a narrow stare, but it wasn't her usual mean-spirited sneer. Perhaps that had been a childhood construct, something I'd built in my own head to explain the cruel things she'd said to me over the years.

"Grandma, this is my fiancé, Eamon. He's from Ireland."

He offered his hand so readily I almost wished I'd warned him she might bite it off. But I hadn't, and she didn't—tiny victories. "Nice to meet you. Katherine has told me a lot."

A tut left her lips and she rolled her eyes like a bratty teenager. "Whatever Katherine had to say about me is undoubtedly highly unflattering. But I appreciate you wanting me to think otherwise." Her sights immediately returned to me, which was its own particular kind of surprising. Nobody ever stopped looking at Eamon to look at me. "Katherine. I am just..." She shook her head, still staring, and I realized what she was about to say. "You look exactly like her. Exactly."

Tears welled in my eyes. If there was an invisible tether

between the women in my family, it was pulling on me hard right now. All the years gone, all the regret and resentment, and I still wanted her to love me. I needed it like air and water and my whole life I'd felt as though I didn't deserve it. "Funny, isn't it?" I laughed quietly, desperate for something to lift me out of that place where I felt unworthy of being my mother's daughter, of looking like her.

"I had no idea. I think the last photograph I saw of you was from your high school graduation. Lucy showed it to me. And it was taken from a distance. I could see the resemblance then, but not like I see it right now."

I knew exactly what she was saying because I lived with it every day. The resemblance was uncanny and it had grown stronger with every birthday, as I crept closer to the age my mother had been when she'd died. I'd learned not to think about it too much. Amy knew not to talk about it. Dad didn't even mention it anymore. "Can I sit with you?"

Beverly lunged to move the stack of magazines sitting on the cushion next to my grandmother—all of them true crime. "I'll leave you three alone," she said.

I took my spot on the couch and Eamon stood near me, hands behind his back. "So, Amy's getting married," I said. "To a really nice guy. His name is Luke Mayhew. Comes from a nice family. A big family. They're very much in love."

"You told me. Over the phone."

"Right. I did." I silently begged Eamon for some encouragement or ideas of what to say next, but all he did was momentarily distract me with how dang nice he was to look at. Not helpful. "And as I also said on the phone, Amy would really like to wear something of our mother's on her wedding day. Which makes sense, right?"

"I suppose."

"That's why I'm here today. The wedding is on Saturday.

And I know you said no before, but I was hoping I could convince you to change your mind."

"So your sister sent you to do her bidding?"

"Actually, no. She has no idea that I'm here. I woke up this morning and thought I should try one more time. Eamon and I just went to the train station and came up."

"You make it sound so easy. Almost like you could come and visit regularly." She casually smoothed her pant leg with her hand. The guilt was never laid on directly in my family. It was always merely implied.

"If you had given me any indication at all over the phone that you wanted me to visit, I would've come earlier. You weren't exactly kind to me." I wanted the necklace, but I wasn't going to sugarcoat her behavior. She'd lashed out at me and I still didn't feel as though it had been deserved.

Grandma cleared her throat. "You caught me off guard, that's all. Just like today. If you'd given me some warning, I could've had coffee waiting for you."

It took serious willpower not to point out exactly how full of shit she was. "I don't need coffee. I don't even need you to be nice to me, Grandma. I know how you feel about me."

She pressed her lips together and looked down at her lap again, this time picking at a spot on her pants with her nails. "You're still mad about that day in the hospital."

"Honestly? I don't have the strength to be mad about it any more. It just makes me sad to think about it. I needed you that day, and you turned your back on me."

She raised her head and looked me straight in the eye. "What do you say to a ten year old girl who's just lost her mother? Especially when you're blinded with grief and guilt."

I was stuck on what she'd said. The grief I got. But the guilt? Wasn't that all mine? "Why would you ever feel guilty?"

"I think I know why your mother did what she did. And it wasn't because she'd fallen in love with the wrong guy."

"I have no idea what you're talking about."

"If she learned that behavior, she learned it from me."

Now I was even more confused. "Learned what?"

"I did the same thing to her and Lucy. Let them spend time with a man who wasn't your grandfather. A man I was involved with."

If ever there had been a moment where I had absolutely no idea what to say, this was it.

"I'm not proud of it," she continued. "But I did."

"I had no idea."

"The situations were different though." She sounded as if she was forming her defense. "It wasn't the same. I wanted to get caught. Your mother did not. Your mother was torn between two men."

"I don't even know what that means. You wanted to get caught?"

Her eyes were pleading, as if she wanted mercy from me. "I was barely eighteen when I married your grandfather. My parents were so ready to be rid of me. They said I had too many ideas in my head. Things were different then. Your grandfather got to pursue his interests. But I was expected to stay home and have kids. He put everything he had into his work. I felt ignored." She shook her head and blew out a deep breath. "So I strayed. But I only let your mother and Lucy meet the man because I was hoping they'd tell your grandfather. Of course, they never did. And I couldn't stomach the thought of what I was doing, so I called it off. Still, I let it go on for nearly two years. Long enough to make a real impression on those girls."

I glanced over at Eamon who seemed equally flabbergasted. "I had no idea, Grandma."

"Of course you didn't. But that day at the hospital, all I

could think about was that you'd actually had the nerve to go through with it. And look at what had happened. I'd lost my own daughter because of it. My granddaughters had lost their mother. I couldn't stand the thought of the example I'd set."

"Nobody could've known what was going to happen that day. Nobody. It was a freak accident." The words had erupted from my mouth, and just like that, I realized that I now truly believed what everyone had been saying to me for twenty years. It *was* an accident. A patch of ice in the wrong place. A scream at the wrong time.

She was crying now and although I didn't want to, I felt a duty to watch her process this. "Do you forgive me, Katherine? For that day at the hospital? I was out of my mind. Truly. And I couldn't see it. That's half of the reason your aunt Lucy didn't want me living with her. I couldn't let it go and she couldn't take the endless talk of her dead sister. It's really only been because of the endless hours I spend by myself in this place that I've been able to think some of it out."

A person could get help from the unlikeliest of sources. "Of course I forgive you." I said it as if it was of little consequence, but it was a big deal to me. I'd carried around the hurt from that day for a long time, but I was so tired of the weight of it. I wanted to send it back to the year it had happened and never see it again.

"Grandma, what did you think of Gordon?"

She shrugged. "She dated him in high school. I thought he was a loser then, but she apparently couldn't stay away from him. I never saw the appeal, but there's no accounting for taste. Sometimes you meet somebody and they're just the right person for you. It doesn't have to be any more complicated than that."

I nodded, reminding myself that so much of this was so, incredibly simple. A chain of tiny events that when strung together, made for a tragedy. But that day could just be part of our lives. It didn't have to be everything.

"You really like this guy Amy is marrying?"

"I do. And believe me, I didn't want to. I have to say that I always felt like our family was cursed when it came to marriage. Amy and I had a pretty good run at being single, just the two of us. It seemed stupid to tempt fate."

Eamon cleared his throat and when I turned back, he unleashed that pointed "you're so full of it" look. He was right. I was full of it. But I had a lot of it to get past. I was doing my best.

"Perfectly understandable," Grandma said.

"Luke is very sweet to Amy, and kind. He loves her very much. I can see it on his face when he looks at her or talks about her."

"Like the way this one looks at you?" She turned to Eamon. "How do you say your name again?"

"*Aim-un*."

She nodded, but didn't try to repeat it. "Katherine's grandfather used to look at me like that."

And Eamon looked at me like that. I hoped he knew I was looking at him the same way.

"We had our problems," she continued. "But it was only because I couldn't separate my need to love him and my need to be myself. That was always the battle. I think your mother was fighting that same thing. It takes a strong person to love someone and stay true to yourself. I hope your sister can do that."

That was one of the most insightful, normal things I'd ever heard from a member of my family. "I think Amy will do great."

"I suppose it's time to talk about the necklace, isn't it?"

A flicker of excitement appeared in my chest. I didn't want to embrace any truly optimistic thoughts, but at least I hadn't had to bring it up. "If you don't mind. It would make Amy so happy. It would make me so happy."

"I'll only get it for you if you promise to come back and see me again."

"Really? You want me to visit?"

"Of course. You're my granddaughter."

I wanted to smile and say that yes, of course, I'd love to come and visit, but there were things between us still unsaid. "I spent the last two decades feeling like I wasn't your granddaughter. I need you to know that. I understand why you said those things to me that day, and I forgive you, but they hurt me, deeply." If I could never make peace with my mother, I could at least make peace with hers. "I needed your love all those years. Amy and I both needed you. It would have made our lives completely different to have had you in it."

The hurt was plain in her eyes, and I felt bad for it. I truly did. But it also felt a hell of a lot better to stop taking all of the blame for every dysfunctional thing. Everyone needed to accept their share. "I made a lot of mistakes, Katherine. I'm hoping God can forgive me for some of them. Some day." She reached out and took both of my hands. Her knuckles were large and bulging, her skin crepe-y and thin. Still, it was smooth and soft. They were a grandmother's hands. I'd never felt so thankful to hold them. "I loved you and your sister all those years. I really did. It was in my heart. Probably buried under everything else that kept it closed off. I'm sorry that you ever had to live a day not knowing that I loved you."

"And I'm sorry I didn't reach out to you sooner. I shouldn't have let the years wear on forever."

She patted my hand and let me go. "Your mother's jewelry is in a shoebox up on the shelf in the closet. Maybe your fella can get it down for me."

"I see I'm not needed for anything but my brute strength, but I'm okay with that." Eamon flashed his lady-killer smile and stepped into the closet, which was already open. "What color is the box?"

"Red. Or blue. Maybe it's blue."

He poked his head out of the doorway. "Which one do you want?"

"Blue."

Eamon retrieved the box and presented it to her.

She lifted the lid and surprise crossed her face. She quickly replaced the top. "Oops. Wrong one." She giggled and handed it back to Eamon. "No peeking."

Good Lord. There was no telling what was in that box and I certainly didn't want to know. Some secrets really are better kept buried. Eamon was back quickly with the red box.

She glanced inside. "This is the one." Unceremoniously, she plopped the whole thing in my lap. It was like she was handing me a bag of groceries. "There you go."

I stared down at the box, not comprehending what she was saying. "Do you want me to go through here and find it?"

She shook her head. "Take the whole thing. If I start getting sentimental about what's in that box, I'll fall apart and that's the last thing I want to do today. I've got a bridge tournament this afternoon and I want to stay sharp."

"Are you sure?"

She placed her hand on the side of my face. "A bitter woman took that jewelry. I don't want to be her anymore."

Eamon stepped forward. "If you don't mind me asking, why the change of heart?"

She gazed up at him and I swear I saw a glimmer of what I felt in my chest every time I looked at him. "I lost my daughter, but a big part of her is still here. I hadn't fully realized that until she walked into the room. I have to treat that part with love or I'll lose everything I have left."

"Thank you so much." I hugged the box to my chest. "I know it'll mean a lot to Amy."

"I feel sort of bad about RSVP-ing 'no' to her wedding, but I don't like to travel anyway."

I was glad she'd brought it up. I still wasn't sure Amy had actually sent her an invitation. "I'll be sure to have her call you after the wedding. She can tell you all about it." I might have to beg Amy, but I'd get her to do it.

"Or have her come with you when you visit. I'd like to apologize to her in person."

The notion of Amy and I ever making a trip together again was almost too hopeful a thought. "I'll suggest it."

With nothing left to say, Eamon and I bid our goodbyes, promising to return in the spring, when the snow was gone. We ran into Beverly in the hall.

"How'd it go?" she asked.

I held up the box, victorious. "Somewhere in here is the necklace, presumably. If nothing else, it's a box of my mother's jewelry and there should be something for my sister to wear on her wedding day."

"Well done. I'd say your sister is a lucky girl to have you in her life."

I laughed, trying to ignore the irony of that statement. "Let's just say I had a few things to make up for."

CHAPTER TWENTY-FOUR

ON THE WAY back from Connecticut, with the train car rocking from side to side on the track, I dug through the jewelry. The other passengers probably thought I was nuts as I pulled out tangled gold chains and plastic bags of earrings. Grandma Price had not taken particularly good care of my mother's things. In fact, it was almost like she'd stuffed everything in the box the day after my mother died and never looked at it again.

Unfortunately, most of the pieces in the box meant nothing to me. I couldn't even remember seeing my mother wear half of them. If only I'd been paying better attention. Then again, I hadn't known that I would need to hold on to every second with my mom. I'd had no idea our time together would be so short.

"Are the pearls in there?" Eamon asked.

"Pretty sure they're at the bottom. I haven't looked yet." The ivory velvet jeweler's box was in sight, waiting for me to open it.

"Why not?"

"I don't know. Nervousness. Regret. Worry that they won't be nice anymore and I won't have anything to give to Amy."

Eamon placed his hand on my mine. "We came all this way for it. Just look. You'll feel better when you do."

"You're right." I pulled out the box and took a deep breath before opening it, silently making a wish that they would be okay.

Eamon peered past my shoulder. "Pretty."

I didn't have much in the way of words at that moment. I was busy stemming the tide of memories, of the many times I'd seen her wear this necklace—for Christmas Eve dinner, New Year's Eve, her birthday, Valentine's Day, every time she and my dad went out for their anniversary. Judging by all of that, the occasions she'd made an effort to at least look the part of happily married woman, it made me wonder if her heart had ever been in it or if she'd simply been putting on a show.

None of that mattered now. It would just end up being more merciless conjecture on my part, and I'd done enough of that for many lifetimes. I would simply remember the one time I hadn't been there—her wedding day, and the portrait Amy and I had spent hours staring at. Mom wasn't faking a thing in that picture. That much I knew for sure.

"They're perfect. Absolutely perfect." I gathered the necklace in my hand, letting the pearls roll over my fingers. They were still beautiful, and for the first time in several weeks, I had a tiny glimmer of hope about my situation with my sister, however ill advised that might be.

"If this doesn't redeem me, nothing will."

———

THE NEXT DAY was rehearsal day. I was busy packing our things. The necklace, tucked safely in its box, was already in my purse. Everything else was strewn about, but I had a few hours to get it together. Despite Amy's continued refusal to speak to me, she still wanted Eamon and I to stay at Luke's parents' house that night, mostly because she didn't want us to be late for the ceremony, which was at eleven tomorrow morning.

I consulted the packing list I'd made and cross-referenced it with everything I had set out on the bed. From somewhere under a pile of clothes, my phone rang. I would've let it go to voicemail, but I worried it might be the florist. The flowers were my domain. They had to be perfect. I sifted through the pile and found my phone under my pajamas. When I saw the name on the caller ID, I nearly had a heart attack. *Amy.*

"Hello?"

"Katherine?" She hiccuped, then let out a quiet sob.

"Oh, my God. What's wrong?" If Luke dumped her, I was going to walk to Brooklyn in my bare feet and strangle his handsome neck.

"I talked to Bill. It was awful."

"Who in the hell is Bill?"

That just brought out about another wail. "Gordon's brother."

"Oh, shit." I glanced at the clock. It was three hours until we were due at the rehearsal. We were going to have to arrive extra early. "Where are you?"

"We're at Luke's parents' house. I can't face Cindy like this. She's going to ask me a million questions. She's so nosy, Katherine. You have no idea. It's a nightmare."

Eamon appeared, wearing a towel. "Shower?" he mouthed with a sexy bounce of his eyebrows.

"Amy. I can be there in less than an hour, okay? I'm bringing Eamon with me since we both need to be there for the rehearsal. You can tell me everything then. Is that okay?"

Eamon looked truly disappointed, which was its own kind of adorable. Even better when he unwrapped the towel, shot me a pointed glance, and walked away, downtrodden and naked.

Amy sniffled. "I'm sorry, Katherine. I'm a terrible person." The crying started again.

"It's okay. Have a glass of wine and I'll get there as soon as I can."

Eamon reappeared in his boxers, regrettably no longer naked. "Guess I'm postponing my shower. I can see why you get so annoyed when everything revolves around this damn wedding."

I kissed him on the mouth, slow and soft. "Maybe we can take a shower tonight."

"What's wrong with you? You seem so happy."

Huh. I *was* happy. "She needs me. Finally."

Less than thirty minutes later, for the third time in as many months, I found myself in a car on the way to Luke's parents' house. My mind was racing, not knowing what had happened, but certain it was bad. It took a lot to upset Amy.

"What do you think Bill could've said to her?" I asked Eamon.

"No idea. The whole thing is too bizarre to begin with."

"I know. It is."

When we arrived at Tom and Cindy's, Luke practically sprinted out of the house and up to the car. "Thank God you're here. Amy's beside herself and my mother drank a bottle of Chardonnay this afternoon and will not leave her alone."

"Can't we get your dad to distract her?" I asked, rushing into the house with Luke and Eamon.

"He went to go pick up my Aunt Jan at her hotel. I think he got stuck in traffic."

A whiff of familial trouble was in the air, but I couldn't dwell on that now. I had a sister to save. "Where is she?"

"My room. Upstairs. Take the hall to the left. It's the last door on the right."

"Got it." I took a few steps and turned back. "You guys are okay, right?"

Eamon and Luke looked at each other and shrugged. "Well, yeah. We're going to listen to music and start drinking."

"Sounds like you two."

I rushed up the stairs, wondering how in the heck they kept the white carpet runner so impeccably clean. When I reached the top landing, I was huffing and puffing. This house was way too big. There were actually three halls to choose from, but luckily, it was fairly obvious which way I should go. When I reached the door, I knocked quietly.

Amy opened it only a crack at first, peering at me with red-ringed eyes. "Thank you for coming." She opened the door, seeming calmer than she'd been on the phone, so that was good. Luke's bedroom was like something you see in movies or TV shows about the private quarters at the White House. Fancy with a capital F.

Amy plopped down on the edge of the bed and plucked a tissue from the box on the bedside table, which was of course covered in some sort of enamel facial tissue cozy.

"Can I sit next to you?" I didn't want to assume anything at this point. I still wasn't convinced she didn't want to kill me.

She sniffled and wiped her nose. "Yes, of course, Katherine. Don't be obtuse."

Obtuse? I reminded myself that she was getting married in fewer than twenty-four hours. All sense of sanity could very well be out the window for the duration. I took a spot right next to her. "I brought you a present."

"You didn't have to get me anything. You showing up and still wanting to be my sister is enough for me." She peered at me with her sweet blue eyes, which in many ways looked more broken down today than they had the day she got the letter. "Assuming you still want to be my sister."

"Always." I handed her the clamshell box covered in cream velour. "This is my gift to the bride. Eamon and I still got you guys a separate wedding gift."

Amy started crying before she even opened it. When she lifted the lid and saw those pearls inside, she let out a gasp, her shoulders shuddering. "I can't believe you got it."

"Eamon and I went back to Connecticut yesterday. We actually saw Grandma Price. We talked to her and everything."

She closed her eyes and tilted her head back. "I am the worst piece of shit person on the planet, aren't I?"

I grabbed her hands and pulled them into my lap. "No. You are not. It's okay that you got mad at me. I would've gotten mad at me, too. But I hope you see now that I was in an impossible situation. I was damned if I did and damned if I didn't."

Her eyes opened slowly and she dropped her chin to its normal height. "I know. I know that now."

"What happened when you talked to Bill?"

"He said that his brother lost all touch with reality when he got sick and that the letter was the...let me see if I can get this right...he said it was 'the pathetic ramblings of an unwell man'." She made air quotes and everything.

"Wow."

"I know. And then he said that he didn't see any resemblance between his family and me, and that he'd already contacted his lawyer about contesting the will. He hadn't sent me the letter. Someone in Gordon's lawyer's office did. He also told me that he threw out Mom's things, which he called a bunch of old junk."

For as much ill will as I'd harbored for Gordon Stewart over the years, his brother was eclipsing that. "What a jerk."

She crossed her legs and looked down at the floor, sighing heavily. "I don't know what I expected. I never should've contacted him."

"I'll tell you exactly what you wanted. You wanted closure. You wanted some sense that things in the world had finally been set straight. That's what you and I have been looking for since the moment we first saw Mom kissing Gordon in the back room at Taylor & Daughters."

She nodded, staring off, deep in despair. "I guess."

All of the bullshit of our childhood threatened to roll in on me, the way a storm comes in to the shore, like it doesn't give a goddamn care for anyone else in the world. The infidelity, the unsteadiness, that sense that we couldn't trust our own mother—all of it was still haunting my sister and me. I wanted so desperately for it to just be gone. Once and for all, as Dad would say.

"Ames, I think we have to give each other closure. It's the only way. Nobody else is going to give it to us. Mom is dead. Gordon is dead. Dad is..." My voice faltered. Our dad was the most unwitting man in the history of victimhood.

"He's never going to know. I love him, but he will never know what it was like for us. We can tell him what happened that day in the car, but it won't change that he wasn't there." Amy said exactly what I was thinking.

"Which also isn't his fault."

"None of this is anybody's fault. But that doesn't make it much easier, does it? It just makes it this giant clusterfuck of pain."

Amy opened the clamshell box again and ran her fingers over the pearls. "She sometimes seems like even less than a ghost. Every day forward is a step away from her and her memory. And this stupid wedding has brought it all into focus."

"I know," I croaked, my throat dry.

"I mean, Cindy is making me insane, and she's making Luke feel the same way. We both just want it to be over. And all I can think is that if Mom were here and none of that stuff had ever happened, I would be arguing with her like I am with Cindy. Or she'd be making you crazy or making me feel guilty. So what exactly is it that I'm missing so much?"

I knew precisely what she was getting at. "It's the whole stupid myth of the picket fence and the happy ending. It doesn't exist. People hurt each other. We make mistakes. And then we do it all over again. We take each other for granted. We take this moment for granted." Was that our blessing? Out of the rubble, was that the takeaway? That we didn't take things for granted? "All the more reason to get married tomorrow, Ames. You love Luke and he loves you, too. And even if you're only happy for a while, that's better than most people get." I sucked in a deep breath. "I know that sounds horribly pessimistic. I think you two will make it for the long haul. I really do."

"You hated the idea at first."

"I didn't want to let you go. And I was worried you were going to get hurt."

"You can't protect me forever."

An invisible weight tugged at the corners of my mouth. "But I promised to. After the accident. When you were unconscious and I already knew that Mom was dead."

Amy turned to me and cocked her head to one side, like one of those adorable dogs with incredibly expressive ears. "Promised who?"

"I promised God that if he let you live, I would keep you safe for my entire life." We'd never been particularly religious, but at the time, it was the only thing I could think to do. Amy was out cold, head hanging at an ugly angle against the back of the seat. Her eyelids were closed, colored with the palest lavender you have ever seen. She wasn't moving. The cold seeped into the car like a monster, but at least it told me one thing—Mom was gone. And Amy was still alive. The puffs of air that came out of her nose and mouth were wispy little things.

Fragile baby breaths. Not like mine. "I couldn't wake you up no matter how hard I tried. My seatbelt had locked up and I couldn't reach you. To keep us warm. I was pretty sure we were both going to die, so I made a deal with God that if he let us live, I would always keep you safe, no matter what." Tears ran down my cheeks, but I wiped them away.

"You never told me that."

"I know. It's so silly, but I always held onto it. I always felt like I had to abide by that promise or something bad would happen. I swear that's the very last secret. You know everything now. Everything."

She collapsed into my arms and we both let go. Of everything. The years of pain and torment, of asking a million little questions that started with "what if" and "why". With buckets of tears, we said goodbye to the quiet moments when we'd doubted the world could ever be a good place for us. We buried the twists of fate that had been haunting us both for too long.

"I love you so much," Amy said.

"I love you, too."

"I don't want to have the wedding tomorrow."

"Did something happen with Luke?"

"No. I still want to get married. I just don't want to have this stupid wedding. It feels like it's all about making other people happy." Amy pulled a hunk of tissues out of the box and handed me half. She had so much mascara smudged around her eyes that she looked like a raccoon. Surely I was worse.

"Ames. Come on. You have that beautiful dress. Don't you want that moment when you start walking up the aisle and everyone turns and starts saying how beautiful you are?"

She twisted her lips. "Yeah. That'll be fun."

"The flowers are going to be incredible. Dad and Julia will be here. Fiona. It's going to be amazing. I promise."

"Will you dance with me at the reception?"

"Try and stop me."

She smiled sweetly. "Okay then. We get through the rehearsal tonight, then we have a wedding."

"Tomorrow is going to be perfect. I promise."

CHAPTER TWENTY-FIVE

THE MORNING OF THE WEDDING, I woke to a scream.

You cheating bastard!

I grumbled and sat up in bed, dry-eyed and cotton-mouthed, feeling more than a little rough. Amy and I got plowed at the rehearsal dinner. The specifics were fuzzy at best, but I am positive there was Bon Jovi karaoke in the family room when we got home from the country club. I don't remember much more than Eamon and Luke begging me and Amy to stop. But when your sister has been hating you for weeks, the appeal of "Livin' on a Prayer", one more time, is too great to ignore.

More yelling came. *Get the hell out of this house! I can't even look at you!*

"Who was that?" I asked.

Eamon stirred. "Not sure, but it doesn't sound good."

The voice was definitely female, but I was fairly certain it wasn't Amy. "Should we see what's going on?"

Eamon pried open one eye. "Or we stay out of it."

A door slammed so hard the house shook. A car started. Our room was on the front of the house, so I climbed out of bed and sifted through the layers of draperies until I found the window. Tom's big black SUV was pulling out of the gate.

"Tom is leaving."

"Probably running some wedding errand."

I glanced at the clock. "It's seven A.M. Seems early for that."

Eamon propped himself up on one elbow. "If we're lucky, he's gone to get donuts."

A tentative knock came at our door. "You guys awake?" Amy whispered.

I quickly opened up, finding both her and Luke out in the hall, still wearing their pajamas. "What's going on?"

Luke looked like he was about to be sick. "Can we come in?"

"Yes. Of course," I answered.

Eamon climbed out of bed and grabbed a sweatshirt. "Did something happen?"

"I don't even know where to start." Luke had lost his happy veneer. He was visibly upset.

"Cindy kicked Tom out of the house. He and Aunt Jan have been having an affair," Amy said.

I clasped my hand over my mouth, but inside I was saying *I knew it*. There's always dirt. Always. "I'm so sorry."

"I always thought my parents had an amazing marriage. I just..." Luke ran both hands through his hair. "I don't even know what to think anymore."

"I think we should cancel the wedding. Luke and I can get married on Monday morning at the county clerk's office."

None of us said anything in response to that. Even my arguments yesterday for forging ahead as planned seemed to fall flat. The groom's parents were in the middle of a marital crisis. Having a wedding hardly seemed like a good idea.

"No." Luke sat a little straighter. "Fuck that. I don't want to wait, we've already sunk a bunch of money into this, and I want to see you walk down the aisle. If my parents are having problems, that's just too bad. If they can't deal with it, that's their problem. So they don't sit together. Or they fake their way through it. It's not about them, anyway."

Amy shook her head. "I don't know. It feels like the universe is trying to tell us something."

"Maybe it's trying to tell you that if you can get through this, you can get through anything." I didn't want to sound like Pollyanna, but Luke clearly wanted to move forward as planned, and I wanted him to know I had his back. Plus, I didn't want Aunt Jan to ruin anything for anyone. Knowing her, she'd find a way to brag about it.

"Eamon, what do you think?" Luke asked.

"I'm Irish. We tend to use even the worst of excuses to throw a party."

Luke took Amy's hands in his. "I love you too much to put off our future any more. I say we move forward and see what happens."

Amy dropped her chin and her lower lip popped out. "I love you, too. I do. And if you're okay with today, then I am, too."

"So we're doing this?" The excitement in Luke's voice made a triumphant return in four words. Now that there was a happy plan ahead, he looked so much more like himself.

Amy nodded eagerly. "Yes. Let's do it."

"Looks like there's going to be a wedding today." I stood and gave Luke a hug. "I'm really sorry about your parents, but I'm so glad you're going to be my brother-in-law."

He squeezed me extra hard. "I'm glad, too."

"Okay, then." Amy clapped her hands and I knew she was about to dole out our marching orders. "Eamon, you're heading over to the country club with Luke in an hour. The bridesmaids are all getting ready here and we head over in the limo an hour after that so I can get dressed. Any questions?"

The three of us shook our heads in unison.

"Let's get this show on the road." Amy and Luke made a swift exit.

"I guess I'd better hop in the shower," Eamon said.

"I'd join you if I didn't think we'd get distracted and you'd end up being late."

"For once, I have to agree that sex is not the proper course."

I kissed him on the cheek, his stubble scratching my lips. "There's always tonight."

Eamon swatted me on the butt, then disappeared into the bathroom. I pulled his tux and my dress out of the closet and was inspecting for wrinkles when my phone rang. "Hello?" I pinned the phone between my ear and shoulder and started packing up my jewelry and makeup.

"Yeah. Hi. This is, uh, Max with Maggie's Floral. You're listed as the contact for the Fuller-Mayhew wedding."

"Yes. Hi. Are you at the country club already? I know it says no deliveries at the front entrance, but they assured me it's okay for flowers."

"No, ma'am. There's been an accident."

"An accident?" It felt like the bottom of my stomach dropped out. Eamon was out of the shower and had stopped scrubbing his hair with the towel when that word came out of my mouth. "It's the florist," I whispered to him. I didn't want him to worry it might be Fiona.

"The delivery truck got sideswiped by a pickup," Max said.

"Oh no. Was anyone hurt?"

"I'm a little roughed up, but that's not why I'm calling. I'm very sorry, but your flowers are toast."

"Toast?"

"Ruined."

An apocalyptic vision of my sister's bridal flowers popped into my head. I saw those beautiful dark purple calla lilies and deep red roses strewn all over the Saw Mill River turnpike, motorists unwittingly crushing them with their car tires. "I know what 'toast' means. Nothing can be saved?"

"Afraid not. The truck is on its side in the middle of an intersection about two miles from the wedding venue. I'm waiting for the police."

Two miles from the club wasn't far. "Can you send me your location?"

"For what?"

"I'm coming to get whatever flowers I can salvage. Is that okay?"

"I'm sure Maggie will give you a refund. Insurance will probably cover it."

"It's not about the money. My sister is getting married in a little more than two hours and we have to have flowers. We have to."

"Okay, okay. I get it. I'd get here quick though. The tow truck is on its way. And prepare yourself for the worst."

"I'll be there. Don't let them tow off my sister's flowers." I hung up the phone and sprang into action. This was no time to freak out.

"What's the plan?" Eamon asked.

I was already requesting an Uber from my phone. It was only a few minutes after eight o'clock, and the ceremony wasn't until eleven, but I needed to have the flowers at the venue and looking perfect no later than ten. "You get dressed, find Luke, and think up some reason you and I are going over to the club on our own." I glanced down at my phone again. "The driver will be here to pick us up in seven minutes. I'll get us packed up."

"Don't you need to take a shower?"

"There's no time. I'll have to go with dry shampoo and a ton of deodorant. I'll do my hair and makeup at the club."

"Do I tell Luke what's happened?"

"No. We don't need to give him or Amy any more reason to

be spooked about today. Tell them we had to go meet Fiona. It's not a lie if we call Rachel from the Uber and tell her to have her dropped off at the country club instead of at the house."

He nodded and smiled. "You're a good sister."

"I've spent my whole life trying. It had to kick in at some point."

Lickety split, Eamon and I met the driver and we were on our way to the location Max had sent me. I was wearing my bridesmaid dress with my black Chuck Taylors. Eamon was wearing his tux. My hair, which still sort of smelled like last night's booze, was pulled back in a ponytail. Everything was already pretty much a disaster, but I decided to be optimistic—things could not get worse.

The accident scene was indeed catastrophic. Vehicle glass scattered over the blacktop, crumpled metal littering the inter-section, and cars trying to drive around it all. The van was on its side and a red pickup truck with its front smashed in was a good twenty yards away. But no one was injured, so that was good news. I was going to squeeze every good thing out of today if it killed me.

After a quick talk with the police to make sure I could take our flowers, Eamon and I ventured over to the back of the van. He opened the door, the metal groaning in protest. I crouched down and duck-walked inside. I ignored my impulse to cry when I saw what we were working with—the white boxes holding the bouquets were strewn about, the flowers themselves arranged like someone had been playing pick-up sticks.

"Is it bad?" Eamon called into the van.

"Toast was a pretty good way to put it."

"Is there anything we can save?"

"The boutonnieres and bouquets are in boxes. Hopefully they're okay. It's mostly the flowers for the ceremony and recep-tion that went flying." I sidestepped puddles of water, glad I'd had enough sense to wear sneakers. I knew then that I had to channel my mom, something I quite frankly had never done. Not once. But if she were here, she would've gone to work. There was a wedding happening today and a bride in need of flowers. There was nothing to be done except to make it happen.

A stack of three gray plastic tubs sat off to one side. I'd have to borrow those and use them to carry the flowers. Most of the vases were broken, but a few weren't, and I was pretty sure they'd have some at the club. Luckily, a spool of the silver satin ribbon we'd chosen was sitting among the debris, still shrink-wrapped. "I'll grab everything I can and we'll figure it out when we get there." I started handing Eamon the white boxes and when that was done, I picked through the flowers and gently placed them in the tubs. Max, the delivery guy, had finished talking to the police and was still waiting for a tow truck, so he helped. Fifteen minutes later, Eamon and I were back on our way.

We pulled up in front of the country club, and I flagged down some of the catering folks to help us get the flowers inside and help find me a workspace. We set up a banquet table in a back hall by the kitchen. We found a few pair of scissors, and some extra plain glass vases for the centerpieces. It was going to have to do.

Eamon's phone beeped with a text. "The car is dropping off Fiona. I'll be back in a minute."

I decided to start with the bouquets and although it was a terrifying prospect, I knew that Amy's should be first. If anything needed to be perfect, it was that. My pulse was pounding in my throat as I lifted the flap of the box, which was crushed on one corner and wet on the others. *Please be okay. Please be okay.* I opened it and could hardly believe what I was looking at. It looked perfect. Absolutely perfect.

"No. How is that possible?" I muttered to myself, quickly opening the bridesmaids' boxes to see if I would actually be that lucky.

I wasn't.

Those bouquets all had at least one snapped stem. Some had several. But I took the state of Amy's as a good omen and since there were no extra flowers, I started removing those that were broken.

I hadn't realized just how much I was running on adrenaline until I looked up and my heart came to a stop. Eamon and Fiona were walking toward me, both all smiles, holding hands. Fiona was wearing a lovely deep purple dress with an empire waist and full skirt, along with black Mary Janes. I hadn't taken the time earlier to fully appreciate how ridiculously handsome Eamon was in his dark gray tux. The two of them stole my breath away.

Fiona let go of her dad's hand and ran up to me to give me a hug. "I've missed you," she said.

My heart melted right then and there. "I've missed you, too. You look beautiful in your purple dress." I smoothed back her hair with my hand and kissed the top of her head. How I loved this child. "Did you see how handsome Daddy looks today?"

"I did. It even looks like he combed his hair."

"I clean up pretty well." Eamon's off-kilter grin said that he knew that he was doing far better than pretty well.

Fiona eyed the array of empty vases and odd collection of flowers on the table. "What happened?"

"Can you keep a secret?"

"Of course I can."

"We have to fix all of the flowers before Aunt Amy gets here." I glanced up at the clock on the wall. "Which will be in about a half hour."

"I'll help," she offered.

"Me too," Eamon added.

And so I issued instructions. Eamon and Fiona sorted the flowers, dividing them up by type and discarding whatever wasn't usable. When they were done with that, they filled the containers with water, like an adorable daddy-daughter fire brigade, and I went to work arranging. With handfuls of flowers in my hand, it was hard not to see a vision of my mother working behind the counter at Taylor & Daughters, humming to herself and happy to be doing the thing she so loved. I didn't try to banish the thought, nor did I let it wander to other memories of her. I simply let it play in my head while I did my best to do what she would have done if she were here today—I fixed the flowers.

In the end, a few centerpieces ended up being thin, but I figured we'd put those at the back of the reception hall and Amy would hopefully never notice. Fiona helped me tie new bows on the vases while Eamon went to meet up with Luke and keep him away from the floral disaster.

My dad found us just as Fiona and I were finishing. There were flower stems and scraps of ribbon littering the tabletop. There was no escaping what had happened. "What in the world went on back here?" He pulled me into an embrace then greeted Fiona. "There's my princess. I hope we can sit by each other during the ceremony."

"No magic while they're getting married, Grandpa Mark. It would be rude."

"But of course."

I turned and acknowledged the mess on the table. "There was an accident with the flowers, but I think we got everything fixed. Please don't tell Amy. I'll tell her later. After the wedding."

"Or never. Never works, too." He took survey of our work while one of the staff began loading the centerpieces onto a cart.

"But well done. You clearly learned all of this from your mother. Glad it came in handy."

"Yes. Me, too." I sighed happily feeling like a weight had been lifted. Or to be more precise, many weights. "Let's go see if Amy is here yet."

Fiona and I walked double-time down the hall back to the bride's room.

Amy was just arriving, her massive dress still wrapped up in the garment bag. Talk about cutting it close. "There you are." She unsubtly eyed me up and down. "Katherine, you look like hell. You're sweating and your hair and makeup aren't done. We have less than a half hour. What have you been doing?"

"Playing with me. It's my fault," Fiona said.

Amy bopped Fiona on the nose with her pinky. "Nothing could possibly be your fault."

"Don't worry," I said. "I'll get cleaned up right now."

"I can curl your hair, Katherine," Fiona said.

"You can?"

She nodded. "I can. I practice on my mam all the time. I curled it that day we met at the park. I'm not half bad."

I was going for better than half bad, but at this point, I was interested in saving time. "Wow. Okay."

Fiona followed me into the bathroom and she stood on a chair, spraying my roots with dry shampoo, brushing out sections, and carefully curling my hair. There was no telling what the final product would look like, but all I could think was that the girl had some skills.

I started to put on my makeup, looking into the mirror, blending concealer and foundation. Today, my reflection didn't bother me. I liked seeing a glimmer of my mom somewhere on the other side of the glass, knowing that yes, she was part of me, but she most certainly was not all. I mostly saw myself looking back from the mirror, with Fiona by my side. For as many moments as we'd spent teetering on chaos lately, this was the best I'd felt in a long time.

Still, there was one thing I could do to make things even better.

"I love you, Fiona. You know that, right?"

She unleashed her sweet smile. "I love you, too."

"I love your dad very much. I want to ask him an important question today. I want to ask him to marry me. But I want to know if that's okay with you." I wondered if she'd be confused by the notion of me essentially asking for her father's hand in marriage, but she didn't bat an eye.

"It's perfectly okay with me. A girl should be able to ask a boy just as much as a boy can ask a girl."

"That's what I think, too."

"Do you think he'll say yes?"

It hadn't occurred to me that Eamon might say no. And that was when I truly understood how much of a blow it must have been when I'd turned him down. He'd probably never seen it coming. "I can only hope that he loves me and forgives me enough to say yes. But if not, we'll figure something out."

Fiona let the final curl go and spritzed my entire head with a cloud of hairspray while I covered my face with my hands. "There. Done," she proclaimed.

I peeled back my fingers and turned my head to check out my hair—long perfect spirals of blonde. I had to admit the nine-year-old had done a much better job with the curling iron than I ever could have. "It's perfect. Thank you so much."

"I'm excited you're going to ask Daddy the big question. I'm rooting for you. Just so you know."

"I appreciate that, sweetie. More than you know."

Fiona and I walked back into the bride's room to see Amy in her dress. I was so glad for that day at Vera Wang, when I'd completely lost it and sobbed like an idiot. It saved me from messing up my makeup now. "You look amazing." Standing behind her, I placed my hands on her shoulders and kissed her cheek.

Amy looked back at me through the reflection of the dressing mirror. "I do look pretty good, don't I?" She ran her hand over the double strand of pearls. "Thank you for getting the necklace. It wouldn't have been right if Mom wasn't here in some way."

I swallowed hard, not wanting to cry. Later, maybe tomorrow or when she and Luke got back from Peru, I would tell her that Mom had absolutely been with me when I fixed the flowers. I was pretty sure she'd been watching over Amy's bouquet, too. "She's here. In the best possible way."

Dad poked his head into the room. "Ladies. They're ready for us to line up." He caught sight of Amy and his lower lip started to tremble. "You are the prettiest bride that ever was."

Amy popped up from her seat and wrapped her arms around him. I followed and hugged them both at the same time. I was not about to miss out on this moment. None of us said a peep. I sensed that we were all fighting back the tears. Today was a big day and not only because Amy was about to get married. Today showed how far we had come. We were a family and we were stronger together. That was all that mattered.

Fiona started to worm her way into the middle of the huddle. "Guys. Make some room."

Dad laughed and stepped back. "I will always make room for you. But first, we need to have a wedding."

"Showtime." Amy took a deep breath, then led us out into the hall and down to the ballroom entrance.

"You go sit up in the front row next to Julia, okay?" I said to Fiona. "Grandpa Mark will come and sit with you after he gives Amy away. Dad and I will be standing right there at the front."

"I know how weddings work, but thanks." She marched up

the aisle on her own, greeting guests as she went, admiring one woman's hat and getting a bit flirtatious with a good looking guy sitting at the end of one of the rows.

The bridesmaids were gathering when I spotted Luke's mom, Cindy, heading in. I knew I had to say something, but what do you say to a woman who has just learned that her husband is sleeping with her sister? I tiptoed over in time to see her tucking a silver flask into her beaded bag. "Hey, Cindy. I wanted to say congratulations and well done."

She unleashed a wry smile that made me wonder exactly how long she'd suspected her husband was having an affair. "Thank you for saying something nice about the wedding, rather than treating me like I've been struck with an incurable disease."

"Of course."

"You know, I have never liked my sister. She has always felt this need to outdo me. I guess she outdid me in the ultimate way this time." She shrugged. "Be glad you have your relationship with Amy. It's special."

"Thank you. I love her a lot." I went in for a hug. Cindy needed more than a pat on the shoulder today. "And thank you for being so kind to me. You've raised some amazing kids."

"I did, didn't I?" A wide pink lipstick smile crossed her lips.

"Yes, you did."

I rushed back and took my place right in front of Dad and Amy. I took the chance to straighten Dad's boutonniere. "You two ready for this?"

Amy nodded and kissed Dad's cheek. "I love you, Daddy."

"Me, too." I stole a kiss on his opposite cheek.

He blushed, smiling with his eyes. "You girls are the best. I love you both more than you'll ever know." There was no telling how many more teary moments we would have today, but I had the distinct sense that we were all cherishing every one.

The music started and we snapped to attention. One by one, the bridesmaids began their march, sashaying in silvery satin. When it was my turn, I set my sights on Eamon, standing one away from Luke, with his hands behind his back. He was more than my salvation. He made me my best. It wasn't that I'd only been *Sunny Girl* because I'd kept my past from him. I was *Sunny Girl* when I was with him. And I had to make sure he knew how much that meant to me. Today. No more waiting.

I reached the front and he winked at me, sending a tidal wave of warmth through my body. Did he know what he could do to me with just a glance? He probably did.

I turned and watched Amy walk up the aisle. My heart, in all its patched-up glory, was so filled with love it was almost impossible to understand. And to think I'd spent so many minutes worrying about this day, fretting about whether or not she would be happy or safe without me. Now I knew she could find her own happiness, and she'd done a damn fine job of it, too.

The crowd settled back in their seats and the ceremony began. It felt as though I was watching it all happen through an entirely different lens than I'd imagined. Not rosy. Just clear. This was what love looked like, and I was humbled to be in its presence. Amy and Luke exchanged their vows, and I let myself soak up every good feeling around me. There was so much of it that the entire room glowed in gold. Even with all of the drama, everything had come together. Everything was right. Especially when the minister pronounced them husband and wife, and my sister got to kiss Luke. The knot had been tied. And I couldn't have been happier.

Luke and Amy embarked on their trip down the aisle, and his oldest brother, who was best man, stepped forward and offered his arm. This was exactly as we'd practiced. The trouble was, I didn't want him. I wanted the guy behind him. So I stepped aside and let one of the other bridesmaids go first.

"Making trouble, I see," Eamon whispered into my ear when he took my arm.

It felt like my cheeks were going to burst as we walked down the aisle together. "I had to have you. I don't know how else to put it."

He was still laughing a bit as we stepped out into the hall. We were supposed to stop, but there was one more thing to do. I grabbed his hand and kept going.

"Katherine, the receiving line..."

"We'll congratulate them later. I need to do something." I ducked into the reception hall with Eamon. Everything was set —the tables, the dance floor, the lovely, albeit sparse in the back of the room, flower arrangements. This was as close as I could come to a romantic setting on this cold December day.

"I don't think we're supposed to be in here yet," he said.

"I'm not worried about rules right now, Eamon."

I marched him out to the middle of the parquet dance floor and took his other hand. I looked into his eyes, much as I had that first night we met, when I was just as much in awe of him as I was now. Was this really happening? And would it work out the way I wanted it to? I wanted to believe it would. It had to. Nothing else made sense.

I dropped down to one knee. The look of shock on his face was totally worth whatever embarrassment I might suffer if he said no. "I love you, Eamon. I love you and I want to spend the rest of my life with you. I don't ever want to let you go. I want us to get married. If you still want to."

"Katherine, are you proposing?" He stooped lower and looked me right in the eye. "Do you realize what your sister will do to you if you get your dress dirty before the pictures?"

Was he stalling? Why wasn't he blurting out an enthusiastic

yes? "I don't care about the dress. If it gets dirty, I'll stand behind one of the other bridesmaids. And yes, I'm proposing. I'm asking you to marry me." The full realization of what I was doing hit me. It stuck in my throat and practically turned sideways. "I asked Fiona's permission. I wanted to know she was okay with it and I knew that would be important to you."

He shook his head and smiled. "You are unbelievable."

"Is that a yes or a no? Because right now, this feels a bit like a no. And I need you to know that I understand why you might want to get even with me, but it would really make me feel a lot better if you didn't."

He tugged on my hands. "Stand up, so I can kiss you."

I obliged, mostly because my knee was killing me and as Amy and I had once discussed, no one would turn down a kiss from Eamon. He reined me in with his arms, warm and comforting. Secure. "That was the most romantic thing ever. Thank you." He pressed a soft but oddly chaste kiss to my lips.

"You already asked me three times. Well, two and a half. That time at my office wasn't really a proposal so much as you were pointing out the solution to a problem. I figured it was my turn."

"Are you ever going to stop talking?"

"Are you ever going to answer me?" Voices came from the other side of the room. Guests were filtering in and finding their seats. "We're kind of operating on borrowed time here. There's no telling how long it'll be before people start trying to make conversation with us."

Eamon grinned. "I'd love to make you wait, but I don't have it in me. I will marry you, Katherine. It's all I've wanted. Truly."

If there was an Olympic event for smiling, I could have not only competed for the gold right then and there, there would have been no beating me. "Perfect." We fell into the most amazing kiss, the sort of kiss that makes everything else around you go warm and fuzzy. Only Eamon could do that to me. Only he could blur out the rest of the world until all I could see was him.

"Ahem," a familiar girlish voice said.

We let go of our kiss and Fiona was standing right there, rolling her eyes. "Guys. You're embarrassing me."

Eamon scooped her into his arms. "Sorry, darling. Katherine and I are going to get married. That's why we were kissing."

She pushed on his chest until he had no choice but to set her down. "I already knew all about it."

"And are you happy?" he asked.

"Of course. Nobody reads to me like Katherine and she always has the best snacks around the house, like those cheese crackers I love." She turned and looked up at me. "Plus, I love her. So that's good."

Both Eamon and I got a little choked up at that. We put her in the middle of a hug to mark what felt like the true beginning of our little family.

Amy and I made eye contact and she said something to the person she was speaking to then wound her way through the crowd. "What the heck, Katherine? Two minutes after I get married and you're making out with your boyfriend in the middle of the reception?"

"Fiancé." Eamon corrected her and took my hand.

"We just got engaged."

I expected the ultimate look of surprise, but she simply looked pleased. Her eyes were content; cheeks flush with the blush of true love. "Engaged to be married?"

Of course she'd asked that. Amy would never give up a chance to give me crap, not even on her wedding day. Not even when we were all nothing but giddy fools. "What other kind of engaged is there?"

"Daddy," Fiona said. "Can you take me to get a glass of lemonade?"

"Of course." He kissed me quickly on the cheek. "Be right back."

Amy and I watched as they wandered off. "God, you're a lucky bitch," she said.

"Thanks. I know." I slung my arm around her. I didn't want to rub it in, but she wasn't wrong. I was really lucky. "Congratulations. You did it."

"Yes, I did. And now it looks like you're next."

THE END

———

Thanks so much for reading! If you have a moment, please leave a review on your favorite retail website or Goodreads. For more information about Karen Booth, visit karenbooth.net.

ACKNOWLEDGMENTS

It takes a village to raise a child, and this book was my baby for two years. I couldn't have done it without the support, time, and thoughtful following people: Melissa Jeglinski, Patience Bloom, Margaret Ethridge, Piper Trace, Karen Stivali, Val Skorup, Jo Ann Gagnier, Sheli Dile, and Donna Soluri. At some stage of this book, you all had your hand in it. I couldn't be more thankful for my first-line feedback squad.

Thanks to author friends who get me, encourage me, work with me, and bitch with me: Joanne Rock, Sarah M. Anderson, Kat Cantrell, Reese Ryan, Catherine Mann, Louise Bay, Serena Bell, Jenny Holiday, Tiffany Reisz, Elisa Lorello, Jennifer Gracen, and Sasha Devlin. Also a huge shout-out to the Backstage Antics and Seasoned Romance groups on Facebook.

My best gal pals: Sara, Evette, Ashley, Lisa, Stephanie, Frine, Cara, Donna, and Jennifer.

Much love to my family. My husband, Steve, who is endlessly patient and encouraging. My kids, Emily and Ryan, who still think I'm cool and and want to hang out with me. Ella, our cat, who spends many hours curled at my hip while I write.

Lastly, thanks to my readers. I do this because I want to create a world for you to get lost in. I do this because I believe in love. Reach out any time. karen@karenbooth.net.

xoxo
Karen

ABOUT KAREN BOOTH

Karen Booth is a Midwestern girl transplanted in the South, raised on '80s music and repeated readings of "Forever" by Judy Blume. An early preoccupation with rock 'n' roll led her to spend her twenties working her way from intern to executive in the music industry. Now she's a married mom of two and instead of staying up late in rock clubs, she gets up before dawn to write sexy contemporary romance and women's fiction.

Thank you for reading! If you enjoyed this book, please leave a review with your favorite online retailer or on Goodreads. Even if it's only a few words, it means so much!

And don't forget to sign up for Karen's newsletter at bit.ly/kbnews. You'll get info on new releases and exclusive giveaways!

28874201R00174

Made in the USA
Columbia, SC
18 October 2018